THE EARL'S INDIFFERENT DAUGHTER

Sisters of Ember Hall
Book 3

Elizabeth Heights

ARE YOU SIGNED UP FOR DRAGONBLADE'S BLOG?

You'll get the latest news and information on exclusive giveaways, exclusive excerpts, coming releases, sales, free books, cover reveals and more.

Check out our complete list of authors, too!

No spam, no junk. That's a promise!

Sign Up Here

www.dragonbladepublishing.com

Dearest Reader;

Thank you for your support of a small press. At Dragonblade Publishing, we strive to bring you the highest quality Historical Romance from some of the best authors in the business. Without your support, there is no 'us', so we sincerely hope you adore these stories and find some new favorite authors along the way.

Happy Reading!

CEO, Dragonblade Publishing

Additional Dragonblade books by Author Elizabeth Heights

Sisters of Ember Hall Series
The Scot's Secret Love (Book 1)
The Lord's Reluctant Lady (Book 2)
The Earl's Indifferent Daughter (Book 3)

The Earls of the North Series
Gambling with the Earl (Book 1)
Forced to Marry the Earl (Book 2)
Taming the Earl (Book 3)

PROLOGUE

Year of Our Lord 1315
Egremont House, English Borderlands

S HAFTS OF SUNLIGHT filtered through the high window in the armory to form dappled patterns on the plastered walls. Adam was slowly and meticulously polishing swords; holding each one up to the light and examining the surface for nicks or marks. He had only a sennight left in the service of Rory Baine, but was determined to be diligent until the very end. Everything was quiet, save the soft sound of rubbing and the occasional rasp of metal. The room was foursquare and sparsely furnished, with just one small window for light, but Adam had always enjoyed the sense of peace and purpose down here.

Overseeing the armory had been one of the first jobs granted to him when he joined the household. It was a weighty responsibility for a wee lad with narrow shoulders that still sagged with grief, but Adam, the only son of a tenant farmer, was well used to doing the work of a man. Now, ten summers later, he had grown half a head taller than the mighty Rory Baine, with shoulders that were broad and well-muscled, thanks to the strict regime of training at Egremont House. His skin was tanned from long hours outside and his eyes shone with hope for a future that was nearly within his grasp.

He hummed tunefully as he admired the intricate engravings on the hilt of a particularly fine broadsword. This belonged to Rory's son, Callum; a bright and kind boy some years his junior, whom he had trained as a swordsman and in so doing, grown to love almost like a brother.

Adam recalled the day that Rory had presented the sword to Callum. It was the same day that the strapping youth had first bested Adam in a sword fight. Beaming with pride, Adam had clapped Callum on the shoulder and proclaimed that his work was done; he had taught him all he knew. Rory promptly strode away from the training ground, causing Adam to fret that he had somehow displeased his ofttimes irritable mentor. But when Rory returned, a smile flickered at the edge of his thin lips. He held a long package out toward his son.

"'Tis time for you to have this," he'd said.

Callum had slowly pulled the sword from its sheath and held it high, admiring the gleam of fine-crafted metal in the noontime sun.

Just as Adam was doing now.

He pursed his lips. He would miss Callum most of all when he left Egremont House. But the lad was already away in Lindum, training to be a knight. For all of Adam's expert swordsmanship, that honor would never be accorded to him.

"And nor do ye want it," he told himself severely.

Nay, he would never be a knight.

He would be a farmer, like his father before him.

He balanced the weight of the sword in his hand, imagining in its place a hefty hoe or pitchfork, and he laughed aloud, the sound ricocheting around the bare walls. Happiness bubbled in his belly, making him as lightheaded as a man well into his cups.

"A farmer," he said, liking the solidity of the word. He took a breath. "A husband."

The words fitted together, like hand and gauntlet.

He put down the sword and placed his palms on the smooth wooden work table. "Clara will be my bride."

The dream he had longed for was now close enough to believe in. In mere days, Adam would wed his childhood sweetheart and become the happiest man in all the land. They would live with Clara's parents, in the farmstead that had been in the Gowen family for generations. His days would pass in hard, honest toil. God willing, they would be blessed with children. It would be a simple life, but one filled with laughter and love.

He replaced Callum's sword, his hand lingering only a moment over the hilt. He had never coveted the status or coin of the family that had taken him in. In truth, he pitied young Callum Baine for the pressures exerted on him by an ambitious father.

Adam wiped his hands on a leather cloth and put everything away tidily, before closing the door of the armory and climbing the narrow steps to the courtyard. Heat enveloped him and he blinked until his eyes adjusted to the harsh sunlight. A few chickens scratched amongst the cobbles, but no one was about, save the lookout guards on the gate.

Before this summer, Egremont House had been a regular hive of activity. Lady Elizabeth, Callum's mother, enjoyed nothing more than a steady stream of house guests who would hunt over the moors or picnic on the hills. The evenings would see laughter and music fill the feasting hall, and even Rory would crack a smile and tap his foot in time to the lute. But now, Lady Elizabeth's health was failing: the shutters to her bedchamber were closed against the summer sun and her husband's brow seemed creased in a perpetual frown.

Adam paused at the stop of the armory steps, his hands on his narrow hips and his dark hair mussed by the breeze. The silence was almost visceral and after a moment he realized what was so strange.

There was no birdsong.

He cocked his head to the side and listened closely, but the usual melody of woodland birds calling from the trees surrounding Egremont House had ceased.

A gust of wind blew grit into his face and in the same moment a cloud passed over the sun, casting the courtyard into shadow. As Adam rubbed at his eyes, someone shouted and the guards pulled open the main gates. Two riders trotted through the archway, both looming overly large: their horses moving as if in slow motion. He opened his mouth but struggled to catch a breath of the warm August air. One of the men spoke, his voice shrill with urgency, but before Adam could make sense of the words, his companion shot out an arm to silence him.

It was Rory Baine. His dark eyes were fixed on Adam as he rode toward him, his scarlet cloak billowing over his horse's hindquarters.

Adam ordered himself to straighten up. He reached behind him for the granite wall of the armory and tried to take comfort in the sun-warmed stones, but there was something about the expression on Rory's face that reminded him of that terrible day when he was but a wee boy.

A wee boy waiting in the barn for the physician to come out of the house and tell him that all was well.

Instead, it was his father's old friend, Rory Baine, who appeared in the barn doorway and told Adam, not unkindly, that he was now an orphan.

"Adam." Rory reined in his warhorse and jumped neatly onto the cobbles. "I have grave news."

The exact phrase he had used back then.

Adam could not speak. Behind the horse, he saw the wide eyes of Rory's manservant.

"Milord," he managed.

Rory was not a tactile man. When he reached out and touched Adam's shoulder, Adam knew for certain that something was terribly wrong.

"'Tis the Gowen farm."

Adam's mouth went dry. "What of it?"

Rory shook his head, greying hair bouncing on his broad shoulders. "I am sorry, lad."

A sharp pain rippled through Adam's chest. "Tell me."

"We rode past on our way back from Rossfarne. 'Tis ruined."

"Ruined?" Adam blinked, not understanding. "How?"

"Raiders." Rory voiced the word that every man on the borderlands dreaded hearing, and more so since the Battle of

Bannockburn. "They set fire to the house and barns. There is little left standing."

Adam's knees gave way, so that it was only the fierce grip of Rory's hand on his shoulder that kept him upright. Wretchedly he tried to form his next question.

"None survived," Rory said gently. "We searched and made certain."

Adam's lips formed the name *Clara*, but no sound came out.

"I shall go back with several men, and we shall give the Gowens a decent burial." Rory bowed respectfully. "But 'tis best you stay here."

The idea of his beloved Clara disappearing under the earth brought Adam out of his stupor. Breath returned to his body and he all but shook Rory's hand away.

"Nay. I must go to her."

"She is dead, lad." Rory's gaze was unflinching. "She and her sisters and her ma and pa. All of them killed whilst out in the fields. 'Tis a mercy they did not burn alive."

Adam's stomach recoiled. "Mayhap you are wrong. Mayhap she is only injured." He pushed himself away from the wall. "I must see for myself."

"'Tis no sight for a lover's eyes."

Rory shook his head firmly, but Adam had no care for his concerns. Cold sweat beaded on his brow and his body pulsed with desperate desire to be with Clara. He pushed his dark hair from his eyes and tried to steady his breathing. The Gowen farm was a long walk from Egremont House.

He would have to run.

"Forgive me, milord." He bowed hurriedly then set off at a jog.

"Wait." Rory's command reverberated through the courtyard and Adam forced himself to a halt. "If ye are intent on doing this, take my horse." He held out the reins whilst Adam blinked in surprise.

"Thank you."

Adam jumped into the saddle and urged the horse back the way he had come. Just one wide cart track wound over the moorland hills, which were purple with heather and buzzing with insects. The way was as familiar as the back of his hand. As he passed the mound of rocks, where he and Clara would ofttimes sit and plan their future, he decided that Rory must be mistaken.

Not about the fire. Nor about the raiders. But about Clara.

She could not be dead.

God could not be so cruel as to take her from him. Not when Adam had already lost both his mother and father. Not when Clara was so good and kind and beautiful.

But as he crested the hill, he smelled smoke drifting on the breeze. And as he galloped down the farm track, the taste of it turned acrid in his throat. Blackened rafters, still smoking, stood open to the sky. No hounds barked from the stable yard, no cattle watched his progress. Pain wrapped long arms around his ribs and squeezed his chest until it was difficult to breath.

He halted the horse, dismounted, and looped the reins over a lone stoop—still standing, despite the devastation all around. His heart was heavy, but still he pressed on, needing to see the truth for himself.

It was a truth that changed him forever.

Clara was laying in what had been the hayfield. The Gowens had brought in the harvest just days earlier, and the ground was stubby and hard. It was no place for peaceful repose. Blood pounded in his ears as he tried to make sense of it.

She was face down, but Adam could not deny the familiar hue of her corn-colored hair, and the shape of her slender body, still clothed in her work apron. A plume of blood had dried between her narrow shoulder blades and a distant part of Adam registered, almost gratefully, that her death had been quick.

His vision blurred with tears as he lowered himself to his knees and cradled Clara's head. But the tears did not fall. Instead, as he gazed over the sun-bleached field and took in the terrible shape of another body, Clara's father, some distance away, something inside Adam shifted. A part of him that had been tender with hope and love, instead grew hard and cold.

He was but twenty years of age, and fate had delivered a second cruel blow.

Whatever Adam loved, was lost.

Whenever he hoped for a future, it was taken from him.

He vowed that he would never love—nor hope for it—ever again.

CHAPTER ONE

Year of Our Lord 1330
Wolvesley Castle

"ESME, THAT IS the fourth man you have declined to dance with this eve." Her mother spoke from the side of her mouth so the russet-haired knight walking dejectedly back to his friends would not hear her reprimand. "Are you determined to refuse them all?"

"Not every one of them, Mother." Esme craned her neck but still could not make out the man she desired to see above all others. The great hall of Wolvesley Castle was thronged with revelers, all clad in their brightest and best. Pearls and rubies glittered in the candlelight, and the wooden floor vibrated with the stamping and shuffling of so many booted feet. Esme and her parents were atop the dais, enjoying an uninterrupted view of their guests, from the circling dancers in the center to the groups of chattering knights on the sides.

Crispin is not amongst them.

Esme clenched her hands in frustration, before hastily unfurling them to accept the solicitations of a portly gentleman whose ascent to the dais had brought wine-red pools of color to his jowls. He bowed over her gloved fingers, and she forced herself to smile.

"Lord Ashville," she chirped. "My father will be delighted to see you." She had to raise her voice above the troupe of musicians playing a lively jig.

"'Tis not your father's company I seek, Lady Esme, but your

own. Would you care to join me on the dance floor?"

With alacrity honed by several months of practice, Esme instantly demurred. "Alas, I am in no mood for dancing, milord. Allow me to walk you over to my father." As she spoke, she took determined steps to where the Earl of Wolvesley was ensconced in his elaborately carved wooden chair. He raised a bushy brow beneath his thatch of grey-gold hair as she approached. "Father, I have brought Lord Ashville to see you," she said sweetly.

Taken by surprise, Lord Ashville could only bow and mutter a greeting as Esme skipped back to her mother's side.

"That was verging on rude," the countess stated calmly.

"Rude but necessary." Esme smoothed her voluminous skirts. "Surely you would not see me wedded to a man old enough to be my grandfather?"

"Your reputation for indifference makes it increasingly unlikely that we shall see you wedded to anyone at all." Her mother took a deep breath, her green eyes bright with worry.

"Esme, you do not have to marry. But if your life does not have a sense of purpose—"

"I know, I know." Esme sighed dramatically. "Without purpose, my life will be dull indeed."

This was not a fate which Esme feared. Her life was brighter and more intricately layered than the rose-pink gown threaded with pearls which she had been laced into earlier.

The countess softened her gaze. She will still an attractive woman, though her thick hair now shone more silver than gold. She wore a well-cut gown of emerald green and her slender fingers flashed with jewels. "We only want you to be happy."

Esme could have gnashed her teeth with impatience. If only she could show her mother how very happy she was. For months now, she had been planning the statement she would make at tonight's ball. By refusing to dance with any and all suitors since Beltane, she had intended to cause quite a stir when she finally took to the floor with Crispin.

But Crispin is not here.

'Twas almost as if he had sensed the upcoming twists of her cunning plan.

Where is he?

Esme resisted the urge to pull off her glove and nibble on her fingernail. She bade herself to stand still and upright, her shoulders back and her lips curving into a smile. She might be the youngest of the five de Neville siblings, but she was every inch her parents' daughter; tall, golden-haired, and resolute.

True, her resolve may, outwardly at least, be oriented around fun and frivolity. She certainly wasn't wise, like Frida her eldest sister. Or strikingly beautiful, like Isabella, who was closest to her in age. But Esme had no intention of allowing her life to drift without purpose.

Purpose pumped through her veins like heady wine. She twirled a loose pearl at the cuffs of her sleeve as her mind raced to put together a new plan. Most certainly she could not stand here idly until the end of the ball. If Crispin would not come to her, she must go and find him.

Esme curtsied to her mother. "May I be excused for a moment?"

The countess gave her a searching look. "Will you return?"

"Of course." Esme affected surprise.

"Please be sure of it." Her mother tightened her lips. "This ball is, after all, for your benefit." She reached out a hand and laid it, hesitantly, on her daughter's arm. "I would have you know the meaning and joy of true love, Esme."

Esme smiled.

If my mother only knew the truth!

With a final curtsy, she lifted her skirts and did her best to pass through the busy dance floor without attracting more unwanted attention. She had discovered at an early age that the best way to do this was to keep her eyes fixed firmly ahead and to walk without hesitation. In this fashion, she reached the marbled entrance hall of the keep and passed through the high arched doors into the cool night air. Here she paused. The last of the harvest had been brought in more than a sennight since, and the breeze whispering through her hair carried the first bite of winter, but she did not have the patience to go all the way up to her bedchamber to fetch a cloak. Instead, she gave her arms a brisk rub and tripped down the stone steps, giving the splashing fountain a wide birth as she took the path to the stables.

Darkness had fallen some hours since and the quiet outside was a marked contrast to the brightness and bustle of the great hall. Esme found her way by the light of the stars but was still grateful to reach the wattle-and-daub outbuildings which housed the many knights and men-at-arms in her father's service. Most of them were inside the keep, dancing, feasting and making merry. Esme stepped into the glow of the wall-torch and lifted her hand to rap on the door.

But some inner instinct held her hand. She was out here all alone and knew not who might answer her summons. Suddenly unsure, she stepped back into the darkness and gave a sharp intake of breath when she came up against a warm, solid surface.

"Lady Esme." The voice was gruff and deep. "Forgive me. I did not mean to startle you."

She put a hand to her fluttering heart and spun around, exhaling with relief when the man held up a lantern and identified himself as Gerrault, the longtime stablemaster of Wolvesley and a firm favorite of her mother's.

"Gerrault," she said weakly. "I am glad it is you."

The stablemaster smiled, but it failed to reach his grey eyes. "What are you doing out here at such a time, Lady Esme?"

The question was boldly put, but Gerrault had known her all her life; he had taught her to ride and bathed her knees when she fell.

Esme bit her lip as she tried—and failed—to think of a reason why she might have left the gaiety of the ball to pick her way through the darkness and stand outside the knights' barn.

"I am looking for Crispin," she said bravely, opting for the truth. "Sir Crispin de Gough."

Gerrault's face remained carefully neutral, but Esme imagined a glow of disapproval in his steady gaze.

"I have business to discuss with him." She lifted her chin defiantly.

An owl hooted overhead, as if calling out her untruth, but Gerrault only heaved a sigh. "If that is the case, I must tell you where he is. You'll find him in his horse's stable, getting him ready."

"Ready for what?" Esme frowned.

"That I cannot say." Gerrault fixed his gaze on the soft earth beneath their feet. "If you'll take my advice, milady, you'll return to the ball. Where you belong."

Esme folded her arms protectively. "I shall return to the ball forthwith, Gerrault, have no doubt." She smiled at him but knew by the set of his shoulders that he was not reassured.

"As soon as I have delivered my message to Sir Crispin."

Gerrault held his lantern out towards her. "You will be needing this then."

His kindness affected her more than his caution. Esme put her hand over his for a moment. "Thank you."

He nodded stiffly.

"Gerrault?" She bit her lip once more. "You won't tell anyone about this, will you?"

"I play no part in castle gossip."

"You won't tell my mother?" she burst out. "Please."

"If you return to the ball, Lady Esme, as far as I am concerned, there will be naught to tell."

She would have thanked him again, but the ageing stablemaster had already turned away and melted into the darkness. Esme held up the lantern in front of her face and ignored the buzzing of nighttime insects as she found her way to the cobbled stable yard. Sure enough, a torch blazed beside the stable of Crispin's destrier.

Her heart thumped inside her restrictive bodice. *What was he about?*

Esme's legs turned to jelly, and she clung to the shadows of the barns. Crispin loved her. He had said as much. So why had he not come to the ball as promised?

She stifled a sob as a dozen answers sprang to mind. Her sister Isabella, long since married to the elderly Earl of Felsham, had spoken scornfully to her about men and what they truly wanted from a woman.

And that *thing* that they wanted, was the only thing Esme had ever denied Crispin.

She swallowed and gripped the lantern harder. Surely that didn't matter? Not when they had been secretly courting for over a year.

Not when he called her his faerie queen and promised to love her forever.

Esme could have told her mother that she already knew the joy and meaning of true love.

True love was like a fever. It was a racing heart and a mind that could concentrate on one person alone. It was a pair of brown eyes that made her stomach churn.

Esme had long taken joy from the fact that Crispin wanted her for who she was, not for her position or coin. Whereas other men fawned over her father's title; Crispin urged her to keep their relationship quiet, even when Esme wanted to tell the world.

Soon, Crispin had said.

Tired of waiting, Esme had concocted her plan to announce their relationship in a more indirect fashion. And mayhap Crispin had rumbled her, was displeased with her, *was planning to leave her*.

She pushed herself away from the rough granite of the barn and marched to the stable, pausing only to place Gerrault's lantern on the cobbles.

"Crispin?"

His chestnut stallion swung his head towards her, but there was no sign of Crispin.

She stepped closer, placing her hands on the half wooden door and leaning over to look right and left. The horse was busy at his hay rack. The stable was clean but apparently empty. Then she made out a gleam of blue amidst the shadows at the back of the stall.

"Crispin?" she called again, louder this time.

The knight had been dozing, curled up against a soft pile of straw. He started at Esme's voice, a familiar slow smile breaking across his handsome face when he recognized her.

"Dearest girl. I sent up prayers that you would come to find me."

Momentarily confused Esme could only frown. She must not allow herself to be distracted by his chiseled cheekbones or beautiful brown eyes. "Why were you not at the ball?"

Crispin nudged the stallion aside and came to stand at the other side of the door. He smelled of hay and his finely stitched blue tunic was creased. His large hands covered hers, making her realize how chilled she had become.

"Alas, dear one. Events have overtaken us." He shrugged his muscular shoulders, his full lips curling into a regretful smile beneath his nut-brown locks of hair. "But I am pleased that at least we have this opportunity to say farewell."

"Farewell? Why? Where are you going?" She took a breath, realizing how plaintive she sounded.

"I am summoned to a friend in need." He lifted his hands and cupped them around her cheeks. His eyes widened with regret. "'Tis a summons I cannot ignore."

"But you are sworn to my father." Esme's frown deepened. None of this made sense.

"Which is why I must slip away unseen at first light." Crispin put his head to one side. "There is much I cannot tell you, Esme. You must trust me when I say that I have not come to this decision lightly."

She grasped his hand, pressing it harder against her cheek and leaning into the heat of his palm. "I trust you," she promised. "But when will I see you again?"

"I cannot say."

"My father may not welcome you back to Wolvesley." As the words left her lips, Esme realized their importance. "'Twould be better if you spoke to him first and explained the situation. He's the King's man. You can trust him with anything."

Crispin stilled and his face grew unreadable. "I know 'tis hard for you to accept. But there are some things that go beyond your father's jurisdiction." A note of mockery had crept into his voice.

In the heat of the moment, she had forgotten to tread carefully. Crispin was a proud man, but his pride was easily wounded—as Esme had long since learned.

"Hard for me to accept that you are a skilled, trusted knight of much renown?" She took one of his hands and placed it over her heart. "Nay, never." She shook her head so vigorously her hair threatened to break free of its pins. "Though 'tis nigh impossible for me to accept that you are set to leave Wolvesley with no plan to return." Her vision blurred with genuine tears, and she lowered her head so he would not catch them shining in the torchlight.

"My dear, sweet girl." He wiped the corner of her eyes with his thumbs. "Look at me."

Hesitantly, she met his gaze.

"My departure wounds me just as deeply as it wounds you."

She sniffed in a most unladylike fashion. "Then do not go."

To Esme, it was all very simple.

Crispin took a step away from her and dragged a hand through his tousled curls. "This is unanticipated."

Esme let a beat pass. "How so?"

Crispin appeared to be wrestling with something. "Truly, Esme. I did not know you cared so deeply."

"Of course I care," she protested.

His fists clenched. "And yet you spurn me at every turn."

Was that the gleam of *his* tears which she could now see?

"I do not spurn you," she protested, but he had already turned away.

"'Tis mayhap for the best. I will say goodbye now, Esme. In

time, I hope I am able to return to Wolvesley, but you will no doubt be married by then."

"Nay." She wrestled with the door, bolting it behind her and crossing the straw-strewn floor to stand behind him. Her hands flew around his broad shoulders; her face pressed against his back. "I shall marry none but you, Crispin. Do you not know that?"

His body fairly bristled with tension. "You would turn down all the titled and wealthy lords your father has lined up for you?" His voice was choked as he gestured angrily in the direction of the keep.

"I already have," she replied steadily.

Crispin's destrier clopped over to investigate this disruption, exhaling warm breath over her face and neck before losing interest and returning to his hay.

Crispin still resolutely faced the back wall of the barn.

Esme's thoughts were tinged with panic. What could she do to show him how much she cared?

Her hands slipped from his shoulders, down towards his tapered waist. As if they had minds of their own, they glanced over his taut belly and up towards his muscular chest. She felt a new kind of tension enter his body; one which matched with the awareness building deep inside her.

And just like that, she knew what she must do.

She pressed herself against his back, relishing the sparse solidity of him before she rose onto her tiptoes and pressed a kiss to the warm skin where his neck met his shoulders.

He turned around and linked his fingers with hers.

"What are you about, Esme?" His voice had become throaty.

"If you do not know how much you mean to me, then I have done you a great disservice." She paused, breathless with a heady combination of daring and desire. "I must put that right."

Crispin's brown eyes met hers and she thought for a moment he might voice some dissent. Before he could utter a word, she rose up again and touched her lips to his.

The familiar tinderbox sparked deep inside her belly, and she felt herself smiling as he hauled her closer and ran his hands down the length of her spine. His hands went to her hair, snaking through the careful styling and scattering pins as he gently tugged it free.

"And how do you intend to show me how much I mean to you?" His voice was husky, the words interlaced with butterfly kisses which traced a tingling path from her jawline to the lace of her bodice.

Esme tipped back her head, closed her eyes and deliberately silenced her rational mind. In the past, at times such as this, notions of propriety had prevented her from taking full pleasure in Crispin's caress. But now, as his palms skimmed her breasts and his breathing became heavier, she didn't allow herself to fret about what was and was not appropriate behavior for the daughter of an earl.

She only thought of here and now. Of Crispin, and how she could not let him leave Wolvesley whilst thinking that she did not love him.

When he fumbled with the pearl buttons at the front of her gown, she did not stay his hand. She did not flinch, not even when his impatience caused the silk to tear, and two buttons pinged off to become lost in the straw. As he fumbled beneath her skirts, she leaned into his muscular shoulder and ensured the pace of her breathing matched with his. When he lifted her chin and gazed into her eyes at the same moment his fingers found her curls, she smiled to show him how much she liked it.

It was halfway true. She didn't *not* like it. In truth, she didn't know what this was meant to feel like. Isabella spoke with distaste of *duty*, but Esme had heard tales of women going weak-kneed with desire when men touched their secret places.

She certainly hadn't thought it would all be so *physical*.

Nor that it would take so long.

She pressed her lips together and endured the embarrassing probing, wondering what she might do to make it stop. Was Crispin taking pleasure in doing this to her? She sneaked a look at his flushed face and concluded that yes, he possibly was. When he finally withdrew his hand, she wanted to sigh with relief.

Instead, Esme smiled, ready to kiss him again and hear his familiar declaration of love. But without letting a beat pass, Crispin swept her into his arms and carried her to the back of the stable where the clean straw was stored.

"I have wanted you for so long, Esme," he said as he carefully laid her down.

The straw smelled sweet but sharp strands stuck into the thin fabric of her gown and made her squirm. She opened her mouth to protest but Crispin took this as an invitation to kiss her once again. This time, his kiss was hot and deep. His tongue swept into her mouth, exploring urgently. Esme found herself sinking downwards into the straw, even more so when Crispin's solid weight landed on top of her. Before she could gather her wits, she realized that he had penetrated her with something far more substantial than his finger. The white-hot rasping pain of it took her breath and she fumbled at his shoulders, but Crispin's face was screwed up in concentration. He thrusted several more times before letting out a deep, guttural moan and collapsing into the straw next to her.

Esme's foremost feeling was relief that his weight was no longer pinning her down. She flexed her hands and feet experimentally, pleased that they still reacted to her instructions. It seemed as if she had been sawn in two, like a tree cleft by lightning. She dared not try to stand up, for fear her legs would not hold her.

"My darling girl. My faerie queen."

She turned her face to the side, to find Crispin briskly straightening his tunic and jumping to his feet. Esme smiled weakly, unable to think of a response.

"Here, let me help you up."

She wanted to protest, but Crispin's strong fingers had already grasped her wrist and hauled her upright. She leaned against him until she found her balance, trying to ignore the soreness at the top of her thighs as well as the warm trickle of… something… down her calves.

She glanced down to see the red bloom of blood on her rose-colored skirts.

"Oh." She blanched awkwardly.

"It always happens the first time." Crispin kissed the top of her head. "Do not worry, sweet Esme."

Her thoughts scrambled but her eyes were drawn once more to the blood. "We must marry."

"Of course." Crispin's reply was smooth. "As soon as I return from my mission."

"Are you intent on leaving Wolvesley still?" She sagged against him, feeling tears of uncertainty pricking at her eyes.

Have I made a mistake?

"I must. I explained this to you already." A note of impatience crept into his tone.

"I'm sorry." Her tears were harder to staunch now. She had given herself to this man but still he planned to ride away from her.

"Nay, 'tis I who am sorry." His voice gentled. "We will marry, Esme. I give you my word."

She tried to smile. His word should be enough.

"But if the word of a knight does not satisfy you, I will give you my ring."

At once, her heart soared. "Truly, Crispin?"

"Of course." But instead of reaching into his pocket to withdraw a piece of jewelry, Crispin strode over to the fresh straw. He plucked several long strands and began twisting them together.

"A ring made of straw?" Esme blinked.

"'Tis the ring that is of consequence, not the substance it is formed from."

She pressed her lips together as he slid the hastily fashioned ring over her finger. It was too large, and she clenched her fist lest it fall to the floor.

"This is my promise to you." Crispin closer his hand over

hers. "I will return, and we shall marry."

It was the assurance she had longed for, but her heart still beat hollowly in her chest. She stepped into his embrace and pressed her cheek against the rasp of his stubble.

"Will you do something for me?" he whispered, his breath warm against her neck.

"Anything."

"Leave Wolvesley yourself on the morrow. Wait for me at your sister's home."

"Ember Hall?" She tipped back her head and looked at him in confusion. "Why?"

"Because if you remain here, your father will marry you off before I have chance to come back for you."

Salty tears blurred her vision once more. "I will not allow that to happen."

"Please, Esme." His voice was urgent. "Do this one thing."

His worries were unnecessary, but she could see how they troubled him. "I will." She nodded, to show her assent. "I will find a reason to visit my sister, Frida."

"Then all shall be well." His smile was radiant.

Esme was not convinced. This night had not turned out the way she had planned.

"Just be sure to come for me soon," she said, forcing an answering smile through her tears.

CHAPTER TWO

E SME SAW THE messenger approaching Ember Hall through the narrow window of her bedchamber. She sank onto her cushioned window seat, one hand pressed to her heart, as the guard stood back to allow the rider through the gate.

Within moments, she would know.

Her heart fluttered like a small bird trapped in a cage, even as she told herself sharply that the message was most likely meant for someone else in the house. She took up her embroidery in a futile effort of distraction, but the decorative swirls of colored thread had never interested her less.

Is Crispin on his way to me?

She put the embroidery down and clasped her hands together in a silent prayer. It had been more than a sennight since the ball at Wolvesley Castle, when Crispin had asked her to be his bride. She deliberately did not dwell on the exact circumstances of his proposal; merely the fact of it.

"I have always loved you, Esme," he had said that night in the hay-scented stable, whilst the flickering wall torches outside sent shadows leaping around them.

Esme frowned; her gaze fixed on a brightly patterned tapestry hung on the opposite wall. Was that right?

Nay, she realized, wrapping her fingers around the space where—briefly—a ring made of straw had rested. He had not said that.

"I have always wanted you, Esme." That was what he said.

She bit her lip, wanting to believe it was the same thing.

It had led to the same thing, in any case.

Enough. She could not sit around here like some meek creature, waiting to learn her fate. She gathered her shawl against the early autumn chill and walked from her bedchamber, taking care to slow her pace as she proceeded along the gallery. The children's nursery was at the end of this hall, and she did not want to draw the attention of her niece and nephew. The wooden stairs squeaked as she descended, disturbing two hounds slumbering by the fire in the great hall.

But aside from the hounds, the room was empty.

Esme swirled around, her scarlet skirts flying outwards. In her mind's eye, someone—preferably not Frida—had been waiting here to receive her, their hands outstretched to pass on the message she longed to receive.

A log crackled in the grate, mocking her folly.

She took a deep breath. Just because the scene was not as she envisaged did not mean that Crispin had not written to her; nor that the message was not making its way through the house. She smoothed her voluminous skirts and took a seat by the hounds, talking to them softly and trying not to flinch as her voice broke the near silence of the large room.

She had grown up amidst the noise and bustle of a great castle and consequently, had always found the tranquility of her sister's home unsettling. 'Twas pretty enough, with glossy wooden paneling, high vaulted ceilings and mullioned windows framing sweeping views of the English countryside. But Esme was accustomed to musicians, men-at-arms and gossip.

Not this infernal peace and quiet.

She did not enjoy hearing herself think.

As if answering her prayers, footsteps sounded along the corridor and a moment later, her sister Frida appeared.

"Esme, there you are. I have a message for you."

Esme blinked in surprise that her fancies had become real, but she recovered quickly, knowing she must take care to guard her emotions around Frida. Her eldest sister had once been gifted with the Sight and, even though an accident some eight winters past had dimmed her powers, Frida still possessed an uncanny ability to read people.

But Frida smiled warmly and held out the rolled parchment as if naught were amiss. She was a tall and attractive woman who moved briskly through life with a strong sense of purpose. The same accident that had claimed her sight had turned her golden blonde hair to a shimmering silver, enhancing her air of wisdom.

Six summers stood between them—the oldest and youngest of the five de Neville siblings. For as long as she could remember, Esme had always been a little in awe of her eldest sister.

"Thank you," she said, affecting nonchalance and folding the parchment into a pocket of her skirt.

Frida eyed her speculatively. "Aren't you going to read it?"

Esme made a show of rotating her shoulders, making her shawl slip down to her elbows. "I long for some exercise. Yesterday's rain kept me too long indoors."

"I see." Her sister clasped her hands over the simple bodice of her grey-green gown.

"I shall go for a walk and find a quiet spot to read my message. It will be naught of import, I am certain." Esme turned away from Frida's all-seeing blue gaze and strolled toward the window, noting the nodding pink rose heads climbing outside. "Mayhap I shall walk to the standing stones," she trilled. "You have always found them a good place to think, have you not?"

I must stop talking.

Frida always had this effect on her.

"Is that what you want to do, Esme? Think?"

The question was quietly asked, but Esme's knees began to tremble all the same. Whilst she scrambled for an appropriate answer, Frida came to stand beside her. Together, they looked out of the long, narrow window, although Esme was no longer paying attention to the green hills beyond.

"Methinks you are at a crossroads, dear one. And you must choose your path carefully."

How much has my sister already divined?

"Do not rush into anything," Frida continued. "Certainly not anything so lasting as marriage."

Esme froze. Her mouth opened and closed but no sound came out.

"I know that is what Father wants for you," Frida added softly.

The rush of relief made her audibly exhale. "He has been lining up suitors for me all summer long." She echoed Frida's posture and clasped her hands over the pearl buttons of her bodice. As she did so, she couldn't help but notice the difference between Frida's practical day dress and her own, flouncy gown. "Many of these suitors are older than Father himself."

Frida put a gentle hand on her arm. Esme could feel the warmth of her touch, even through her fine woolen shawl. "Father will not force you to do anything against your will. It is for you to decide your future. And that is why you are here, isn't it? To give yourself time to think things over?"

"Aye." Esme smiled, as if Frida were her confidant.

And how she wished that was true.

But she could not confide the truth of the matter to her respectable older sister. Frida would be shocked beyond words if she learned what Esme had done.

A rush of envy washed over her. Frida was settled in life, with a good husband who all but worshipped the ground she walked upon.

Esme tightened her lips. "If there is naught else?"

Frida stepped back, lowering her head so Esme could not read her expression. "Enjoy your walk. I hope you find good news in your message."

Her pulse pounded at that, but Frida was already making her graceful way up to the nursery. Esme exhaled slowly, her fingers tracing the outline of the parchment in her pocket.

Had Crispin been the one to write and roll this parchment? If so, 'twas the closest she had been to him in many days.

Esme straightened her shoulders and walked briskly toward the front door, leaving the lavender-scented calm of the hall behind her as she stepped into a chill wind which whipped up her skirts and made her grasp at the ends of her shawl. For a moment, she considered going back inside, but the unsettled conditions matched her heart's tumult, and she ploughed on through the courtyard, scattering chickens in her path. Her long legs ate up the path over the hill, even as her eyes began to water. Her hair, hastily secured this morn by a somewhat reluctant housemaid, pulled free of its pins to lash about her face.

Esme was not well attired for a walk in the country. She paused atop the cliffs, gazing down at the blue-green waves rushing furiously onto the sandy cove. The sea looked anything but inviting. Naught would be inviting on this day, save a warm drink by a crackling fire. But Esme had made a show of wanting a walk and could not turn back now. Besides, she longed to read Crispin's words someplace no one was likely to interrupt her.

She struggled on, pleased when she first glimpsed the harsh granite of the standing stones—a circle of rearing stones, some of them the height of a middling child. This had always been a favorite retreat of Frida's, but Esme had never understood the appeal. There was something off-putting about the loneliness of the location, and the stones themselves exuded a forbidding air which made Esme feel almost as if she was trespassing. But today, they provided welcome shelter from the cruel wind. Esme made a beeline for the widest stone and sank down onto the springy grass behind it.

'Twas a blessed relief to be out of the wind. She dragged a hand through her tousled hair and straightened her skirts as best she could. She must look a sight. So be it, the only witnesses to her dishevelment were the gulls circling overhead.

For a moment, she fixed her gaze on the endless expanse of rolling fields ahead of her. Autumn had brought the first hint of russet and gold to the treetops, and even Esme could not deny the beauty of it. Now that she was out of the wind, the rolling of the waves and the calling of the gulls lulled her into a sense of calm.

Crispin had written to her. Perchance he was on his way. All would be well. But when she unfurled the parchment, 'twas her father's familiar writing she saw. Sudden tears made his words crabbed and she all but flung the message over the cliffs. She loved her father, aye. But disappointment made her inwardly rage at him. After several deep breaths, she was composed enough to read the missive, which contained no further surprises. The Earl of Wolvesley wished to know when his youngest daughter would return. He had several suitors asking for her hand and would give her the pick of them, if she were present.

Esme crumpled the parchment, gazing blindly into the distance. She knew she was fortunate to be offered a choice in the matter. Moreover, she was blessed with the freedom to come and go, much as she pleased from Wolvesley. Many of her peers were not permitted such liberties, but Esme had been raised to think and act for herself. Since early adulthood she had been accustomed to joining her brother Tristan on jaunts up and down the country, visiting friends and family.

But Tristan was no longer her willing accomplice. He was married now, to their father's ward, Mirrie. Indeed, he had eyes for no one but his bride, especially now that she was expecting their first child. The two of them had excused themselves from the latest Wolvesley ball, claiming they wanted to spend the evening quietly together.

Esme wrinkled her nose, unable to deny a second stab of jealousy that morn. She was pleased her brother had found love. But must he make such a show of it? He was another example of a sibling who had waltzed, untroubled, into a happy state of matrimony. Neither Tristan nor Frida could have any idea of the torment she endured.

What a mess.

She hugged her knees and allowed tears of self-pity to roll down her cheeks. Without word from Crispin, all she could do was wait, as he had requested. She sniffed in a most unladylike fashion, wondering for the hundredth time what business was so important it should take him away—not only from his station at Wolvesley, but from *her*.

There was another question lurking at the back of her mind, one that she had not dared give voice to. But out here, with the waves and the gulls and the disappointment, she could no longer ignore it.

Does he truly love me?

She gritted her teeth. That was only a small part of it.

Do I truly love him?

Releasing the thought she had suppressed all these long days was oddly exhilarating. Esme tipped her head back against the ancient stone and closed her eyes.

How was she to know if she was in love? 'Twas not like learning Latin; there was no text to follow. Her brother Tristan and sister Frida had seemed to slip effortlessly into the state. But Isabella made no pretense of happiness in her marriage. As Countess of Felsham, Isabella enjoyed wealth, status and comfort. But she showed naught but middling affection for the man by her side.

What would Esme enjoy as Crispin's bride?

She cared little for wealth or status, but comfort was important. A feeling of being cared for. Cherished, even.

Ever since they began their *affair*, Esme had rarely gone a day without experiencing the thrill of a forbidden kiss. Their time together had been imbued with secrecy and drama, right from the start. And Crispin was so handsome, with his chestnut curls and deep brown eyes. Whenever he looked at her, she could hardly hear reason above the pounding of her pulse.

Secrecy, drama, giddy excitement. *Was that love?* Esme wondered if love was perchance something stronger and more steadfast than the tumult of emotions that had infected her like a fever.

She swallowed painfully, unwilling to follow her thoughts further. Either way, these days apart from Crispin had broken the spell of attraction and intrigue. Now her desire to be with him was murkily entwined with the painful knowledge that she *should* be with him, because of what they had done.

Esme sighed deeply and looked back down at her father's message.

Impossible.

Even if she wanted it, she could not return to Wolvesley as the prospective bride of some great lord. Esme did not claim to understand all the workings of the world, but she knew the men bidding for her hand expected two things of the match.

Her dowry and her virginity.

She could bang her head against the stone and rail against her stupidity, but it would achieve naught but further pain.

Nay, she had no choice but to make the best of it. She must bide her time and wait for Crispin to come for her.

Esme pushed herself to her feet, buffeted once again by the strong wind coming over the cliffs. She would return to Ember Hall and write a reply to her father. 'Twas not fair to keep him waiting. Praise be, her reputation for cold indifference to suitors may mean her rebuttal would not come as a surprise.

She would be like Jonah, her youngest brother, who had claimed sanctuary at Ember Hall for almost as long as Frida had lived here. He said the peace and quiet soothed his soul and eased the pain in his wasted leg. Mayhap she would also come to find some reprieve from her troubles in these lonely hills.

Though right now, Esme was not willing to count on it.

As soon as she walked back through the front door, she knew something was amiss. A great clamor of voices came from the great hall, as if many people were speaking at once. Loudest was Callum, Frida's husband; a man who did not usually raise his voice.

"Our lives need not all be uprooted by this," he declared as Esme entered the room.

Wide-eyed, she took in the scene. Frida and the children stood in a huddle by the fire; the youngest, Merry, in her mother's arms. Callum paced opposite them. His rugged face had turned a paler hue than Esme had ever seen it. Jonah sat awkwardly on one of the tapestried chairs, studiously ignoring a small black cat who was winding around his legs.

And upon the furthest-away window seat, perched a man all in shadows, whom Esme did not recognize.

"What is happening?" she interrupted.

Callum waved a brawny arm in her direction. He was dressed in breeches and a heavy tunic, as if he had just come in from work in the fields. "Naught of note. I shall be away a few days, that is all."

Frida huffed and shifted the weight of the babe in her arms. Her silver hair was in danger of coming loose as Merry patted and tugged at it. "Naught of note indeed. Your father is ill, mayhap dying. 'Tis a matter of enough import to merit discussion."

Callum folded his arms across his muscular chest. "I shall go to him and say my goodbyes." His voice broke, betraying the distress he was trying hard to keep at bay. Even Esme could see that her usually unflappable brother-in-law was upset. He fixed his gaze down at the floor until Frida went to stand by his side, then he leaned against her in a momentary display of vulnerability.

"We shall come with you," Frida said quietly.

"'Tis too far. The children are too young."

"The children are healthy and so am I." She lovingly pushed back a tendril of his dark brown hair. "Would you deny me this last chance to meet your father? Or your father this last chance to meet his grandchildren?"

Callum grasped her hand as if he were drowning. "I tell you, Frida, 'tis not like that. Kielder Castle is not Wolvesley. My father is not yours." He glanced toward the man on the window seat. "Adam will confirm that my ancestral home is no place for our children."

The man sat back so he was even further overshadowed, but he said nothing.

"You can speak freely, Adam," Callum persisted. "There is no man's opinion that I take greater heed of."

Even the children looked toward the window seat in expectation, but Callum's plea was met with continued silence. Esme's eyebrows shot up. Was this man a servant or relative of some kind?

Frida allowed a moment to pass, before briskly taking up where she had left off. "We shall pack a few things and be ready to leave by first light on the morrow."

Callum opened his arms wide, his gesture taking in the vast hallway as well as the courtyard and fields beyond the windows. "I cannot ask that we abandon our duties here."

"You have not asked," Frida interrupted. "Besides, the harvest is all brought in, and our stores are full. 'Tis not even Michaelmas and we are already set for winter."

Frida and Callum locked gazes in a battle of wills.

Into the silence, Esme spoke. "You are right Frida. You should go." She had racked her brains to remember the location of Kielder Castle and concluded it was somewhere in the highlands. There had been some unpleasantness, she dimly recalled, when the truth of Callum's Scottish ancestry was first discovered. In fact, the more she thought on this, the more certain she became that Callum's father was some great warlord. A rift had sprung up between father and son after Callum's marriage to Frida. Which was all the more reason for them to make peace, whilst the opportunity still remained.

Her heart twisted in sympathy. She had no real concept of the distance involved. She only knew that if it were her father that was gravely ill, she would move heaven and earth to see him.

"You should all go to Scotland." She met her sister's gaze and smiled, noting that Frida appreciated her support.

Little Flora stepped forward and wrapped her arms around Callum's leg. "Can I go to Scotland?" she asked, her sweet, five-year-old voice piping around the room.

"Me too?" Her brother Christopher would not be left out.

Frida scarcely hid her smile. "'Tis what your children wish."

"My wife as well?" Callum gazed down at her, with so much love shining from his brown eyes that Esme felt her own heart turning over.

"Your wife as well," Frida murmured.

In another moment, they would be kissing one another. Esme could not bear it. She clapped her hands to capture their attention. "That is just as it should be. Jonah and I will take care of Ember Hall in your absence."

'Twas the wrong thing to say, she realized this almost immediately. Frida's blue eyes widened with anxiety and Callum shook his head.

"Nay, lass. You cannot stay here. You must return to Wolvesley Castle, where you will be safe."

"I will be safe here." She spun around to look entreatingly at Jonah, the brother she had scarcely seen since her arrival. "Tell them, Jonah."

But her brother only shrugged, his face creased with pain. "I have not been well these last weeks," he said, resting his golden head on the back of the chair. "Mayhap Callum is right, Esme. You should go home."

Esme's mind was racing. "If you are unwell, 'tis better that I stay here and look after you." She looked at him with new concern. "Is it your leg?" Her brother was elegantly dressed in spotless breeches and leather boots which hid the fact that, from the knee down, one leg was narrow and twisted. "You should rest, that's what Mother always says. I shall fetch and carry and ensure you have all you need." She rubbed her hands together, as if the matter was settled.

"I am not quite so feeble that I cannot take care of myself," Jonah said distastefully, narrowing his blue eyes.

"Then I shall give you all the space you need, whilst being here if you need me." Esme was well accustomed to her brother's moodiness. She would not let him spoil her plans.

"Esme, it cannot be done." Frida passed the babe to her husband and crossed the room to stand beside her. "You are always welcome here, you know that. But without Callum's protection, it is simply not safe."

Esme looked into her sister's earnest face and saw the prospect of sanctuary rapidly disappearing.

But if I return to Wolvesley, I will be pressed to accept a suitor.

"You have always said that Jonah is as skilled with a sword as Tristan." She made her voice light.

"Has she?" Jonah looked almost interested.

Here is my chance.

Esme nodded vigorously. Her skirts swirled as she playfully mimed a sword thrust.

"Even Tristan admits it."

Jonah gave her a strange sort of smile. "You think that between us, Esme, we could keep vagabonds and thieves at bay?"

"I do," she declared, feeling victory within her grasp. "Forsooth, Jonah, 'tis most unlikely we will encounter any."

"The fact remains that Jonah is not in full health right now." Frida held up her hands as if forbidding further discourse.

Esme could have stamped her feet. "There are guards," she began.

"None that I would trust with such a precious assignment." Callum smiled over at her from his position by the fire as Merry cooed in his arms.

Under different circumstances, Esme might have smiled back. Frida's husband was a handsome man. But right now, she felt more inclined to scowl.

"I do not wish to return to Wolvesley," she declared. "I wish to remain here."

"We cannot always get what we wish for," her sister retorted, calm as ever.

Frustration surged inside her, but Esme knew she could not allow the full extent of her feelings to surface. Giving herself time to recover, she wandered over to the window and had all but arrived there when she remembered the mysterious man sitting by it.

It was too late for her to alter her path.

Esme continued to walk steadily forward. The man was tall, she realized. Taller even than Callum, which was no small feat. And he was wide. His broad shoulders took up almost the whole width of the window. His hair was long to the nape of his neck, and the light streaming in behind him picked out strands of silver shining amongst the dark curls.

Their eyes met briefly before he turned away.

His eyes were green. His cheekbones were sharp. His hands, resting lightly on the cushioned seat, were large and clean.

Esme paused uncertainly, she had been intent on ignoring him, as he had ignored them. But now that she was standing so close, his magnetic presence was hard to snub.

"I am Lady Esme de Neville." She dipped into a small curtsy, thinking that a show of good manners might unsettle him.

Slowly, he turned his head to their eyes met once again. He did not appear unsettled.

"Adam Hawker," he said, his voice rough with lack of use. He did not rise up from his seat or even offer her a bow from his seated position.

Callum cleared his throat. "Adam has served my father since I was a boy."

Not a relative then.

"You are a warrior, sir?" she addressed the large, silent man.

He nodded.

"And you rode here to inform Sir Callum of his father's failing health?"

She received another nod.

"A trusted warrior, I dare say?" She fixed him with her brightest smile.

"I believe so, milady."

A frisson went through her as their gazes clashed. He clearly had not wanted to respond to her questions, but Esme was yet to encounter a man who could resist her smile.

She turned that same smile back toward Callum. "You said earlier that there is no man's opinion that you take greater heed of, did you not?"

Callum nodded. "I stand by every word."

"And you trust him, just as your father does?"

"I do."

Esme put her head to one side, pretending to think it through. "Well then," she said brightly. "Why not leave me in the safekeeping of your man, Adam?"

CHAPTER THREE

*T*HE LASS IS *the very image of Clara.*

Adam wanted to close his eyes against the swell of painful memories. The last thing he needed was this living, breathing reminder of his lost love.

His body already ached with tiredness after his long journey south from the highlands whilst his mind was troubled by his mission. Aye, it was right and proper to inform Callum of his father's illness; but nonetheless he balked at taking a man—who had not long since found happiness—far from the source of that happiness and back to a place of cold and steely disapproval.

If he was being strictly objective, Adam would admit that Lady Esme's hair was a more golden hue than Clara's had been. And perchance this lovely young woman had seen a couple more summers than the lass who lived through less than twenty of them. 'Twas the bright, restless energy emanating from her that put him so in mind of Clara. The radiance of her smile. Her shimmering determination.

Belatedly, he realized the whole family were staring at him as if waiting for some kind of response. The roaring of blood in his ears, which started when Lady Esme first entered the room, had grown louder still when she conversed with him. Whilst imprisoned by her brilliant blue eyes, he had answered her questions. But as soon as she turned back toward her family, he had lost himself in the past.

Lady Esme put her hands on her slim hips and frowned.

"The idea displeases you, sir?"

Adam's opinion was rarely called upon at Kielder Castle. He was accustomed to receiving orders and acting upon them. Anyone who had spent time around the great warlord, Rory Baine, knew that it was safer to keep one's opinion to oneself.

Wearily, he rubbed a hand across his brow. "I beg your pardon, milady."

She lifted her chin. "What do you say? Aye or nay?"

Callum passed his bairn to a servant before joining their little group by the window.

He had grown contented since Adam saw him last. With a beautiful wife and strong, healthy children. And a home filled with laughter and lively conversation.

I should not have come.

"My good man, you are not obliged to remain here as personal guard to Esme whilst I am away. Though I know my sister-in-law is a hard woman to refuse."

Adam lowered his head, resting his gaze on his worn leather boots which were coated with dust from the road.

Did he wish to return to Kielder Castle? To the backstabbing and constant air of acrimony?

Nay, I do not.

Did he wish to stay here, to be tormented by memories of Clara?

Nay, I do not.

Adam's life had been dictated by the whims of others since his youth. He had long since stopped attempting to wield control over the tides of fate.

"Whatever pleases you most, milord," he said. "'Tis little difference to me."

He heard Callum puff out a breath. From the corner of his eye, he saw him shake his head to restrain Esme's celebration.

"Come now, Adam. We do not stand on ceremony here. Moreover, you have never addressed me as milord. There is no call to begin. But I see we have placed you in an impossible situation. Let us retire to the solar and discuss the matter without further interruption."

Adam lifted his head. As ever, the gaze of Rory's only son was unflinching and honest.

Callum offered his hand, and Adam realized it would be churlish to refuse it. He allowed the younger man to haul him to his feet, feeling again the deep ache in his calf muscles.

"Thank you," he said gruffly.

Callum clapped an arm around his shoulders and turned them both in the direction of the solar.

"I shall bring in some wine." Callum's bride smiled warmly.

When he first caught sight of her, Adam had been taken aback by Frida's waterfall of silvery hair. But now he saw that her face was that of a younger woman. Her eyes were bright, and her movements were quick and light.

Callum is fortunate indeed.

They tramped together across the wooden floor. Adam was relieved to enter the solar and hear the squeak of the door closing behind them.

"Sit." Callum flung himself down into a tapestried armchair and indicated a comfortable-looking couch opposite. The room was long, narrow and flooded with light from a large window. A writing desk and matching chair were pulled up by the window, as if to make best use of the light. "Frida's brother, Jonah, likes to sit in here and write," Callum explained, nodding toward the desk.

Adam had no response to this. He was overly conscious of his travel-stained clothing and the impeccably clean furnishings. He had washed his hands upon entering Ember Hall but would have paid more attention to his ablutions had he realized he would be spending so much time with the family.

Though Callum had always treated him like family. And Adam had once thought of Callum as the little brother he never had.

So much had changed since Callum left Kielder Castle that final time. None of it good.

As if divining his thoughts, Callum leaned forwards, clasping his hands together. "Tell me everything that you could not say in front of my wife."

Adam dampened his lips with his tongue. He was parched with thirst and wished he had not been so quick to turn down the offer of refreshments when he first arrived. But he had wanted to deliver his message as soon as possible, without the hindrance of niceties.

"It is much as you would imagine," he answered carefully, biting back 'milord.' "Your father's health has been failing this last year. At the harvest supper he took to his bed and has been unable to leave it since." At Callum's questioning expression, he offered more. "When I left, he was still able to take some bread and drink some watered wine. But the physician said you should be sent for."

"I do not question your motives in coming for me," Callum said quickly.

"I would not do so lightly."

Adam paused to meet Callum's eye, waiting for his nod of understanding.

"And what of Kielder Castle? What of my old comrades, Andrew and Arlo?"

Adam's chest ached, though he had anticipated the question. "Andrew has moved away from us. He married a lass from the islands. I told him to grasp his chance of happiness."

Callum smiled. "I am glad of it, though I am sure he is much missed." He drummed his fingers on the arm of his chair. "And Arlo?"

"He was kicked by a horse last yuletide. His leg was broken, and I am afraid he has not fully recovered."

Callum almost jumped from his chair. "Ye Gods. I had no idea."

"He did not want to cause you any concern."

"Has my father sent the physician to see him?"

Adam paused for a moment, then settled for the lie. "Aye. More than once. He made a splint for his leg and Arlo can get about tolerably well now. But his days of wielding a sword are behind him."

In truth, Adam had summoned the physician and paid for his services with his own carefully saved coin.

"He has taken some other position in the household? Or has my father granted him a pension?" Waves of agitation rippled across Callum's face.

This time, Adam could not bring himself to lie.

"There is little in the castle coffers to allow such a pension," he said diplomatically. "Arlo helps in the stables." He paused. "When he is able."

Callum dragged a hand through his hair. "I know the rebuilding of the keep drained our reserves." He referenced the siege some six years prior which had seen Kielder Castle all but razed to the ground. "But Arlo has served our family most faithfully. I do not like to think of him working when he is injured."

Adam said nothing. The situation was more dire than he could aptly give voice to. Rory Baine had retreated further into spiteful parsimony since his son's departure, and it was not unknown for the servants to go long weeks without receiving the coin they were due. But with no other settlement for miles around, many had neither the wealth nor health to consider leaving.

And others, like himself, felt duty bound to stay and do what they could to help. The siege of Kielder Castle had left its scars: children without parents; warriors without limbs; and farmworkers with wounds—physical and mental—that refused to heal.

He fixed his gaze on the dapples of sunlight covering the plastered wall ahead of him. Laughter came through the adjoining wall of the great hall and outside in the courtyard, someone was singing.

A woman's voice. *Perchance it was Esme?*

He shook his head to dislodge the notion. Foolish fancies for a young woman, some years his junior—*and many ranks his better*—would not aid him in any way.

Callum sat back in his chair. "What of this request from my sister-in-law? That you remain here whilst I visit my father?"

He was temporarily lost for words.

"'Twas impertinent, I know. But she is a lass who speaks her mind." Callum grinned, clearly unaware of the impertinent steer of Adam's thoughts. "I wondered if you might appreciate the chance of some days at rest?"

Adam lifted his brows. "Days at rest?" he repeated stupidly.

"Should you be of a mind to chop some firewood or exercise the horses, none would stand in your way. But as my wife said, we are ready for winter." Callum shrugged. "You can take some rest. Or else renew your acquaintance with the land. 'Twas not far from here you were raised, I believe?"

Adam swallowed painfully. The lure of someplace called home had ceased to tug at his heartstrings many years since. When Clara was killed and Adam, mired in grief and twisted with desire for vengeance, followed Rory Baine north to the Highlands.

He had become a man who served, who followed orders. Even though he had once hoped for more.

"Do you have friends or family still living nearby?" Callum cocked an eyebrow, oblivious to the tumult of emotion his question caused.

"Nay." Adam did not elaborate.

"More chance for rest then." Callum crossed his long legs and smiled. "Take some rest, man. I am certain you deserve it."

A beat passed. "Why do you offer me this?"

Callum's face lost some of its benevolence, but Frida chose that moment to step into the room, balancing a well-stocked tray in her hands.

"This is long overdue for a man who traveled so far to reach us," she murmured, settling the tray on a low table and passing

Adam a cup of warmed wine. "Your news took us all by surprise. But please, eat and drink your fill."

Adam took a sip, pleasantly surprised by the rich taste and subtle spices. He recalled his manners before he drained the cup.

"Thank you, milady."

"Frida," she corrected him, smiling slightly. "Callum has spoken to me of a man named Adam who first taught him to fight with a sword. You are that same man, I believe?"

The simple fact that Callum had remembered that time—and saw fit to share his memories with his wife—made Adam choke up with emotion.

"Aye, 'tis the same man," Callum answered for him. "I had seen mayhap ten summers. Adam here was a strapping youth. If it were not for his early lessons, perchance I would not have been accepted at Lindum."

A long look passed between husband and wife. "Then we never may have met," Frida said simply.

Callum glanced at Adam. "I trained alongside Frida's brother at Lindum," he explained. "Tristan de Neville. Mayhap you have heard his name?"

Adam nodded. Tales of an English knight named de Neville had indeed reached as far as the highlands. But nonetheless, he hoped they would not dwell overlong on this subject. Callum may have spent happy years at Lindum. But for Adam, those same years were tinged with darkness.

"I will leave you to talk." Frida threw another smile at her husband and walked gracefully from the room.

"Eat," Callum encouraged him, nudging the tray closer. Adam's stomach rumbled with hunger, but he would not give in to it before he had his answer.

"Pray, answer my question. Why do you offer me this chance to reside in your home and do naught for it?"

"Not naught. You forget, the primary purpose is to ensure no harm befalls my wife's sister."

"And is harm likely to befall her?" He thought of the young

woman with hair as golden as ripe corn and eyes as blue as the sea. She looked to have never known a day of hardship in her life.

"She is the youngest child of the Earl of Wolvesley. A prize many men would like to claim." Callum scratched at his arm. "In good conscience, I cannot leave her here undefended. But in truth, nay, I do not think it likely she will be approached."

"Why does she not wish to return to Wolvesley? Is she ill-treated there?"

Adam eyed the freshly baked bread which exuded a most alluring aroma, but in his mind's eye he saw the cheerless stone halls of Kielder Castle and heard a woman sobbing.

"Not in the slightest," Callum answered firmly. "The earl adores her."

Adam exhaled. "Then I cannot make sense of it. Why should she wish to remain here? And why do you want me to remain here with her?"

"I cannot answer the first. Perchance you should ask her yourself. 'Twill be some whim she has. Or a quarrel with an admirer, mayhap?"

"She has many admirers?" Adam found himself asking.

"There is a long line of suitors asking for her hand. But the lady is indifferent to them all." Callum half smiled. "The de Nevilles are a close family. Esme visits us often; Ember Hall is a second home to her. I would prefer not to turn her away." He opened his arms, indicating he had nothing to hide.

"And the second?"

"More complicated." Callum scratched at his growth of beard. "In part, 'tis because I trust you with the task." Adam raised his eyebrows and Callum laughingly continued. "Come now, you must have seen for yourself how things are. Esme is an uncommon beauty. Not just in looks, but in character. She could charm the very birds from the trees. And her dowry is sizeable."

Adam clasped his hands and focused his gaze on his fingernails. Anything to avoid Callum's honest gaze. "And you trust this flower of England to my safe keeping?"

"I would trust you with my own daughters," Callum said, his voice serious. "But that is not all of it." He sighed deeply. "I have some idea what your days must be like."

Adam stilled before slowly lifting his eyes to Callum's. "You mean, at Kielder Castle?"

"I mean with my father," Callum said gruffly. "He is not an easy man to be around."

"Nay indeed." 'Twas easy enough to agree with that.

"You can take no pleasure in serving him. Since my mother passed, he has become a bloodthirsty Scottish warlord. You were raised in England as the son of a farmer."

Adam could deny none of this.

"Have I remembered that correctly? You came to my parents following the death of your own?"

He nodded. His parents had been tenant farmers; their land adjoining that once farmed by Clara's family. But he was unwilling to reawaken such memories.

He closed his mind to thoughts of his lost love. "My parents were taken by a fever when I was but a youth. My father and yours once served alongside one another and Rory was quick to offer me a home."

'Twas a rare example of generosity from Rory Baine.

"I can scarce remember a time when you were not at Egremont House." Callum smiled. "I hope you found at least some small happiness there?"

Adam was happy to provide such assurance. "I did. Your mother was a lady of great kindness."

"But then she also died." Callum's face darkened. "You must have had some reason to follow my father to the highlands. Whatever that reason was, you stay with him now because of a sense of duty."

Adam was finding it hard to swallow. Harder still to formulate a response.

"Moreover, your sense of duty is to the villagers and servants. Not to my father."

"I have never moved a finger against him." Adam's pulse pounded.

"I do not accuse you of it," Callum swiftly interjected. He sat back in his chair. "The only thing I accuse you of, Adam, is having a big heart. You care for those unlucky enough to live within my father's walls. You have picked things up where I left off some years hence."

Callum could always see straight through to the crux of a matter, even when he was a young boy. It was one of the many qualities Adam admired in him.

"But I am Rory Baine's son. Perchance it is time for me to take on this burden."

Adam shook his head. He carefully placed his cup down on the table before his trembling hands caused wine to spill on the rug. "You have a wife and family. Your home is in England. 'Tis as your mother would have wished it."

Mayhap he should not have uttered those words. But it was the truth as he saw it.

"I am not abandoning them. Forsooth, my wife and family are determined to go with me." Callum tipped his head back and stared up at the vaulted ceiling. "Though I question even Frida's abilities to bring peace to the troubled halls of Kielder Castle. But that is not a matter to discuss now. In all honesty, Adam, I have been anticipating this summons for some months. It is time for me to return." His expression turned bleak, but only for a moment. "Why should some good not come out of this? Stay here, man. Enjoy the rest. We have a good wine cellar, and you are unlikely to be much troubled by visitors."

Adam was halfway to being convinced. He tore off a hunk of bread and chewed it ruminatively.

"You will return here?"

"Indeed, I hope so." Callum rubbed again at his arms. "If not I, then Frida and the children will. This is their home. I will not rip them from it, whatever may occur at Kielder. But I must accept there will be much to do in Scotland, whatever the outcome with my father."

Adam nodded and reached for a glistening red grape. "I would like to be of help to you, when that time comes."

"And I would be pleased to accept." Callum grinned, once more the boy Adam had known.

"You will not leave me to fester in this lonely corner of England?" He wanted to be sure, especially given the ghosts of his past which still haunted these lands.

"You have my word." Callum rose from the chair and clapped him on the shoulder. "Though you should not speak in such haste. This lonely corner of England has brought me much peace and happiness."

"Aye, well." Adam found his lips twitching up into a smile. "I do not aim so high as that."

"A few days' rest, making sure no churl carries off my wife's sister. I dare say you should grasp this opportunity. Who knows what perils await us all if that man, Roger Mortimer, has his way? This tentative peace between England and Scotland would not long survive." Callum shook his head.

Adam had long ceased to follow the intricate twists of English politics, but he knew of the man Callum referred to.

"He is too power-hungry." *Much like Rory Baine*, he reflected.

"Whereas we both know the power that peace can bring." Callum offered his hand. "Do we have an agreement?"

A few days rest.

The chance to sleep easily in my bed.

Adam clasped the man's forearm with an iron grip of his own. "We have an agreement."

CHAPTER FOUR

FRIDA HAD NOT been exaggerating when she said they would be ready to leave at first light. Indeed, the first rays of dawn had scarcely permeated the darkness when Esme was woken from her slumber by hurried footsteps and shouted instructions. She pulled her blankets all the way over her head and determined to stay in bed for as long as possible, but a tentative knock sounded on her chamber door.

Quelling a deep surge of irritation, Esme sat up and rubbed her eyes. "Come in."

The door creaked open, and a hovering candle appeared, floating less than three feet above the ground.

"Ye Gods." Esme clutched at her blankets, recalling Frida's past dalliances with the spirit world and fearing the worst.

"'Tis only Flora," someone piped in a familiar voice.

Esme blinked and slowly the scene came into better focus. Her young niece stood in the doorway, holding both a candle and the small black cat that had been pestering Jonah yesterday.

"Come in." Esme beckoned her in, yawning widely. She lit a taper and put a flame to her own night light, pleased to banish the shadows.

Flora balanced her candle on the trunk at the foot of the bed and clutched the cat closer. "Aunt Esme, can I ask a favor of you?"

"Anything." Esme sat back against her pillows and smiled vaguely. The last vestiges of sleep still muddled her thoughts, though she had resigned herself to wakefulness.

"Will you take care of Felicity whilst I'm gone?"

Felicity?

Esme blinked.

"My cat," Flora clarified, her big blue eyes fixed on Esme.

"Your cat?" Esme stretched her arms above her head and rotated her head. She had slept well enough but was accustomed to a softer mattress and thicker pillows. "Do cats do not fare very well for themselves?"

"Not this one," Flora insisted. She had lost a tooth recently and spoke with a bit of a lisp. "Mama said she's the runt of the litter and would have likely died if we didn't look after her. She's still not fully grown yet."

Esme switched her gaze to the purring black cat in her niece's arms. The cat gazed back without blinking.

"Mama says the journey is too long and it wouldn't be fair to take her. Also, that she might run away and get lost." Flora pressed her face to the cat's fur, obviously disturbed by the idea.

"Felicity." Esme straightened her blankets and tried to gather her thoughts. "That's a very grand name for such a small cat."

"Mama said I should name her for what I wanted her to be."

Confused, Esme could only raise her eyebrows questioningly.

"I wanted her to grow big and strong," Flora lisped. "And grand." She smiled at the notion. "She was so little when I found her."

"I see." Esme swung her legs out from under the covers, wincing as her bare feet made contact with the wooden floorboards. Back home at Wolvesley, her bedchamber was laid with thick rugs and her lady's maid would have put out goatskin slippers ready for her.

Here, she must fend for herself.

"Can you pass me my shawl?"

The child obliged, dragging the finely spun garment across the floor and then perching up on the bed beside her. Esme had no sooner pulled the shawl over her shoulders than Flora unceremoniously dumped the cat onto her lap.

"She likes you." Flora was delighted.

"Does she?" Esme looked dubiously down at the small creature, who had begun to knead her night rail with sharp claws. "Ouch," she exclaimed.

Flora giggled. "She only does that to people she likes."

Esme fought an instinctive urge to tip the cat off her knees. She thought of her fine silken gowns and the damage this creature would wreak upon them. Then she looked down at her niece—with her shining golden hair and neatly tied travelling cloak—and knew that she could not refuse her.

Flora stroked the cat's jet-black fur. "Felicity does not like many people. Only Mama and Papa and me."

"Not Jonah?" Esme flung out, more in hope than expectation.

"Felicity likes Uncle Jonah. But Uncle Jonah says she disturbs his writing."

"I see." Resigned to her fate, Esme joined Flora in stroking the cat's smooth fur and was gratified when Felicity arched her back in pleasure.

"Will you take care of her for me?" Flora tipped her head upwards and Esme saw glassy tears reflected in the candlelight.

"Of course I will." She circled one arm around the little girl's shoulders and drew her closer. "I will take the very best care of her. Until the day you return. Then, you and Felicity will have both grown bigger and stronger." The cat now rubbed its cheek against Esme's fingers, purring loudly.

"Do you think she might forget me?" Flora rested her head on Esme's arm, and Esme's heart turned over.

"Most certainly not. Cats have very long memories," she invented quickly.

Mayhap they did? Esme had very little experience of the matter. Back home at Wolvesley, cats were kept only in the barns, helping to keep them free of vermin.

But this particular creature seemed to possess both intelligence and personality. It sat primly on Esme's knee, looking up at her as if claiming her.

"Do not worry about us, Flora. Felicity and I will be just fine."

Flora bit down on her lip. "Can I take her now? Just until we get into the carriage?"

"Of course."

Flora scooped up her cat and walked toward the door.

"Thank you, Aunt Esme."

"You're welcome."

Flora closed the door behind her and Esme sighed.

The care of one small cat was a small price to pay for the chance to stay here, just as she had wished.

A triumph she owed to the mysterious warrior from Callum's past. He had showed neither charm nor manners in the great hall, but his acceptance of her request had granted her a reprieve. More time away from Wolvesley, to wait for Crispin's arrival.

More time to consider your options, her mind whispered traitorously in her ear.

Grimacing, Esme paced over to the window and moved aside the oilcloth. The darkness of night had morphed into the milky light of dawn, allowing her to make out the shape of a carriage and pair waiting by the front door. Behind it was a cart, half-filled with luggage. Voices floated up from the courtyard and a dog barked with excitement. A lone figure barreled through the front door holding an enormous trunk against his chest.

"Steady there," someone cautioned. Esme recognized the voice as Callum's.

"I have it," came the reply.

It was the mysterious warrior, Esme realized. He had lifted a heavy-looking trunk and was carrying it with ease. He walked with long strides over to the waiting cart and deposited it in the back.

"Is there much else?"

His deep voice did something to her insides. His accent was not dissimilar to Callum's; the broad vowels of north England mixed with just a trace of Scottish lilt.

She must thank him, for this reprieve he had granted her.

Esme released the oilcloth and spun from the window, newly filled with resolve. She would don her loveliest gown and ensure she looked her best to make this speech of thanks. She recalled the warrior's disinterest yesterday; the way he had not responded to Callum's entreaties, even though Callum later claimed that Adam was as close as kin.

Well, kin ofttimes ignored one another. She knew that well enough.

Still, Adam's detachment meant he was a puzzle she was keen to solve.

But no sooner had she pulled a suitable gown from her closet than she realized her mistake. She needed a maid's assistance to lace it, and 'twas unlikely any maid could be spared this morn. Even yesterday, when all was calm, the housemaid had helped her dress with an ill sort of grace.

Mayhap I should make more of an effort with the servants at Ember Hall.

What was the maid's name? She looked familiar and perchance had served Frida for as long as Frida had resided here.

Esme frowned with effort. Frida always referred to her servants by name.

Jennifer. That was it.

But knowing her name altered naught. Frida and Callum were soon to depart, and Esme could not bid them farewell in her night clothes. She selected a simple day dress in muted green which buttoned down the front, splashed cold water onto her cheeks from the pitcher, and dragged a comb through her long hair, wincing at the tangles. There was not enough light to judge her reflection in the looking glass, so Esme had to assume her efforts were satisfactory. Picking up her candle, she left the quiet of her bedchamber and stepped out into a house transformed by unfamiliar bustle.

The housemaid, *Jennifer,* scurried past, holding a pile of linens and muttering, "Beg pardon, milady."

Grateful for the width of the gallery, Esme darted to the side and narrowly missed her nephew, Christopher, who was on his hands and knees by the paneled wall.

"Good gracious." She put a hand to her racing heart.

"I'm looking for my ball." Christopher looked entreatingly up at her.

Esme had rarely been called upon to be so helpful so early in the morning.

"What color is it?" She picked up her skirts and dropped to her knees beside him. Wall torches cast pools of light onto the gallery, but very little daylight came through the arched window at the end of the gallery.

"Blue."

"How big?" she asked incredulously.

Christopher opened his hands, miming a ball the size of a chicken.

Esme remained skeptical. "I shall help you look."

His smile of thanks melted her heart, despite the hardness of the floor beneath her knees. She made slow progress crawling down the length of the gallery, running her hands over the notched floorboards in the hope of encountering Christopher's lost ball. She kept her eyes trained downwards, and did not notice the booted feet standing at the end of the gallery until she was almost upon them.

"I believe I have something of yours," someone spoke with a deep, gravelly voice.

"My ball!" Christopher cried.

Esme was conscious of her undignified position on the floor, but she had no choice but to look up and see Adam proffering a gaily painted wooden ball toward the small boy.

"Thank you." Christopher clutched the ball to his chest as if it was treasure.

"May I help you up?" Adam sounded partway amused.

"I can manage, thank you." But she regretted not accepting

his assistance as she staggered to her feet. "Good morn, Adam," she said with as much grace as she could gather. Her skirts were twisted around her legs and would have to remain so, for now.

"Good morn, Lady Esme."

He had tidied his appearance since yesterday, she noticed. His boots were polished, his breeches were spotless, and his waistcoat was buttoned neatly over a pale shirt.

A shirt which served to emphasize the hard lines of muscle running down his arms.

Esme took a breath. "Let us put titles aside if we are to spend so much time with one another."

She may have imagined it, but the warrior appeared to blanche.

"So much time?" His voice raised with the question.

"Meals and such like," she trilled, summoning her brightest smile. "I wanted to say thank you for agreeing to stay here with me. It means a great deal."

Adam inclined his head. "You are welcome, milady."

Perplexed at his continued use of her title, Esme held out her hand to Christopher, but her nephew was already running towards Adam, who scooped the boy into his arms and swung him around so he squealed with laughter.

"Your mother and father are looking for you," Adam said.

"I am here." Christopher was indignant.

"Let us reunite you." With a faint smile in Esme's direction. Adam began walking back down the gallery, his booted feet treating heavily on the wooden floor. Esme had little choice but to follow, tugging at her skirts to straighten them.

They arrived in the great hall to a scene of heartening domesticity. Frida, Callum, and the children were seated at the long trestle table, breaking their fast with cold meats, fresh fruit and rounds of soft cheese. Flora sat with the cat on her knee, seemingly telling it a story as she fed it with torn off strips of ham. Merry burbled happily from her mother's knee and Callum had his hand pressed atop of Frida's. They turned smiling faces toward the incomers.

"There you are, Christopher," Frida exclaimed mildly. "Come and eat. 'Twill be some time before we have the chance for more refreshment."

Adam set the little boy down and put his hand to the small of his back as he straightened up. "Will you break your journey at Novum Castellan?"

"Aye, that is our plan," Callum beckoned them over to join the family. "Is the inn there still tolerable?"

Adam inclined his head, standing back to allow Esme to precede him. "Tolerable enough for a man travelling alone."

"I do not require fine and fancy things," Frida demurred, helping Christopher to fill his trencher.

"That will serve you well for the days ahead," Adam jested, surprising them all with a fleeting smile.

His eyes were a most attractive color, Esme realized. Emerald green, like long grass in a meadow. They shone even brighter when he smiled.

If only he smiled more often.

"Frida is well warned over what awaits her," Callum said.

Esme took her seat and plucked off a grape. "Why? What is it that awaits you?"

Her question was met with a tense pause. Frida and Callum exchanged a look and belatedly, Esme realized they might not like to discuss the details in front of inquisitive Flora.

"Kielder Castle is my ancestral home, but it does not offer the home comforts of Ember Hall," Callum answered diplomatically. "Nor the warmth and welcome of Wolvesley."

"To say the least," Adam muttered. He spoke quietly, but his position, directly to Esme's left, meant that she heard every word.

"When we first came here, Ember Hall was neglected and unloved." Frida smiled genially at the table. "It did not take long to turn it around."

"May good fortune shine upon you." Adam bowed his head.

"All shall be well," Christopher intoned gravely. At the look of surprise from the adults around him, his bottom lip quivered. "That is what you told me," he beseeched his father.

"Aye, and I stand by it." Callum patted his son on the head. "Eat up, lad. We must make haste."

Frida got to her feet and extended a hand toward Flora. "Let us go and wait in the carriage."

As Flora looked about to protest, Esme took her cue and quickly walked around the table to crouch beside the little girl.

"Is it my turn to hold Felicity?"

Flora nodded bravely, passing over the cat as a tear snaked down her rounded cheek.

"Goodbye, Felicity," she sniffed.

"Safe travels, Flora," Esme mimed in a squeaky voice which made her niece smile. She straightened up in time to catch a surprised expression on Adam's usually immobile face.

Holding the cat meant that Esme's hands were no longer free to pick at the tempting foodstuffs on offer, which was most inconvenient as her stomach was rumbling. But she did not think she was capable of taking a seat and settling the cat on her knee under the watchful gaze of Adam.

She did not wish to lose her dignity for a second time that morn.

There was a second flurry of greetings as Jonah arrived in the great hall. Her brother was walking with a stick, which was most unusual. Since childhood, Jonah had eschewed crutches, even if that meant his progress around their childhood home was slower than it could have been.

Vanity, Esme had always assumed.

Finally, Christopher had eaten what his father deemed sufficient, and they all trooped out to the waiting carriage. Esme hugged her sister goodbye, somewhat awkwardly because of the cat.

"Can she go outside on her own at all?" she asked Flora, working to take the plaintive edge from her voice.

Flora nodded sagely, giving Felicity a final stroke. "But not at night."

With relief, Esme bent her knees to set the cat down, but the creature had other ideas, digging her claws into her shoulder until she relented.

"You're a clingy thing," she told her, as Felicity purred in victory.

Callum hugged her briefly. "Take care, Esme."

"Of course," she demurred.

"I have told Adam that 'tis unlikely you will encounter any trouble."

"Most unlikely," she agreed, closing her mind to thoughts of Crispin and what might happen if the young knight did indeed return for her, as he had promised.

Callum lifted his son up the carriage steps and swung himself inside after him. He was about to close the door when Frida called in protest.

"My jars and herbs."

"Do you need them?" Callum asked from inside the carriage.

"Aye, I must be prepared." Frida's voice was firm. "Who knows what ailments and injuries we may encounter in the days ahead. I gathered some salves into a box. But the box is not in the cart. Is it there." She must have pointed outside the opposite window, but Esme could not see her.

Before anyone could react, Adam came forward. "I will fetch them."

"The box is heavy. You will need assistance," Frida called, but Adam was already stalking across the courtyard. He shifted the makeshift box into his arms and a noise of clanking jars came from it.

"Be careful," Frida cautioned. "Callum, go and help him."

"There is no need." Adam made steady progress back to the waiting cart, his muscles bulging and he lowered the box into an empty corner.

Esme was openly staring, safe in the knowledge that no one was watching her.

Yet with some sixth sense, Adam must have felt her eyes upon him. As soon as he had positioned the box of salves, his gaze met with hers.

Esme looked away, blushing.

Ye Gods, she had not anticipated this pull of attraction toward a man who was different in every way to Crispin.

Callum gave the signal, and the carriage moved off to a chorus of goodbyes. Soon Esme, Jonah and Adam stood in an empty courtyard. Jonah turned to go inside, complaining of the cold.

Esme directed a smile toward Adam. "Would you like me to show you around?"

Adam looked discomfited. "There is no need, milady. Callum already showed me all I need to know."

Before Esme could demure, the tall man melted away in the direction of the barns. Esme's lips puckered with disappointment and the cat shifted in her arms.

"Let us go in," she said.

I am already talking to a cat.

How would she fare after several days of isolation?

Feeling dejected, she returned to the hall, mildly cheered by the soothing scents of lavender and woodsmoke. Jonah was seated at the trestle table, spreading a heel of freshly baked bread with soft cheese. An expression of irritation crossed his fine features when he beheld Esme.

"You must not look so fretful, Jonah. I do not bite." She deliberately chose the furthest chair from her brother, firmly placing Felicity on the next chair along.

He chewed and swallowed before he answered. "I do not fear your teeth, sister. You have not bitten me since you were a child in the cradle."

She met his sarcastic smile with one of her own. "Then why look so peevish?"

He scowled in reply. "What consequence is it to you?"

"I cannot guess," she said airily as she indiscriminately filled a trencher with food. "Mayhap I care about your happiness. Have you ever considered that?"

"Nay, I cannot say I have." He got up abruptly and reached for his stick.

"Jonah." Despite her conviction that she had said naught amiss, she was contrite. "Please do not go. If we are to reside here together, we should at least be able to make polite conversation."

"You forget, sister, this situation was not of my choosing." He hobbled from the table.

"Can we not make the best of it?" she tried again.

He turned to face her. "That is precisely what I am doing. I shall be in the solar for the rest of the day. Pray, do not disturb me."

Esme sighed as she watched him depart. Jonah's mood was even sourer than usual. Perchance she should give him the benefit of the doubt and put it down to pain? Either way, it would not make for cheerful living.

"'Tis just you and me, Felicity," Esme said to the cat.

Felicity purred and butted her head against Esme's palm.

Whoever thought I would be grateful for the company of a cat?

CHAPTER FIVE

THE HORSE HE had chosen from the stables was surefooted and fleet. Before he fully realized what he was planning, Adam found himself cantering up the overgrown cart track which had once led to Clara's farm.

He had not intended to travel this far, but an urge to flee had come upon him when his eyes met with those of Lady Esme over the fully laden luggage cart.

There had been danger in the look that passed between them.

Danger rooted in the first flicker of desire, that he must extinguish before it had chance to take hold.

Still, he was cross with himself. 'Twas the first day of his duties in guarding Lady Esme, and already he had neglected her. But Callum had departed Ember Hall only this morning. Surely word would not have spread about the lady's unprotected status?

He must hope and pray that it had not.

He reined in the horse as it crested the hill, allowing his gaze to roam over the landscape of his childhood.

A landscape that was so much altered it caused him actual, physical pain.

The Gowen farm had once nestled in a wooded valley, smoke billowing from the chimney, chickens clucking in the yard. Joe Gowen was an honest farmer, up toiling before daybreak and not hanging up his tools till long after sunset. His wife raised five daughters without ever losing the gleam of love and light in her eyes. Clara was the eldest, born the same year as Callum. Both sets of parents had approved of the match between them. Even when Callum went to serve Rory Baine at Egremont House, there was no question that he and Clara would one day marry.

Adam had visited the farm whenever he had a day free. Which was not often.

"All of this will be yours, one day," Joe Gowen would tell him.

Adam had never planned to spend so long in the service of Rory Baine. He was raised a farmer's lad and longed to swap his broadsword for a hoe. His father's lands had been reclaimed by the estate upon his death, but Adam hoped to earn them back.

More than a dozen summers later, Adam's heart beat hollowly in his chest as he looked down upon the smoke-blackened ruins of the once foursquare farmhouse.

The whole Gowen family had been slaughtered whilst he, unaware, polished swords in the armory and dreamed of a future that would never be.

Egremont House was less than an hour's ride from here. He knew the way like the back of his hand. If someone had raised the alarm, he might have been able to offer assistance. Alas, the Gowens had neither the coin nor the will to hire guards. Not even after the Battle of Bannockburn, when retaliatory Scottish raiding parties had grown indiscriminate in these parts.

Although Adam had never thought this raid was indiscriminate.

The Gowen's were recognized as hard workers; their lands known to be fertile. The harvest had only recently been brought in.

Adam could not think that any of this was a coincidence.

As if sensing his distress, his horse enacted a side-stepping dance, flinging his head up and down.

"Steady there," Adam soothed him.

But his own eyes were glassy with tears as fresh memories assaulted him. Up ahead was the oak tree, where he and Clara used to meet. Beneath its boughs they had exchanged their youthful promises, and he had stolen kisses from her willing lips.

That and more besides.

They had been but a sennight from their wedding day.

Enough.

There was a reason he kept such memories firmly locked inside his heart. Emotion had no place in the life of a warrior.

Gritting his teeth, Adam turned the horse around and pointed him back toward Ember Hall. He would return to his duties and not neglect them again.

The September sun was beginning to descend behind the hills as he turned into the gates of the hall. The guards recognized him and stood aside to allow him through without a word. He trotted up the well-trodden path, feeling the familiar ache in his legs and back. In all his five and thirty summers, he had never felt so weary.

The horse knew well which stable belonged to him. Adam was obliged to dismount rapidly, before the horse carried him all the way inside. A passing stable lad laughed at his misfortune.

"He'll be wanting his oats," the lad opined. "Shall I take him from you, sir?"

"Nay, do not trouble yourself. I shall see to my own horse." Adam smiled to take the sting from his words. It was nice to hear the accent of his childhood, even though he had grown well used to the highland brogue spoken at Kielder Castle.

He led the horse into a good-sized, well-swept stable and removed the saddle and bridle, calculating how long it was since he last stepped on English soil.

Those painful months immediately after Clara's death were all a blur to him. Lady Elizabeth, Callum's sweet-natured mother, was taken from them at a similar time, leaving Adam with no one to turn to.

No one but Rory Baine, who was determined to return to the highlands.

They had left Egremont House some four and ten summers

since. At first, Adam had journeyed north with the full intention of taking revenge for Clara's death. Rory's relentless insistence on training meant he was battle-ready and strong. His body was fit and his blood burned for vengeance. But the Scots, he soon learned, were just normal people going about their normal lives. He could hardly butcher an innkeeper and call it retribution. Before he could turn about, they were at Kielder Castle, where Adam had remained ever since.

In place of hatred, bonds of friendship and loyalty grew toward the men he served alongside, every day. He ate with them, sang with them, grieved with them. When Kielder Castle was razed by English troops, he shared his comrades' anger and despair. He gazed upon the bloody pile of lifeless bodies inside the curtain wall, and did not think those deaths were any less senseless because of their Scottish descent.

It was not until he beheld the youthful beauty of Lady Esme, that he realized how much time had passed by; how old he had become.

Adam patted the horse, who was diligently eating his way through a bucket of oats, before picking up his saddle and carrying it out of the stable.

Despite his misgivings, he had been right to visit Clara's old home and remember exactly why he had barricaded his heart.

He must take care to ensure those defenses remained in place.

Adam took the horse's tack to the harness room and nodded to the grooms gathered there. Lips tightening with purpose, he walked through the arched front door of Ember Hall, stepping into a different world.

Heat and light enveloped him, making him blink after the gathering darkness outside. His mouth watered at the scent of roasting meat and garlic which was wafting from the kitchen. But the most transformative element of all, was the singing.

He sagged against a carved dresser in the stone-flagged entrance hall as the emotions he had tried to lock away instead burst free and enveloped him. With every sweetly sung note, more of Adam's defenses crumbled. Tears pricked at the corners of his eyes when the lady's voice soared high, and when she finally drew to a close, he was done for.

Praise be, no one was there to witness his temporary vulnerability.

Adam straightened his back and waited for his customary calm rationality to take over. Once he was sufficiently composed, he continued his path to the great hall, where domesticity awaited.

Orange flames flickered in the hearth. Esme sat on a tapestried chair, drawn close to the fire. On her lap was curled the little black cat of this morn. Esme still sang, only quietly, as if to herself. One hand stroked the purring cat whilst the other supported her head. Her hair, golden as the sun, rippled down her back.

Adam wanted to melt away, to preserve this vision of beauty without spoiling it with his big boots and sullenness. But Esme was already turning towards him, her rosy pink lips turning up in the bright smile he had come to associate with her.

"Adam," she said warmly as if they were old friends.

He made an awkward sort of bow. "Lady Esme."

"I am so pleased to see you. Felicity and I have been longing for some company. Come and sit beside me." She indicated another chair, close to the hearth.

Adam's legs carried him forward, even as his mind conjured myriad reasons why he should walk away.

"Have you had a pleasant day?" she asked innocently.

Adam gave her another glance as he perched on the chair. She did not seem cross at her abandonment, only happy that he had returned.

"Pleasant enough." His voice was too rough for this room, for this lady.

"The day has dragged for me." She threw him another smile. "Tell me, do you know how to play chess?"

The question startled him. Aye, he knew. 'Twas one way to pass the long hours of darkness in a highland winter. He shifted uncomfortably in the grand chair.

He should lie.

But her cornflower blue eyes were fixed upon him, and he could not tell an untruth under her all-seeing gaze.

"I do."

She clasped her hands together, startling the cat who gave a quiet mew of protest.

"Excellent. There is a set in the solar. We can bring it in after dinner."

"Do you play, milady?"

He couldn't help himself. He was curious.

And her smile is radiant, and life is short.

"Badly." Her expression grew mischievous. "Perchance you can instruct me in how to improve my game?"

He cleared his throat, telling himself that the warmth in his cheeks was due to his proximity to the fire.

"I am hardly skilled enough to be your teacher. I am certain your brother, Lord Jonah, must be a better player."

She waved a hand dismissively. "Jonah is far too clever to waste his time on a dullard like me." She stroked the cat who resumed its loud purring. "Besides, my brother has stated his intentions of remaining in the solar. You will have to forgive his rudeness; Jonah has always been a law unto himself. I'm afraid 'tis just you and I, Adam."

Just you and I.

Whilst Esme's attention was fixed on the cat, Adam allowed himself to glance in her direction. Now that he had spent more time in her company, he could see that her resemblance to Clara was spurious. They were both slender young women, with golden hair and winning smiles. That was the beginning and end of it.

What had put him so in mind of his lost love, was the way Esme made him feel.

'Twas the way Clara had once made him feel.

Light of heart. Hopeful. As if life was his for the taking.

He leaned back against tapestried head rest and tried to recall why he had been so adamant to stay away from her.

"I am glad to discover you play chess. You do not have the appearance of a man much used to rest and relaxation."

Surprised, he swung his gaze to meet with hers. "How so?"

"Even sitting in this chair, you are not relaxed. Your body is braced to flee."

He could not tell her the truth.

That my wariness is on account of her beauty.

"There is little room for relaxation in the life of a warrior."

She considered this with her head to one side, as the logs crackled in the grate and the setting sun cast a fiery glow about the distant hills, still visible through the open shutters.

"Even now? With peace declared between England and Scotland? My brother Tristan is a knight through and through, but even he has lain down his sword and embraced the life of a happily married man."

Her words stung like saltwater on a fresh wound.

Adam avoided her gaze and closed his mind to what he might have enjoyed as a happily married man.

"I would argue that now is as fraught a time as any, milady." His voice showed his strain. "England has a young, impressionable King who stands in the shadow of an ambitious interloper, ever greedy for more."

"Roger Mortimer." Esme nodded. "He has dined at Wolvesley, with my father."

But Adam was no longer thinking of Roger Mortimer. He considered instead that he was an ambitious interloper, daring to converse with the daughter of an earl as if he were her equal.

When his duties were to guard her, as a servant.

He abruptly rose to his feet, making the startled cat jump down to the floor.

"I will bid you good night, milady."

Esme's eyes opened wider. "But the sun is barely setting. We have not yet eaten."

"'Tis not my place to eat beside you," he said gruffly.

Esme stood up, graceful as a dancer. "You must eat, Adam."

He was gauche and awkward at her side. "With the servants, in the kitchen."

"Nay." She made an impatient gesture. "You are a personal friend of Callum's."

"I serve his father." He fixed his gaze on the knots of wood in the floor.

"Must I beg you for your company?" She folded her arms across her chest and smiled sadly.

Nay, my fragile resolve would not withstand that.

"I beg you not to."

He must walk away from her; else he might sit back down in the comfortable chair and forget all that held him upright in life.

Adam bowed awkwardly and strode from the room.

CHAPTER SIX

ESME HAD NEVER spent so long in her own company.

As the sun began to set on the second full day since Frida's departure, she stood at the window of the long gallery and felt such a swell of frustration rise in her breast that she thought she might scream.

The days were endless, and neither Jonah nor Adam saw fit to offer her any sense of reprieve. She had never been one to settle to sewing, and the weather was not conducive to long walks. At luncheon, she had been so desperate for company that she stood outside the solar door, ready to knock and face Jonah's wrath. But something stayed her hand.

Her brother was famous in her family for his sour moods, but usually Esme could break through his defenses with a combination of teasing and cajoling. Something was different this time. Perchance he really was unwell?

Shall I send for a physician?

And say what? That her brother was refusing to entertain her?

Esme slunk away from the solar, but Jonah's wellbeing still played on her mind. If she were in a better temper, she might attempt to gain entry to his private lair and pester him until he admitted what ailed him. But on this day, her temper was near enough as foul as his own. Any attempt at discourse would most likely lead to an argument.

At least I am not with child.

Esme put a hand to her abdomen, feeling the familiar dull ache in the small of her back. Her courses had begun late last night, and the relief of it had carried her right through the long hours of early morn. But sometime before midday, the paneled walls of the hall had begun to press in on her and the silence to throb in her ears. She had grabbed her bonnet and shawl and scurried out into the courtyard, determined to seek out Adam and press him into some form of conversation. Yesterday evening, seated with him in the great hall, she had imagined they were both enjoying themselves. Words had flowed easily between them. What had she said to make him leave so suddenly?

His expression had been as fixed and sullen as Jonah's when he bade her good night.

The wind had been blustery outside, threatening to whip Esme's bonnet right off her head. She had ploughed on, regardless, demanding of a stable lad where she might find the man called Adam.

"The great big man come down from Scotland?" the boy had asked, wide-eyed.

"The very same." She restrained her smile.

"He's chopping firewood."

In all her days, Esme had never before stood behind a tree and watched a man chopping firewood. But if all men displayed the grace and strength of Adam whilst swinging an axe, she might very well take up the habit.

Her lips had fallen open at the sight of him, shirt sleeves rolled up to his elbows and brows lowered in concentration. The axe rose and fell with rhythmic regularity, so that time slipped away, and Esme was both chilled and stiff when he placed the final log onto the stump.

'Twas then she realized that he knew she watched him.

This knowledge sat in the set of his broad shoulders and the determination of his head never to look to the right. Her cheeks burned with awkwardness, and she slunk back to the hall in a worse mood than when she left it.

Later, stood here at the big window in the long gallery, she had watched Adam walking from the courtyard to the main gate, where he joined the guards on duty at the fortified wall.

His sword had gleamed in the scant afternoon sunlight, and his back was unyielding as he fixed his gaze on the horizon, as if there was every chance a marauding horde might really be making its way over the hills to Ember Hall.

Ridiculous.

He was so pompous, she thought. So joyless. She would do better to ignore him entirely. But then she remembered how he had clung to the dresser, tears shining in his eyes, when he first came into the hall and heard her singing yesterday. The door had been open, and she had a clear view of it all, though she would never mention it—to him nor anyone else.

She had known, instinctively, that Adam's moments of vulnerability were few and far between. Her song had, somehow, unlocked some river of emotion that he usually kept damned.

It was proof that the grim-faced, silent man had feelings after all.

A soft pressure on her calves made her look down, to find Felicity winding about her legs, her black tail waving in the air.

"Are you hungry?" Esme inquired.

The little cat butted its head against her skirts until Esme bent down and scooped her up.

"Let's go and find you something to eat."

She walked carefully down the stairs, pleased that Felicity was content to lay without protest in her arms. Esme had never before had soul responsibility for a living creature, but so far, the role was oddly satisfying.

Mayhap, one day she would make a good mother?

Esme shook the thought from her mind. Her only chance for marriage and a family lay with Crispin.

Crispin, who was noticeably absent.

Crispin, whose long-admired boyish good looks were already beginning to lose their charm in her mind's eye.

She had brought the straw ring he'd hastily made for her all the way here, to Ember Hall, secreting it in a small drawer of her dresser. But yesterday, when she fetched it out, she'd seen clearly that it was not a ring at all. 'Twas only a long strand of straw, grown limp over time.

In a sudden rush of temper, she had thrown it away, and in the hours since she had refused to allow herself to feel ill at ease over this.

But if Esme allowed it, she could grow rather ill at ease about the way Crispin had treated her.

How dare he do…*that*? And then ride away? And then leave her here, waiting endlessly, without so much as a word?

Felicity squirmed and Esme realized she had been squeezing the little cat too tightly.

"I'm sorry," she apologized, rounding the corner into the kitchen.

Agnes, the cook, was wiping down the vast oak table, her long grey plait swinging over one shoulder. She glanced up at Esme and muttered a greeting.

Esme was more accustomed to servants who bowed and curtsied in her presence, but she knew that Frida ran her household along different lines to Wolvesley Castle.

"May I have something for the cat to eat?" she asked, shifting Felicity in her arms.

Agnes smiled slightly. "That was Miss Flora's usual refrain. I understand the creature is fond of cold meats and fish. You can take your pick from the cold store."

Esme looked about her blankly until Agnes pointed her in the right direction. She was slightly put out that the cook had not gone and rustled up something herself. But equally, was pleased to be occupied with a task. She shivered in the chill air as she walked past the dairy and into the stone-flagged cold store, where her first instinct was to squeal in protest at the sight of so much death.

"'Tis only meat, milady." Agnes had come up behind her and

was gently nudging her to one side.

"Not in a form I am used to seeing." Esme put a hand to her mouth and nose, fearing she might gag at the smell. Felicity took this opportunity to jump from her arms.

"Mayhap you'll get along better with fish. This one's already skinned and gutted for you?" Agnes gestured toward a platter of pale fleshy meat.

"Whatever you think." Esme moved toward the platter, but Agnes got there before her.

"Do not fret, milady. I shall fetch it for you."

Feeling mildly chastised, Esme followed the cook back into the warmth of the main kitchen. "You are thinking that little Flora has a stronger stomach than I do," she stated.

"I said naught of the like." Agnes divided up the fish and put some down in the corner for Felicity to inspect.

"You would be right." Esme pushed back her hair and attempted a smile.

Agnes smiled back. "'Tis all a matter of upbringing, milady. And you were raised the daughter of an earl."

"As was my sister Frida," Esme interjected.

"Aye, but Frida came here determined to live a different sort of life." Agnes wiped her hand on a cloth, wincing a little.

"What has happened to your finger?" Esme moved closer, noticing the jagged edges of a clean cut, stretching all along the cook's index finger.

"Naught but a scratch."

"A deep one," Esme countered. "Frida would pack it with honey, I am sure."

Agnes screwed up her nose. "Honey is no good. It sticks to everything, and I cannot get about my work for it."

Esme's mind raced. There were other herbs that Frida would suggest on such an occasion, but she had never paid much attention to her older sister's healing abilities.

She had never thought she would have the need.

"I will go to her store and see what I can find."

Agnes shook her head. "'Tis a kind thought, milady. But I would not put you to any trouble. Besides, Lady Frida took her salves with her up to Scotland."

"She will not have taken all of them." Esme was renewed with purpose. "And in all honesty, Agnes, I would welcome a little trouble. My day has been dull indeed, thus far."

The cook smiled. "As you wish."

Esme pulled her sister's cloak from the hook by the back door and set off into the gloaming. Frida's cloak billowed about her, for Esme was the smallest of the de Neville sisters, but the scent of sage—trapped in the woolen folds—reminded her of times past, when Frida would bathe her childhood cuts and caution her against jumping from the stone basin of the Wolvesley fountain. She found the store quickly, unfastening the door and breathing in the aroma of so many dried herbs. Bunches hung from the ceiling and glass jars gleamed from the narrow shelves, but Agnes was correct; Frida had taken at least half her stock with her.

Esme put her hands on her hips and looked about. She should have thought to bring a candle. It was hard to make anything out in the twilight.

Think, she told herself. *Try to remember.*

She did not want to return to the hall empty handed.

Perchance there was something in here that would help Jonah with his pain.

Esme resolved to return in the daylight. But thoughts of her brother had helped her to recall what Frida used to treat his many injuries.

Mint on an open wound. Comfrey once it had closed.

Esme could not have identified comfrey in a darkened room if someone offered her coin to do so. But mint had a distinctive smell. She stood on her tiptoes and sniffed at the bunches of dried herbs until she was satisfied, she had the right one. Smiling, she lifted it free and all but ran back to the kitchen.

"Here," she thrust the bunch of dried mint toward Agnes.

At the cook's surprised look, Esme shrugged her shoulders. "I am not certain what to do with it. But mint is what Frida would choose in place of honey."

Agnes's eyes creased at the corners as she smiled. "Thank you, milady." She took the herbs. "I shall work things out from here."

More light of heart than she had felt for many days, Esme prepared to leave the kitchen. The sliver of fish in the corner caught her eye as she turned.

"Where is Felicity?"

"The little cat?" Agnes put down the mint and looked about her. "She was here just a minute ago."

"I left the back door open." Esme froze, flooded with horror. Flora had explicitly said that Felicity should not go out at night.

I have failed her.

"I daresay she will come back if you call her." Agnes did not look convinced.

Nonetheless, Esme ran back into the darkening night, Frida's cloak slipping over her shoulders.

"Felicity," she called.

An owl hooted back in reply. She looked about the empty courtyard and felt a fool.

How could she hope to find a small cat who might be any-where at all?

Her exultation at helping Agnes drained away. She would be better off keeping to herself, staying away from people and certainly not taking charge of small creatures. She should have known better.

A gust of wind made her stagger backward and simultaneous-ly, her childhood insecurities rose up to take hold. As a young girl, Esme had known, without anyone telling her, that she would never share Isabella's beauty, nor Frida's wisdom. She had been determined to make the best of it, but who was she fooling?

I have made a mess of everything.

"Felicity," she tried again, her voice echoing around the silent outbuildings.

It was no good. Tears leaked at the corners of her eyes. Felicity was still small enough to be taken by an owl or a fox. Mayhap even another cat. There were several of them living wild in the barns.

I must try to find her.

She stepped further into the darkness, her boots stumbling on the uneven cobbles. Footsteps came toward her and in her state of distress, she feared that one of Callum's mysterious villains was about to steal her away. She swung around to see Adam brandishing a lantern.

Her relief was quickly followed by a hot flush of shame.

"Esme." Concern rippled through his deep voice. "What ails you?"

She gathered what dignity she could. "Naught." She sniffed, wishing she had put up her hood so that her face might be hidden from the yellow light of the lantern.

"You are upset," he stated calmly.

There was nothing to be gained by pretending otherwise.

"I have lost Flora's cat. I left the back door open." She gestured behind her. "She's gone."

Adam paused, swinging his lantern toward the barns and then back to her. "Then let us find her."

Her knees weakened. "You would do that for me?"

"For you, for Flora, for Felicity." He grinned, transforming from a stern-faced warrior to a kindly man. "We can at least try."

"Thank you." She took his arm and smiled up at him, holding on even when he flinched away. His green eyes showed such emotion, on the rare occasions when his face was not fixed in an expression of steel. She cleared her throat. "Where will we look."

He pulled his gaze away from her. "Where would you go, if you were a cat?"

Her eyebrows shot upward. "That is not a question I have ever given any thought to."

He was trying not to smile; she could see his lips puckering. "Still, 'tis a question that demands an answer."

A droplet of rain fell onto her cheek. It would not do to stand about overly long in inclement weather.

"I would go somewhere warm and dry." She was pleased with her deductions. "And mayhap someplace I could hide away." She thought of Felicity's small size and feline instincts.

"The hayloft." Adam began walking towards the largest of the stone outbuildings.

But Esme hung back, assaulted by memories of the last time she had entered a hay store with a man.

Adam turned back in surprise. "Are you not coming?"

He had lifted the lantern high enough to illuminate the rugged lines of his face and the honest enquiry in his eyes.

Esme's worries quietened. She had naught to fear from Adam. Had Callum not said the very same thing?

Callum would never leave her in the safekeeping of a man he did not trust absolutely.

She smiled briskly and joined him, taking his arm so she might better pick her way across the cobbles under the yellow glow of the lantern.

A thought niggled at her brain; one she could not ignore.

Callum would never have left her in the safekeeping of Crispin.

She imagined her plain-spoken brother-in-law eyeing up the knight who had so readily walked away from her.

Callum would have found Crispin wanting.

Adam stood back to allow Esme to enter the stable block ahead of him. "Here, take this," he said, passing her the lantern when she paused in the darkness.

"Thank you."

Esme had a fear of cobwebs, and the musty stable seemed as if it might be full of them. But she could not shrink away and wait outside; not without abandoning yet more of her dignity. She took a deep breath and began to clamber up the wooden staircase to the hayloft, holding the lantern before her like some kind of lucky charm. Once or twice, she stepped on the ends of Frida's cloak and risked tipping backwards into Adam's arms. She managed to save herself, but the idea of it made her smile inside. Without incident, they emerged into the hay-scented warmth of the loft, where Adam was obliged to duck his head beneath the low ceiling.

"Can you see her?" he asked. His hand was on her shoulders, though whether this was to steady her, or to steady himself, she could not say.

She liked the weight of it. Indeed, she fought an urge to move closer to his muscular body. 'Twas hard to see more than mere outlines in the half-light, but those outlines were mighty attractive.

"Esme?"

A beat too late, she remembered why they were here. Turning back to the well-stacked hay, she swung the lantern in an arc.

"Felicity?" she called.

There was no reply, save a slight scratching sound.

Esme raised her eyebrows questioningly, but Adam pursed his lips.

"Rats," he suggested.

"Rats!"

It took every ounce of self-restraint she had not to jump into his arms.

"But that isn't a rat." He nodded over her shoulder. "'Tis a cat."

"Felicity." Relief flooded her. The small black cat was curled up amidst a pile of hay. When Esme stroked her head, she stretched out her front paws and yawned widely. "You had me very worried," Esme told her severely.

"Never was a cat so well-tended." Adam nudged her with his elbow, and she couldn't help but laugh.

"I am only following Flora's instructions."

"As is right and proper." He gave her a little bow. "Shall we return to the hall? Or is there some other animal you wish to locate?"

"We should return." Esme passed the lantern back to Adam

and scooped up the cat. "I will lock you up," she threatened Felicity.

"I shall go down first, then turn around and light your way." Adam brushed past her at the top of the stairwell, making her newly conscious of his height and strength.

He did exactly as he promised, holding the lantern high so that Esme felt quite safe descending the wooden stairs with the cat in her arms. In no time at all, they had reached the front door of the hall. Esme ensured the door was closed behind them before settling Felicity down on the stone flags.

"Thank you," she said sincerely.

But Adam's previous ease seemed to have once again vanished. He stood awkwardly, a few feet away from her, his arms hanging by his sides.

"You are welcome, milady. I'll say goodnight to you now."

This time, she was having none of it. Esme closed the distance between them and took hold of his elbow.

"You will not say good night," she said sweetly. "You will sit with me in the great hall, and we will play a game of chess."

CHAPTER SEVEN

ADAM ADMITTED THE truth to himself. He had wanted to kiss her in the hayloft. Forsooth, he wanted to kiss her now. She was sweet and spirited and kind, a balm to his troubled soul.

She was also the daughter of an earl.

He chanted Callum's name inside his head like a mantra, to ensure he did not forget why he was here.

"I will not take no for an answer," Esme declared, raising her eyebrows in a challenge. Her touch at his elbow sent frissons of awareness all the way through him.

Does she know how alluring she is?

He cleared his throat. "I am not at Ember Hall in the capacity of a visitor, milady. I am here to guard you."

For a moment, he thought she might argue the point, but the lady merely shrugged. The dark-colored cloak she was wearing slipped further over her shoulders, revealing the patterned sleeves of an intricately sewn gown.

Another reminder of the difference in their status. Adam thought of the plain cotton tunic he had changed into after bathing. It had once been a deep blue but had faded with age and was threadbare in patches. Not because he was without the means to dress well, but because he put little store by his appearance.

"You are here to keep me safe." She tilted her head upright, looking at him mischievously. "Mind, body, and soul."

"That is correct."

She leaned closer. "I stand to lose my mind entirely if I do not have the company of someone other than a cat." As one, they both glanced down at Felicity who was weaving about their feet. "You must play a game of chess with me, Adam. To keep my spirits high."

Her logic was hard to counter. Especially when he wanted to agree with her.

"As you wish, milady. But I can only play one game."

"I also wish for you to stop addressing me as milady." Esme threw him a look over her shoulder as she led the way into the great hall. "If memory serves me right, I have already made this request. And if you are here as my servant, rather than my friend, I must insist that you adhere to my requests."

He breathed out sharply. Aye, he had been explicitly—and consciously—going against her invitation. But if he addressed this fine lady only by her given name, yet another barrier between them would begin to crumble.

"Here we are." Esme paused by the flickering fire. "We need to pull up those two chairs and lift this table between them."

Without hesitating, he did as he was bid. Any physical activity helped quieten the warring voices in his head. Moving the heavy furniture caused his heart rate to increase; at least, that was what he told himself.

Esme slipped off her cloak and draped it on the window seat, talking softly to Felicity who promptly jumped onto the cloak and curled up to go to sleep. Esme bent down gracefully and extracted a carved wooden box from a large trunk.

"I fetched this from the solar yesterday." Her eyes danced. "In the hope that we might play."

Adam stood awkwardly by the nearest chair, waiting for Esme to sit down so that he might do the same. But instead, Esme waltzed over to the hearth and pulled on the bell rope.

Finally, she came to join him, sinking gracefully into a tapestried chair and crossing her ankles.

"Will you set the game up?"

He took the box from her, careful to ensure his fingers did not brush against hers. The box doubled as the board, straightening out into a level surface once the pieces had been safely extracted. He lined up them up at one side of the table, noting the exquisite detail in the carving and the smoothness of the wood.

He was not accustomed to such beauty.

"Would you care to be black or white?" he asked, keeping his eyes trained on the board.

"You choose." Esme was nonchalant. "I find it makes very little difference." He felt, rather than saw, the warmth of her smile. "Ah, Jennifer. Thank you. Please could you bring us some wine?"

Wine.

Adam knew he was walking a path that led directly to danger, but he could not seem to alter it.

I do not want to alter it.

He set up the board, so the white pieces were before Esme, allowing her to make the first move. She put very little thought to the game, gazing languidly at the fire and then making space on the table for two goblets when Jennifer appeared with the tray.

This will not take long, Adam told himself. He could decently retire to his chamber before the wine, however fine, muddled his thinking further.

He studied the board as he took a long mouthful, surprised to find that Esme had all but backed him into a corner. His eyes widened as he considered this. Was it a deliberate strategy or an accident?

Esme was now examining a row of pearl buttons at the cuff of here sleeve.

Accident, he decided.

But he had to put down his goblet and think deeply before executing his next move.

Esme seemed hardly to notice his deliberations. She moved her knight and captured his rook with a playful smile.

"Luck is with me, this night."

He eyed her speculatively. "A very good move, milady."

"Esme." She held his gaze and frowned.

"Esme." His cheeks were warm, from the fire and the wine and the beautiful young woman sitting so close he could feel her breath as she leaned over the board.

He took a while to decide on his next move. There were many ways he might win, but he was enjoying the gameplay. No matter how much he chanted the name *Callum* in his head, he could not bring himself to wind things up promptly.

Besides, Callum was a man who appreciated the complex strategies of chess. He and Adam had played many an interesting game; first at Egremont House and latterly at Kielder Castle, before Callum married Frida.

Callum was a worthy opponent, but Adam was beginning to think that Esme was almost his equal.

Still, he had espied a route to success. A sneaky one, that the lady did not notice until it was too late.

"Well done." She clapped her hands as he toppled her King.

With his innate competitive spirit satisfied, a new thought occurred to him. Mayhap he should have allowed Esme to win? But the lady did not seem upset. Indeed, she gathered up the remaining pieces with great equanimity.

"I see I have a lot to learn from you, Adam," she declared. "We must play again so that I can study your technique."

Knowledge slid into him, like a knife through butter. He sat back and rubbed at the stubble on his chin.

"Did you allow me to win?"

A frown darted across her brow. "Most certainly, I did not." She cleared her throat, positioning her chess pieces back in the box. "I am a de Neville, Adam. Winning is in our blood."

He took another mouthful of wine and contemplated this.

"I ask again." He folded his hands and fixed her with a firm expression. "Esme, did you allow me to win."

This time a peal of laughter escaped her. "Only at the very

end," she admitted. "You were so pleased with your strategy; I could not bring myself to disappoint you. And it was a very clever set of moves." She held up a finger, as if disallowing any complaint.

But Adam was sorely vexed. "Never has this happened to me before. Not even when I was a child of ten."

Esme closed the box neatly. "Well, there is a first time for everything."

"I cannot believe it." He drummed his fingers on the table, tempted to demand a rematch.

Esme's lips were working to repress a smile. "I see how this vexes you and I apologize for it. In truth, I did not suspect you would catch me out."

He watched her closely. "You mean you have done this before."

She nodded once, having the grace to look abashed. "I am the youngest of five siblings. Two of which are brothers. *Very* competitive brothers." She paused for emphasis. "I learned at a young age that ofttimes it was easier to let them win, than to deal with the sulking when they did not."

He could not help but admire this. "And they have never found you out?"

Esme put her head to one side. "I love my brothers dearly, both of them, despite their faults." She raised her eyebrows comically. "Tristan and Jonah are quick-witted and smart. They have never doubted their ability to win."

He leaned closer, imitating her air of conspiracy. "That is a failing of sorts."

"Indeed, it is." She nodded seriously, before laughing once again. "But you caught me out, Adam. Clearly, you are a man without failings."

"I would not make that claim."

But he took another mouthful of wine, rather than allow his aggrieved mind to begin listing them.

"There is more expected of brothers than sisters." Esme

gazed into the fire, oblivious of the pretty picture she made, with her golden hair gleaming in the candlelight. "Girls do not have to be quick-witted and smart. They do not have to win. They merely have to smile obediently."

Adam recalled the way Esme had argued her cause for remaining at Ember Hall. "You will forgive me for asking this, but is obedience truly a quality that your family hold dear?"

"To a point, aye." Her expression grew serious. "But I know I have gotten away with a great deal in life, mainly because I am the daughter of a very wealthy man." She met his gaze with something like defiance sparking in her blue eyes. "Perchance that is the quality most sought in a woman, even over obedience."

He had not anticipated such philosophy from one so young and seemingly unburdened.

"Coin?" he clarified.

She nodded. "I have oft thought how much simpler my life would be without it."

He could not answer this. Not without remembering another young woman with a radiant smile, whose family's lack of coin had cost her dearly.

Instead, he made his voice light. "I am but a warrior, who makes his living with his sword. But I have oft thought that the offspring of wealthy men can do much as they please."

He knew this was not entirely true. Rory Baine had once been a wealthy man, but young Callum had been twisted several ways by the dictates of familial responsibility.

Esme matched his more jovial tone, picking up her goblet and taking a long drink of wine. "The sons, mayhap."

"But not the daughters?"

He should bring this interlude to an end, not indulge with banter that was becoming flirtatious.

"You saw yourself what an almighty fuss was made over my simple desire to remain at Ember Hall. When the continued presence of Jonah is never called to question. *He* is one who can do as he pleases."

Adam pictured the young man with a face sharpened by pain. "Do you really think that is true?"

Esme looked away from him, fixing her gaze once again on the fire and sighing deeply. "Nay, 'tis not so simple. Jonah has troubles of his own. We all do." She shrugged.

Adam found himself moved by this show of vulnerability. It tugged at his heartstrings and brought him even closer to danger.

"I am sorry to hear that, milady."

Her response was swift. Immediately she moved her hand so that it covered his. "Nay, do not call me that. You have been doing so well."

He should move his hand away, but Ye Gods, he did not want to.

Esme's fingers were long, slender and warm. The warmth went straight to his heart. As seconds ticked by and neither of them moved, tension began to fill the air between them. Adam dared not raise his head to meet her eyes. He dared hardly breathe.

It was Esme who finally lifted her hand from his and spoke up as if naught amiss had occurred. "Tell me, Adam, what is it that you would do differently, if you could live life as you pleased?"

It took a while for him to find his voice. Even longer for his mind to make sense of the question.

I would leave the service of Rory Baine. The words were on his lips, but loyalty—to Callum if no one else—meant he could not utter them.

"I would work the fields." Instead, he voiced his youthful ambition. "As a farmer," he clarified. "Just as my father before me. With land to pass onto my sons."

She nodded slowly, her eyes widening in surprise. "'Tis not common for a warrior to seek a life of peace."

He thought of his father's readiness to lay down his weapons. "'Tis more common than you might think."

Silence fell between them, but it was not an awkward silence. The log crackled in the fire and occasional footsteps sounded overhead. Adam fancied he could hear the old house stretching and settling itself, ready for the night ahead.

Her next question was more hesitant. "You would like sons?"

Adam swallowed. This was not a matter he had given voice to for many years. "Of course. If I were living life as I pleased."

A pain of some kind flickered in Esme's eyes. But it had gone as soon as it appeared, leaving Adam to wonder if he had imagined it.

"What about you?" He smiled, to relieve the tension. "What would Esme de Neville do differently?"

Ye Gods, he was not anticipating the shimmer of tears in her beautiful eyes.

But her voice was steady as she replied. "Many things, too many to list here."

"Tell me just one." He wanted to see her smile again.

Esme met his gaze levelly. "I will not do that until we have more wine." Before he could protest, she had crossed the room and pulled again on the bell rope.

"'Tis late," he tried, pursing his lips regretfully.

But Esme shook her head, golden hair flying out around her. "You asked me a question and I shall give you an answer." She looked inside her goblet and replaced it on the table with a huff of displeasure. "Entirely empty," she explained.

This time, Jennifer anticipated the request and brought a full pitcher of wine into them. Adam eyed the scarlet liquid and tried to ignore the voice of warning in his head.

Esme refilled their goblets and sat back, cradling hers. "If I could do anything I pleased, I would learn how to wield a sword."

Adam all but choked on his mouthful of wine.

"That is not what I expected to hear." He was pleased to see Esme's customary smile return.

"I am a woman of surprises."

"You are." His mind sounded another note of warning. But the wine was rich and good, and Adam found that he could easily ignore these warnings. "Might I ask why?"

"Why I wish to train with a sword?"

He nodded.

"Is that not obvious?" Esme's fingertips drew imaginary circles on the table. "If I could wield a sword well, I could protect myself."

"You would have no need of me?" The words came from him before he could think better of them.

But Esme's eyes danced as she met his challenge. "I would have need of no man." She put her goblet on the table and opened her arms wide. "I could go wherever I pleased, and no man would say *'tis not safe for you to stay here.*"

"As Callum did?"

"Exactly that."

"But soon you will marry and have a wealthy husband to protect you." His gaze clashed with hers and held it.

Esme did not allow a beat to pass. "Nay, I will never marry."

The shock of this proclamation robbed him again of words. "You are a woman of surprises," he echoed.

"It has been said before." Esme took another long mouthful of wine and Adam, unable to think what else to do, did the same.

I will never marry.

She had stated this with conviction, with no blushing coyness or scarcely veiled irritation at a former suitor.

"'Tis no passing fancy," she broke into his thoughts. "I mean what I say."

"I do not doubt it."

Silence fell between them once again. This time, Adam was painfully aware of Esme's proximity; of the rise and fall of her breasts beneath the bodice of her gown and the sadness he had glimpsed in her eyes.

Something must have happened.

But 'twas no business of his. He must not ask any questions, despite his longing to offer comfort.

But I can offer her a solution.

"Did you know that I was the one to first teach Callum how

to swing a sword?"

Interest flared in her finely-boned face. "I did not." Her fingers danced along the tabletop. "You must have taught him well. My brother Tristan is not easily impressed, but he sang Callum's praises when they trained together at Lindum."

Adam brushed aside the compliment. "That is all due to Callum himself, not my early training."

"Nevertheless." Esme threw him a smile and he knew she wanted him to make the offer that was waiting on his lips.

He breathed through his nerves. "I will do the same for you, if you wish?"

"You will teach me to use a sword?" Esme grasped the tabletop and leaned forward in delight, as if he had offered an introduction to Queen Isabella herself.

"We will see how far we get." Commonsense was taking hold now. Esme was an earl's daughter. Surely, she could not rampage along the moors with a wooden sword?

Esme clapped her hands in delight. "You will find me a fast learner," she promised, darting up from the chair and miming a sword thrust, much as she had on the day Adam first arrived.

He found himself laughing along with her enthusiasm. "That is another thing that I do not doubt."

She grew still and serious. "You have made me very happy."

"You are welcome." He had never meant it more.

"May we start on the morrow?" Her eyes shone with hope.

What have I done?

"We may," he confirmed.

Esme took two quick steps toward him, leaned down and planted a quick kiss on his forehead. The gesture took him so by surprise, he did not react at all.

"Thank you, Adam," she whispered.

By the time Adam had recovered his composure, the lady had disappeared. He was alone by the flickering fire, with a hundred conflicting thoughts warring in his head.

CHAPTER EIGHT

W HAT SHOULD A *lady wear to learn to fight with a sword?*

Pushing aside the oilcloth and gazing out of her bed-chamber window, Esme amended her question.

What should a lady wear to learn to fight with a sword in the swirling fog?

The green hills around Ember Hall were blanketed in grey. Esme could make out little save the hulking shape of the barns. Even the usual sounds of the stable yard were muffled.

She withdrew to her closet, shivering slightly, and rapidly discarded the choice of several flimsy gowns. This was a day for warmth, not ribbons, but she had little that would suit. She considered a day dress of stiffened wool, but the sleeves were too tight for the activity in question.

Esme was not one to readily accept defeat. Fastening a cloak about her shoulders to preserve her modesty, she left her bedchamber and crept along the gallery until she reached Frida's light and spacious room.

I am doing nothing wrong, she told herself sternly. But she felt like a child rummaging in her mother's closet.

Frida had long since learned to dress in accordance with the seasons. She had taken the best of her gowns with her to Kielder Castle, but Esme found several heavy tunics that would suit her purpose. Then, at the very back of the closet, she found something else.

Braccae.

She shook them out, hardly believing her eyes.

When would my decorous sister wear such an item?

At once, a dozen answers presented themselves to her. Frida had always made a point of working out in the fields. No doubt braccae were a sensible choice for herding sheep or hoeing crops, or whatever else she might do. Esme was hazy on the detail.

An outrageous idea was taking shape in her mind.

I could wear these in my lessons with Adam.

What could be better than clothing that allowed her to move about freely, without danger of tripping over long skirts?

Would it be proper?

Esme forced herself to consider this, but then remembered that her own mother, the erstwhile Countess of Wolvesley, often wore braccae when horse riding. Albeit, she had not done so for a number of years. But most certainly when Esme was a child, she could remember her mother striding about in braccae.

That settled the matter. She tucked the braccae under her arm and selected the shortest of the tunics before rushing back to her own chamber. Once dressed, she surveyed herself in the looking glass and smiled at the results.

Had her legs always been so long?

She belted the tunic with a twist of leather, then plaited her hair. What liberty to dress with such speed, without requiring the ministrations of a maid.

She was ready. Which meant she must consider the next important matter.

Will he come?

Esme put a hand to her heart, hoping to steady it. In truth, 'twas not just the lessons in sword-fighting that she was looking forward to. Her heart fluttered beneath her fingertips at the prospect of seeing Adam again.

Last night, in the great hall, conversation had flowed between them as readily as the wine. Beneath his dour exterior, Adam was a man of surprising warmth. She would never have expected to share confidences with someone of such short acquaintance.

Not once had Crispin taken the time to probe at the truth of her heart.

Pursing her lips, she closed her mind to thoughts of Crispin.

She went down to the great hall, where the trestle table was laid ready for her to break her fast. Jonah was nowhere to be seen, as was becoming the norm.

Esme filled a trencher with bread and cheese but found herself too nervous to do anything more than nibble at the edges. She tucked herself onto the window seat and only then remembered Felicity.

She had forgotten her charge!

Esme pushed herself upright, looking about her for the small black cat. She hadn't followed her up to her chamber last night. The last time she had seen her was here, on the window seat.

Acting on impulse, Esme walked through to the kitchen.

"Have you seen Felicity?" she demanded of Agnes, as soon as she was through the door.

If Agnes thought that Lady Esme's outfit was strange, she did not let her opinion show.

"Aye, milady. There's nay call to fret. She was waiting for me in here at daybreak." Agnes chuckled. "I reckon she's worked out where her meals are coming from and decided to settle in." She nodded towards the back wall, where Felicity was stretched out on a blanket which had been folded onto a low shelf.

"You put the blanket out for her?" Esme lifted her eyebrows.

"Well, she's naught but a little thing. And it does no harm." Agnes was defensive.

Esme fought a smile. "'Tis kind of you, Agnes. I'll make sure Flora knows what good care you're taking of her."

"Thank you, milady."

Esme made to walk back to the great hall, but after reaching the passageway, she paused and retraced her steps around the corner.

"Be sure not to let her out at night," she cautioned. "And if she comes looking for me, that's alright. In fact, I will most likely come looking for her."

"Very good, milady."

Smiling, Esme walked around the corner and straight into Adam. Her face cannoned into the hardness of his chest, and she grunted with the shock of it.

"Forgive me." He was the first to recover, but when she looked up at him, his mouth was set in a grim line.

"I believe the fault was mine." She went to smooth her skirts and was momentarily discomfited when her palms encountered only the narrow lines of her braccae. "Are you come to collect me for my first lesson?"

Adam's gaze was studiously fixed someplace above Esme's head. "The weather is not ideal."

"I believe warriors must turn out in all weather conditions," she said innocently.

He still refused to meet her eye.

The man who had beaten her at chess, then teased her about her brothers, had retreated behind a veneer of flintiness.

But Esme's heart fluttered all the same.

"Pray, Adam, do not disappoint me," she persisted. "I have dressed especially for the occasion."

His eyeline did not shift, but a color came to his chiseled cheeks.

"I still say that the weather is not ideal."

"And I say that fresh air and exercise should be enjoyed whatever the weather." She took his arm, as this trick had worked so well for her the night before, and boldly attempted to turn him around.

Alas, Adam was much too tall and broad to be easily turned in a narrow passageway. The two of them became crammed between the plastered walls, scarcely an inch of air separating them.

"I'm sorry," she breathed. Without the layers of protection afforded by a chemise and kirtle, she felt the press of his body all the more. She was far too warm, and it was strangely hard to catch her breath.

Adam's hands skimmed past her hips before settling on her shoulders. "You stay still," he said. He held her in place whilst swiveling around and extricating his limbs from hers.

She wanted to smile at him, to share the idiocy of the moment, but she was hot and embarrassed. And Adam looked more cross than amused.

"We will continue as planned, if that is what you want."

"It is what I want," she confirmed.

He gestured for her to walk ahead, and she proceeded him down the narrow passage, newly conscious of the way her tunic and braccae molded to the curves of her body.

Imagining his eyes upon her.

But when she glanced back, Adam was engaged in gloomy contemplation of the roof beams.

"Where shall we go?" she asked.

This time, his green eyes locked onto hers, but only for a moment. "There is a patch of level ground near the cliffs, by a circle of standing stones."

"You have researched the matter?" She was exultant.

But Adam seemed determined to be distant. "I am here to serve you."

Esme would not be cowed. "'Tis good of you to remind me." She matched his serious tone.

A smile flickered behind his grim expression; she was certain of it.

Outside, the mist settled upon her hair and clothes, making her shiver despite the warmth of Frida's sensible cloak. They walked in silence to the standing stones, which looked even more forbidding this morn, amongst the swirling greyness. The roar of the sea below reached them as if through a long tunnel. Esme might have been sorely tempted to abandon their quest entirely, but for two things.

One, the unrelenting length of her uninterrupted days—

which she did not think she could endure again.

Two, the fact the Adam was here alongside her.

She need not flinch from the perceived hostility of her surroundings with him as her protector. Not simply because he was every inch a warrior; but because he exuded a sense of safety.

And she could not deny those flutters in her belly when his all-seeing eyes glanced upon her. Eyes that had seen things that Esme could only wonder at.

"Wait here," he said, striding past her toward one of the granite monoliths.

She shivered as he was all but swallowed up in the mist, leaving her alone. He returned holding a long wooden stick.

"A stick?"

She was disappointed and her voice showed it.

"Aye. We will not begin our lessons with a broadsword sharp enough to kill a man."

He was mocking her and making little attempt to mask it.

Esme swallowed. "Very well."

Adam handed her the stick, which was more of a whittled down branch, now that she could see it more closely. It was the width of her wrist and the length of her arm. The wood was smooth and somehow warm to the touch, despite the chill of the day.

"Usually, we would use wooden swords for these lessons, but I have none to hand." His voice had relented. "Mayhap I will have the opportunity to fashion one for you. But this was the best I could do overnight."

"'Tis a fine starting weapon," she declared, twirling it in her hands. "Do you not have one for yourself?"

He folded his arms. "Nay. We will not be sparring. Not for some time yet. This is no game, milady."

I am milady again.

"I am aware of that, sir." She countered quickly.

Adam had been about to speak. Now he hesitated, his eyes swinging to hers through the mist. "Sir?"

"You are my teacher." She was beginning to enjoy herself. "I shall address you with the respect you deserve."

He stepped closer, making her belly flutter all over again. "Your respect should be for the weapon you have in your hand. Imagine the heaviness of it. Imagine the sharpness of the blade. 'Tis not a plaything to be waved about. You could take a man's head right off or gut him where you stand."

She lowered the stick to the dampened grass, accepting the reprimand.

"Your sword should become part of you," he continued. "You must accept the weight as part of your own body, 'twill alter your balance and the way you move. You must grow accustomed to it. That is perchance the hardest lesson of all."

Esme nodded, her mind whirring.

"This morn, I will teach you how to hold your weapon. And how to stand—"

"How to stand?" she interrupted.

"How to stand ready for an attack." He raised his eyebrows. "Or does milady already have this knowledge at her disposal?"

"Milady does not." She pressed her lips together. "Sir."

The crashing of the waves onto the sandy cove far below them could not match the roaring of blood in her ears when he reached for her hand. Adam's fingers were warm and strong. They rearranged Esme's grasp of the handle whilst she watched, wide-eyed.

"Like this." He swiveled his head to look at her sharply, ensuring she was paying attention.

She nodded. She had rarely been so attentive in her life.

"Straighten your arm." Standing by her side, he lifted her wrist so that her arm and weapon were at shoulder height. "Do not bend your elbow. 'Tis a point of weakness."

"Yes sir."

Ignoring her jibe, he slowly walked until he was standing behind her.

"Shoulders back." He placed his hands there, tugging gently.

"Widen your stance."

Esme shuffled her feet on the grass, stifling a strong urge to giggle.

"Look up," he instructed. "Never look at the ground, unless that is where your opponent is."

Esme lifted her chin and gazed into the swirling white.

"I cannot see my opponent for the fog."

"All the more reason to be on your guard."

His breath warmed the back of her neck. Esme felt her eyes closing. He was so close. If she leaned back just a little, her body would be pressed against his.

She did not intend to test this theory, but one of them must have moved, because all of a sudden, she was up against him. 'Twas like leaning against solid granite that had been warmed by the sun. Adam was a wall of muscle.

A wall with hands which came again to her shoulders, resting there lightly.

She breathed out, letting the tension leave her body as that delicious fluttering started up again.

"I will leave you to practice, milady."

Her eyes flew open. "You will leave?"

"We have done all we can this morn, in this weather."

His voice came from a distance, and she turned around to see he was already striding away from her.

Her disappointment was acute. But then she twirled her stick in her hands once again and reflected that this was the most entertaining morn she had experienced since arriving at Ember Hall.

Still, I should not have teased him.

He was a skilled warrior taking the time to share his craft with her. Moreover, she had fancied something akin to friendship was growing between them.

Mayhap something more than friendship.

Either way, she should have shown more sincere appreciation for his skills and his time. But he was so darned irritating with the aloofness he seemed to don like a cloak.

For a moment, she considered remaining by the standing stones and practicing her stance as Adam had suggested. But must she remain in the mist to do so?

Nay. She could practice standing up equally well in the warmth of the hall.

Esme wandered back, using the fake sword as a sort of walking stick to aid her over the uneven ground. Her actions put her in mind of Jonah, and when she encountered her brother in the great hall, her smile was genuine.

"Good morn, brother." She removed Frida's cloak and hung it on the back of a chair.

Jonah was seated at the trestle table, munching his way through a trencher of cold meats and fruit. He eyed her with interest.

"Where have you been in such foul weather?"

"Learning to fight with a sword," she answered nonchalantly, propping the stick by the window seat.

"Or with a stick?" He raised his blond eyebrows, questioningly. His hair was neatly combed, and he wore a freshly laundered tunic of green and gold, the colors of Wolvesley.

"I must start somewhere. I was not fortunate enough to have a fencing master assigned to me in childhood."

"I see." Jonah popped a glistening grape into his mouth.

"'Tis nice to see you," Esme said pointedly.

"I am feeling more myself." Jonah sat back in the wooden chair, a smile playing about his lips. "This may not be your only opportunity to converse with me this day."

"Praise be."

Her quip made her brother smile more widely. Esme stepped up to the table and tore off a hunk of fresh bread.

"You are looking mighty pleased with yourself," he remarked, watching her closely with his blue eyes.

"'Tis the fresh air and exercise."

"'Tis the company you keep, I think."

Esme stilled in the action of pulling out a chair for herself. "What can you mean?"

"Callum's warrior friend. Adam is his name. As you know well, sister dear."

Why are my cheeks becoming flushed?

"I must pass my days somehow." She shrugged.

"Games of chess. Sword fighting." When Esme pouted at him, he chuckled quietly. "There is much I can hear from my position in the solar. Much I can see through the window."

"Oh." Esme considered what she had said about Jonah that night by the fire with Adam. 'Twas naught that she would not willingly say face to face.

Except the part about her allowing him to win at chess.

"You have been enjoying yourself," he said accusingly.

"I have been bored half to death," she retorted. "Why must you shut yourself away, day after day?"

Jonah's expression became fixed. "You would not understand."

"Try me." Esme abandoned her heel of bread and leaned over the table toward him, raising her eyebrows expectantly.

Jonah sighed. "What would my beautiful little sister know of unrequited love?"

She was glad she was no longer eating, for she might have choked.

"What does my cosseted brother know of unrequited love?"

He held her gaze until she regretted her unthinking response. "Quite a bit, as it happens. But do not fret, Esme. I never expected you to notice."

She bit down on her lip and voiced a suspicion she'd nursed since their days in the school room. "Mirrie?"

He nodded.

Mirabel, or Mirrie as she was known, was once their father's ward and Frida's closest confidant. She had accompanied Frida here to Ember Hall, long before Frida met Callum. Jonah had followed them soon after.

A fact which Esme had not really registered the significance of until this moment.

Mirrie was now married to their brother Tristan and expecting his first child.

"How long?" she asked softly, wondering if she was correct.

"Forever." He smiled sadly. "But I always knew she held a torch for Tristan. And I never wanted to stand in the way of her happiness. Forsooth, I even worked to bring them together." He shook his head, as if amazed at his own foolishness.

Esme waited for a moment. "You must truly love her, if you put her happiness ahead of your own."

"Wise words indeed, from a lady who has men falling in love with her wherever she goes."

Jonah broke their air of intimacy and concentrated once more on his trencher, but she could tell he was no longer interested in breaking his fast.

"That is simply not true," she said lightly, toying with a bunch of grapes.

"You dispute the fact that you have come here to escape the many suitors clamoring for your hand back at Wolvesley?"

She swallowed, unaccountably tempted to tell Jonah the truth. One confidence for another. "'Tis not only that."

"But you admit to the clamoring suitors?"

"Oh Jonah." She threw a grape at him, but it only bounced off the table. "Aye, I admit to the clamoring suitors. But they are dazzled by Father's coin. Not by me. And if you saw fit to return to Wolvesley, there would be an equally long line of ladies eager for your acquaintance."

"Because of Father's coin?" His mouth was set in a grim line.

"Not only because of that," she insisted.

"Do not feel as if you have to pretend. Why would any woman want to be shackled to me?"

Esme winced at the raw pain shining in her brother's eyes. "Because you are handsome and clever." She thought quickly. "You pen fine poems. I am certain you could woo whomever you wished, if you ever came out of hiding."

Jonah folded his hands on the tabletop. She watched a tremor pass through them. "You are kind, Esme. 'Tis one of the reasons men fall in love with you."

She shook her head, exasperated. "This again."

"I am ofttimes an observer, not a participant. I fancy my skills of observation are sharp enough to be trusted. And I have observed the way that Adam looks at you."

A thrill rippled through her core, which she quickly disguised as a shiver. She wrapped her arms about herself and pulled her legs toward her.

"Interesting outfit," Jonah drawled.

"Practical," she corrected him. "You are wrong about Adam. Perchance he is the only man I have ever met who makes no attempt to flatter me. 'Tis refreshing, actually."

Jonah took a mouthful of ale. "Perchance you are not experienced enough to recognize the signs."

Her cheeks burned at that. "Perchance I am more experienced in the ways of love than you might imagine."

Silence fell between them and Esme fixed her gaze on the grooves in the trestle table.

I should not have said that.

But Jonah's expression was quite calm as he beheld her.

"There was someone at Wolvesley, wasn't there?" His question was gentle. "Someone you became fond of?"

A lump had come into her throat that she could not swallow. She nodded, not trusting herself to speak.

"Did he hurt you?" This time there was an edge to his voice.

Esme put her head into her hands. "He did not mean to."

Is that true?

"Because if any man hurt you, Esme, he should be made to pay for it."

God's blood, she did not want her brother seeking vengeance.

"You have it wrong, Jonah. There was a man at Wolvesley, aye. And I grew closer to him than I should." Her voice wobbled.

"But he did naught wrong."

Jonah did not appear convinced, but as she looked at him beseechingly, his expression softened.

"Fear not, sweet sister, I am not about to ride into Wolvesley, waving my sword and baying for blood."

"I am glad to hear it." She straightened up, reaching for her composure. "Mother would not be pleased if you did."

"Nay indeed." He dragged a hand through his golden hair. "I find this discourse has quite tired me out. You will excuse me for a while."

It was not a question. He was already getting up from the table, his blue eyes fixed on the sanctuary of the solar.

Esme called after him. "You will come out again this day, won't you?"

He threw a smile over his shoulder as he limped across the wooden floor. "I may."

She sighed deeply. Her brother had left her with much to consider. Namely, a question she had asked herself soon after she arrived at Ember Hall.

Did I ever love Crispin?

Was the bitter ache that once lodged in her heart no more than the sting of youthful obsession?

Had she loved Crispin's chestnut curls and sparkling eyes more than she had ever loved *him*?

The more time she spent apart from him, the more she fancied this might be the case. Crispin had never made her feel the way Adam did; safe and excited, both together in a heady mix.

With Crispin, she had felt giddy, aye. And anxious. But rarely was there laughter on her lips, nor flutters in her belly.

Which led her to a second, far more troubling question.

What are my feelings for Adam?

CHAPTER NINE

ADAM WAS BOTH sorry and not sorry that the weather had been so inclement. Four days had passed since Esme's first lesson; days of unending rain, wind and fog. He had told her they could not progress until the situation improved, and he had expected an argument from the feisty young miss, but Esme had demurred as if she did not much mind one way or the other.

But as the days went on, Adam found that *he* minded very much.

He had been out of sorts for that first lesson. Mostly because of her appearance in those snug-fitting braccae. His mind had gone immediately to a place that was entirely inappropriate.

To cover his discomfort, he had been brusque in his instructions. Mayhap even rude.

"Is she avoiding me, do you think?" he asked the black cat who was purring around his ankles.

Felicity looked up at him, her golden eyes unblinking.

He had anticipated a summons to play chess or… something, in the absence of aught else. But Esme had been keeping mostly to her chamber. And so, Adam had kept mostly to his.

The days had grown long with little to occupy himself with. Which was ridiculous, as he was well used to finding tasks to pass the time. But he could not settle to anything. It was too damp and cold to enjoy a ride over the hills. And once he had finished whittling two wooden swords, a sort of lethargy had swept over him.

He missed Esme's company. Missed her brightness and energy.

"I am an old fool, which is worse than being a young one," he told the cat.

Felicity mewed and Adam picked her up, holding her against him as he gazed out of the narrow window of his high chamber. This fifth day had dawned dry at least. Did he dare to hope that things were about to change?

Resolve formed within him. As pleasing as his chamber was, with plastered walls and clean wooden furnishings, he could not skulk about in here any longer. He was a man of action, not philosophy.

A sharp knocking broke into his thoughts. He put down the cat and crossed the floor to open the door, somewhat startled to find Jonah waiting in the narrow corridor beyond. He must have ascended the servant's stairs to arrive here, which would be a difficult climb. But Adam knew to hide his surprise.

He bowed. "How can I be of service, milord?"

The young man was a healthier color than he had been when Adam first arrived. His finely drawn features were no longer pinched with pain, and his shoulders were not so hunched.

Jonah waved his hand. "Please, do not stand on such ceremony. I have grown unaccustomed to it."

Adam inclined his head. "Would you like to come in?"

He was expecting the young lord to refuse. But instead, Jonah nodded and preceded him into his chamber. He did not glance about but stood politely, just inside the doorway.

"'Tis about my sister," he announced with no preamble.

"Esme?" Adam raised his brows.

"Indeed." Jonah pursed his lips, momentarily discomfited.

Is he about to warn me off?

A jolt of adrenaline shot through Adam's belly, surprising him with its intensity.

"I have come to ask a favor." Jonah looked him boldly in the eye.

"Go ahead."

"Please could you resume your lessons?" Jonah winced a little. "Fencing or sword-fighting or whatever it is you were teaching her."

Adam's eyes flared with surprise. His knees went weak with relief. "That is the favor?"

"She is skulking about like a bull with a sore head. I cannot write, nay I cannot even think, with her in such a temper. Please, take her outside and distract her."

Adam found a smile fighting to take hold of his lips. "As it happens, I was thinking that this day would be opportune for our lessons to resume."

"You mean I climbed all the way up here for naught?" Jonah sagged against the doorframe, causing Adam to step forward with alarm.

"Allow me to help you."

Jonah shook his head. "I can manage, thank you. And I spoke partly in jest. 'Tis good to challenge myself, every now and then. Mayhap I will join your lessons myself, one day."

Adam recalled Esme's comments about her brother's prowess with a sword.

"'Tis more likely you will have skills to teach me," he offered.

Jonah clapped him on the shoulder; the gesture had surprising strength behind it. "Your fine words do you credit, my good man, but nay. I am the son of an earl, but I am no fool. How can a man who spends his day writing poems hope to wield a weapon more effectively than a man who spends his days in battle?" He limped past him back to the corridor. "You will speak to Esme?"

"I shall," Adam promised.

Jonah gave him a brief nod and went on his way.

Adam turned back to Felicity, who had curled up on his narrow pallet. "I guess the matter is settled."

Sometime later, he and Esme had returned to the patch of ground by the standing stones. Esme was again dressed in braccae, but this time he did not permit himself to be so affected by it. The lady was a little subdued, certainly more outwardly attentive than she had been on the previous occasion. He demonstrated how to lunge and how to block, and she copied him with pleasing accuracy, but with none of the banter he found himself craving.

"You are doing well," he told her.

She smiled at that, making his heart lift a little.

"I am sorry if I did not give you that impression, the last time we met," he ploughed on.

Esme's lips formed an O of surprise. "'Twas hard work, in the fog," she suggested.

"Aye."

"As you said it would be." Her gaze shied away from his. She lifted her new wooden sword so it rested across her palms. "Thank you for this."

"'Tis nothing."

"You whittled it, especially for me. For us," she amended, blushing slightly. "'Tis not nothing."

"I enjoy keeping busy."

How trite that sounded. And unfeeling. Adam had been too much amongst fighting men these last years. He had forgotten how to be soft and open.

But Esme was still looking up at him, as if what he said had value. "You have made many of these?"

"A fair few." He folded his arms across his tunic, wishing he were not so tongue-tied.

Esme lifted her plait from the back of her neck. "Do you mind if we sit for a while? The sun has surprising warmth to it, and I would appreciate a rest."

"Of course." He escorted her to a level stone where she could sit and rest, all the while cursing himself for his rough manners. "You should have said," he muttered, propping the wooden sword beside her.

She fixed her gaze over the cliffs, at the blue sea sparking in the distance. "I see that you are blaming yourself for tiring me,

Adam. And therefore, I cannot keep up the pretense. I am not tired. I am simply curious about your life and wish to ask you some questions." She shaded her eyes from the sun and offered her most radiant smile.

A smile that was as disarming as her blunt honesty. Much as he disliked conversations about the past, Adam found himself sinking down onto a nearby stone and reluctantly accepting her request. "What would you like to know?"

"I received word from Frida this morn. They have all arrived safely at Kielder Castle. She says it is unlike anywhere she has ever known. What could she mean by that?"

Adam thought for a moment. "The castle itself is a bleak and cheerless place, it's walls have seen neither love nor laughter for many summers now." He paused to throw her an appraising look. "Is this what you wished to ask me?"

"Nay, but Frida's letter made me think more of your situation. How does the son of a farmer find himself training warriors for Rory Baine?"

Despite his trepidation over the subject, he chuckled at her directness. "My father was a farmer, local to here as it happens." He spoke on before she could question him further on this point. "But he was also a Scot." He paused, allowing her to digest this information.

"You are part Scottish?"

"I am." He noted that she did not appear overly shocked.

"Just as Callum is?"

"Just so." He nodded. "My father served Rory's father when he was Laird of Kielder. Rory was his friend. They came down to join a campaign in the borderlands and became separated from the rest of their troops." He pulled at some long grass, letting the stalks fall through his fingers. It was many years since he had last told this tale, and it had somehow grown more painful to think of his father—and of Rory Baine—as those lost young men.

Esme was sitting forward on the stone, her arms wrapped around her knees. Her expression was rapt. "Go on."

"'Twas winter. Not a sensible time for campaigning." He cleared his throat. "Rory and my father spent several days wandering in the mist. They were cold and hungry. Entirely by chance, they wandered into the grounds of Egremont House, where Lady Elizabeth Kerr took pity on them. She was Callum's mother," he added, seeing her look of confusion.

"She showed mercy to her enemies?"

"She was a kind and merciful woman." A brisk breeze stirred the folds of his belted tunic as he recalled Lady Elizabeth's gentle smile and calming presence. "You can guess what happened next?"

Esme wrinkled her pretty nose. "She and Rory must have married. But I always thought that Rory was not a kind man?"

He couldn't help but smile at that, even as a sharp bit of stone dug into his thighs. "That is a fair assessment. But love is a powerful thing. And Rory once loved his wife, very much."

Who knows what kind of man he may have become, had Lady Elizabeth not died when she did?

Perchance Adam's future—and Callum's too—would have turned out very differently.

"What about your own father?" Esme asked softly.

"He also married a local woman." Adam pushed down his emotions. "You said once that it is not common for a warrior to seek a life of peace. But my father was all too happy to lay down his weapons."

"And he farmed land near here?" Esme swiveled her head around, as if she might be able to spy Adam's childhood haunts from where she sat.

"Not far from here." He did not wish to dwell on this. "So, you see, although I am the son of a farmer. My father was also a warrior. And he taught me how to wield a sword from a young age. When my parents passed, Rory took me in."

"And here we are," Esme breathed.

"Here we are," he confirmed.

For a long moment they did not say more. The only sound

was the call of gulls overhead and the rhythmic ebb and flow of the crashing waves far beneath them.

"You are of a noble bloodline? You are the son of a knight?"

"Nay." He shook his head quickly. "My father's family were naught of note."

Her question had unsettled him.

Does Esme wish I was of a more noble bloodline?

No sooner had the idea formed, than he pursed his lips at his own foolishness.

Of course she did. She was Lady Esme de Neville. Their acquaintance—their growing acquaintance—would be so much more acceptable, were he of noble blood.

But he was no such thing, and he would not pretend otherwise.

"That is the end of my story," he said tightly, fisting his hands.

Even if he were the son of a knight. Hell's teeth, even if he were the son of a *lord*, he could not allow this simmering attraction he felt for Esme to develop into anything more.

I am too scarred for one so lovely.

He turned away from her, fixing his gaze at the circle of man-sized standing stones that had stood atop these cliffs perchance for hundreds of years. Since the first time he had come upon them, they had somehow called to him. The stones would have seen people, families, come and go. Battles fought. Hearts broken. An ancient energy shimmered between them, like the thinning of a veil. But it did not alarm him. Forsooth, proximity to these ancient monoliths endowed him with a strong sense of peace; reminding him that there was more in this world than he could ever hope to understand.

His breathing began to slow as his limbs relaxed.

I should not have grown so agitated.

"Forgive my lack of propriety." From the corner of his eye, he saw Esme start to stand.

"There is naught to forgive." The words fell from his lips

before he was aware they were forming.

"I disagree. I have asked personal questions when I have no right to do so. I have even demanded you teach me to use a sword, when a more fitting occupation would be embroidery."

He swung his head at the catch in her voice. She stood a few feet away, her blue gaze fixed humbly on the flattened grass.

Her forthright honesty deserved the truth in return.

"I am of a mind that all young ladies should be taught how to use a sword."

He noted her sharp intake of breath, and the relieved smile that darted across her lips.

"Truly?"

"Aye." He allowed himself to smile back. The sun shone down on them like a blessing.

"That is a comfort to hear." Esme slowly took her seat once again. "How do you hold such daring beliefs? Is it common practice, in Kielder Castle, for women to fight alongside men?"

Her question was innocently asked. He did not permit his bloody memories of the siege of Kielder to derail their conversation.

"'It is not."

She raised her eyebrows questioningly. A dazzling young woman, accustomed to a life of privilege, who had no idea what darkness she was stirring.

Out of nowhere came an urge to unburden himself and explain exactly why he held such daring beliefs. He picked up a flattened stone and rubbed it between his fingers. "I have bored you enough with my stories, this day."

"I am far from bored."

His heart began to beat faster. His was a cautionary tale, was it not? One which Esme deserved to hear?

Adam was unused to dwelling in the past. But her questions had already taken him back there. Would he ever have a better time to share this story than here and now, with the shadows of the standing stones reminding him of all that had gone before—

and all that would continue to be long after his name was but a dim memory?

Does Esme not deserve to know the truth?

His eyes half closed as he recalled how she had kissed him, quickly and sweetly, in the great hall.

"I was once engaged to be wed," he said abruptly.

She gave another sharp intake of breath.

"Clara was her name."

Esme said nothing, but her blue eyes were trained upon him. He could feel the weight of her gaze.

"We were childhood friends." His stomach churned at the onslaught of so many memories. "Then we became something more. I was to take over the running of her father's farm. 'Twas the life I wanted. With the lass I loved." He looked down at the smooth stone, turning it over in his hands whilst his mind galloped backwards.

He had no idea how much time had passed when Esme spoke up again.

"What was she like?"

Her question brought him back to the present. "She was like you," he answered honestly. But he regretted his candor almost straight away; 'twas a leap that he had not planned to make. "By that, I mean that she was fair-haired and fair-spoken; honorable and true. She always wore a smile and could make the best of any situation."

"And you loved her?" Esme's expression had become unreadable.

"Aye." He rubbed at his aching back, compelled to add, "This was many years ago."

"What happened? Why did you not wed?" Esme leaned back on her hands and swung her legs, affecting nonchalance when he knew—from the hard set of her mouth—that she was anything but.

And that was wrong.

This connection between them was real. He knew not what

was fueling the flame—when she had both beauty and wealth, whilst he was a man of advancing years and bitter humor—but he knew that the flame must be extinguished. Left to burn, it would consume too much that was good.

Adam had seen lovers come and go. Esme was young, with her whole life ahead of her.

Moreover, *she was the daughter of an earl.*

Shame on him for allowing this—whatever it was—to continue.

Regret was his familiar companion, and he accepted its return with a deep sigh. "Clara and her family were slaughtered in their own home. They had no guards and no weapons. They were easy prey for marauding Scots."

She sat up straighter. "Scots?"

He made an impatient gesture. "I came to realize that the identity of their attackers did not matter more than the fact of their attack." He bit down on his lip until his rising temper came back under control.

"'Tis a sad tale. I am sorry for you, and I am sorry for Clara." Esme's voice trembled with sympathy.

Adam brought back his arm and flung the stone up and over the cliffs.

I must draw this ill-advised conversation to a close.

"Aye, well. The point of the story is this. If Clara or any of her sisters had learned to wield a sword, mayhap they would not have made such easy prey."

He was unable to sit still for a moment longer. He sprang to his feet as decades-old anger pooled in his veins.

Esme was frowning. "*That* is the point of the story?"

He crossed his arms, keeping his emotions tightly locked inside him. "You asked me why I thought it sensible for women to learn to fight."

She looked down at the wooden sword propped beside her. "I did. But I would not have asked if I had known the pain it would cause you."

Her kindness shone brighter than her earlier smile, but he could not take refuge in it. Adam retreated behind his customary defenses.

"The pain is a part of me now. I hardly notice it." He set his jaw. "'Tis the lot of a man like me, milady."

"A man like you?" she echoed, as he had guessed she might. "Kind, decent, and strong?"

If he met her steady gaze, he would be done for. Already he could feel his high defenses beginning to crumble.

"A warrior, milady. A man who has seen and caused death."

He should not have said that. Not to Esme, who was young and bright and beautiful, who had never been exposed to the horrors of the world.

With a pained gasp, she rose to her feet. Her cheeks were flushed but her voice came out level and strong. "Well, I for one am sorry for it. I shall grieve for you, Adam. And for Clara. And her family."

"There is no need. They are all long gone." He looked out over the white-tipped waves and fought to keep his breathing even.

Esme said nothing, but some wild part of him hoped she might come to stand beside him. Mayhap put her arms around him.

She did not. And he could not blame her for it. Not when their discourse had brought them closer, only for him to push her away at the end.

When he finally turned around, she had gone.

Adam walked to the center of the standing stones, braced his hands around the tallest and let out a loud roar of grief and anger and longing. As the surging emotions abated and he sank down onto the long grass, he reflected that even if he were the son of a knight, he would never have had a future with Esme de Neville.

Too much darkness lived within him to ever be banished, even by a woman who shone as brightly as she.

CHAPTER TEN

THE DAY DAWNED bright, and Esme's head ached all the more for the dazzling shafts of sunlight which blazed through her narrow window and made her squint.

Too restless to remain in bed, she sat upon an upright wooden chair in her bedchamber and rubbed at her temples. When the housemaid knocked upon the door to enquire if milady required any assistance dressing, it took several seconds for her whirring mind to make sense of it.

Frida had always baulked at allocating her youngest sister a lady's maid during her frequent stays at Ember Hall. Esme had been obliged to cajole; even—on occasions—demand. Never had Jennifer willingly offered up her services. The young maid was a hard worker, but she displayed no fondness for dressing hair.

And on this day, Esme could not see the point of it either.

Esme turned her weary face toward the door and shook her head at the hazel-eyed servant.

"Not this morn, thank you, Jennifer."

The maid bobbed a curtsy and withdrew, gently closing the panel behind her.

Esme pulled the folds of her woolen shawl closer and tucked her long strands of hair back behind her ears. Dappled sunlight on the plastered wall told her that much time had passed since the first cock crow, mayhap Jennifer had been sent by Agnes to discretely enquire if milady was well?

Esme was not sure that she was.

Ever since that unfortunate ball at Wolvesley, she had been summoning a smile and making the best of things. She had not allowed herself to skulk about in her chamber, like a fractious child. But the events of yesterday had shaken her fortitude. She could not fasten ribbons to her bonnet, grasp Adam's arm and expect entertainment.

Not now she knew how much anger shimmered beneath his calm exterior.

To think, *he was the man who made her feel safe.*

But she had heard him roar with the rage of a caged bear, driven to torment by memories of the past.

She could not help but feel disappointed. *Bereft*, even. Just like Crispin, perchance he was not the man she once thought he was.

Adam was, as he himself had declared, a man *who had seen and brought about death.*

Esme winced at the patterns of her thoughts. That was unfair. Adam was a warrior, not a man to ride away from a woman he had professed to love. She had seen how much emotion surged within him at the mere mention of Clara, his one-time betrothed. Yesterday, at the standing stones, her heart had ached with pity. But mixed in with this was the bitter sting of rejection, for he had not wanted her sympathy. Had even spurned it.

I am unaccustomed to being spurned.

And she had not anticipated it from *him.*

Esme rested her elbow on the arm of her chair and put her head in her hand. The silvery notes of a ruddock's winter song drifted in from outside; seemingly giving voice to the sadness that had taken root in her soul. Were she in better spirits, she might stand by her window and try to glimpse the red-breasted little bird, who must be perched on a tree nearby; but she did not have the energy to stir herself.

She had not known, before yesterday, that Adam's heart belonged so utterly to another.

To *Clara.*

To a ghost, whose beauty and goodness would never now be challenged by the passing of the years or capricious dictates of fate.

Why does this trouble me so?

Esme could not help feeling a stab of envy toward this unknown Clara. And how ridiculous was that? To covet the life of a farm girl who had met such a sorry—and untimely—end.

But at least she had known true love before she died.

Esme closed her eyes and attempted to quell such unworthy thoughts. But her long-suppressed self-pity was now fully awakened and would not be easily shunted aside.

Would any man ever speak of her with such uncomplicated ardor?

Fair-haired and fair-spoken. Honorable and true.

She reflected, grimly, that she would most likely succeed on one of those counts. Possibly two. But no more.

Perchance that was for the best.

No man could love her truly—nor could she love any man— without confessing what had occurred in the hayloft with Crispin. She knew how much store men put by virginity. Yet even knowing this, she had let hers go with barely a squeal of protest.

And she could never confess it without bringing shame to her family name.

Esme's head throbbed and she fought an urge to sob. A knock at the door made her straighten her back and hastily wipe at her eyes.

"Come in."

She half expected Jennifer again, but it was Jonah's golden head that appeared around the door.

"Are you well, Esme?" he demanded, his blue eyes fixing her in a piercing stare.

She took a trembling breath. "I am not."

"What is it?" He walked more fully into the room and gazed at her consideringly; his arms folded.

"I have a headache," she answered honestly.

"You have not yet broken your fast. Jennifer says you have not been down." His voice was accusing. "You are not even dressed."

She was still clad in her white night rail, but the shawl ensured her decency. Esme would not be made to feel guilty.

"As I said, I have a headache."

Jonah tapped the toe of his boot onto her wooden floor. "Mother always told me, no matter how out of sorts one might feel, 'tis important to rise up and dress."

She shook her head, pouting a little to demonstrate her disinterest. "She never said this to me."

"Most likely because she never had to. You have enjoyed good health and good humor for almost all of your two and twenty summers."

He is insufferable.

"Jonah, I will not be lectured by one who shuts himself away from the world." Esme rearranged her shawl and half-turned in the chair, so she was facing away from him.

Nonetheless, she sensed his chilly disapproval wash over her.

"'Tis precisely because I am so oft afflicted that you should listen to me now." His voice grew hard. "Do not allow yourself to become self-pitying. It does you no favors. Forsooth, sister, I have always admired your resilience."

She was too cross to hear the compliment.

"Am I to be permitted no peace at all? Even when my head aches I am expected to don a pretty gown and smile at everyone?" Esme tossed back her hair and looked fixedly out of the window, though the winter light was so bright it hurt her eyes.

"Exactly that. 'Tis little enough to ask, when others must sweep our floors and fix our fires and bake our bread."

"You are a man of the working people now, are you, Jonah?" She raised one eyebrow, aware of his gaze upon her face.

"I am a man who observes what is happening around me."

Esme was neither inclined nor willing to acknowledge Jonah's fine sentiments. She only wanted him gone.

"Perchance you should look to participate rather than just observe. Then you might find occupation and meaning in your life."

"I have already found both occupation and meaning," he interjected calmly.

But Esme had not finished. "And you might stop meddling in mine," she concluded with a note of triumph in her voice.

For a moment, silence fell between them. Esme opened her mouth to apologize but Jonah held up a restraining hand.

"I have oft said the truth is preferable to a lie. Therefore, I thank you for your honesty, sister."

She rubbed her temples, regret swirling in her stomach. "Jonah, I did not mean it."

She swiveled around in time to catch his short, polite bow.

"I bid you good day, Esme."

Jonah walked from the chamber with surprising alacrity. He had closed the door well before she fixed on a response.

Esme stayed where she was, aware of the futility of going after him. Her brother's sulks were legendary.

A small mew alerted her to Felicity's presence; she must have crept inside whilst the door was open. Glad of the company, Esme scooped up the little black cat and settled her on her knee.

"What a mess it all is," Esme crooned as she stroked the soft fur.

Felicity purred loudly, seemingly in raptures to find Esme not only sitting still but also wearing wool thick enough for a good kneading.

If only I were a cat, thought Esme. It was not a bad life. Sleeping, eating, sleeping again. Felicity only had to mew to gain loving attention.

'Twas not unlike Esme's own life at Wolvesley Castle.

Before I ruined everything.

Hoofbeats outside made her lift her head until she could see out of the window. One of the grooms was leading a chestnut horse out of the stables and toward the mounting block. As Esme watched, her brother Jonah walked steadily from the front door of the hall, checked the horse's girth and took the reins from the groom.

Jonah was going for a ride!

This was not, in itself, surprising. Despite his wasted leg, their mother had insisted that he learned to ride at a young age. Like the rest of his siblings, Jonah had spent much of his childhood in the saddle—making good use of some specially adapted stirrups which meant his disability was scarcely apparent.

But Esme had not known Jonah to willingly get up on horseback for many years now. When he was obliged to travel, he did so by carriage. He had not ridden for fun since his youth.

That was, apparently, about to change.

Esme rose from her chair, much to Felicity's displeasure, and put her hands onto the windowsill, leaning out as far as she dared without attracting notice from the courtyard. She watched the groom link his hands together, offering a boot up into the saddle. And she watched Jonah wave him away.

"Good gracious," she muttered.

The chestnut horse snorted and pawed at the ground as Jonah climbed cautiously onto the mounting block, and Esme held her breath as her brother found his balance for long enough to put his good foot into the stirrup. Even from this distance, she could see what the effort was costing him. He was white-lipped by the time he had finally swung himself into the saddle.

But he had made it!

Esme only just held back from clapping as horse and rider cantered toward the main gates.

Once they had passed out of sight, she put her back against the wall and sighed deeply. Jonah's exploits made her feel idle for staying so long in her chamber, but there was little to tempt her outside.

Not even Adam's company.

"'Tis just you and I again, Felicity," she told the little cat as she returned to her chair. Felicity promptly jumped back onto her lap and Esme, reluctantly, picked up her embroidery.

Mayhap it was because of the cat's constant purring, but Esme found the time went by quicker than expected. It was only when the rumbling of her stomach grew too loud for even Felicity to ignore, that she put her embroidery aside and stretched her arms over her head.

"'Tis time to venture beyond these walls," she said to galvanize herself.

Felicity was none too pleased at this second interruption, but she wound about Esme's ankles as she dressed in a simple pale blue gown, belted at the waist and buttoned at the front. The cat waited at the door, then trotted away down the long gallery, her tail held high.

"Where are you going in such a hurry?" Esme called. "Most likely the kitchen," she answered her own question.

She found no wish to linger in the great hall, which seemed to mock her solitude with its empty chairs and unlaid table. Biting her lip, Esme could not help but remember the bustling great hall at Wolvesley, which was so rarely quiet and scarcely ever empty. But not even the sleepy hounds—usually stretched out by the fire—were present to welcome her today.

Esme gave in to another wave of self-pity. "Everyone has left me." At a loss for what else to do, she followed Felicity's example and wandered through the narrow passage toward the kitchen, deliberately blocking out the memories of when she and Adam had become entangled together. The stone flags beneath her feet rang with her solo footsteps.

She emerged into warmth and light. Agnes was red-faced and perspiring, rolling out pastry on the big wooden table. Even the open door and windows could not mitigate the bellowing heat from a big fire beneath the ovens. Esme sniffed hungrily, scenting roasting meat and something sweet. Felicity, she saw, was delicately nibbling at some cuts of meat which had been placed in a small bowl on the floor.

Agnes straightened up hurriedly. "Milady. Can I help you?"

She had intended to ask for a late luncheon, but now she felt guilty at imposing.

"I would like to help you, Agnes," she said, surprising herself just as much as the cook.

Agnes blinked. "Help me?"

Esme opened her arms. "I am at a loss for occupation and the hours are pressing heavily upon me."

The ageing cook did not exhibit much sympathy. "There is danger in a kitchen," she said flatly. "'Tis all too easy to cut or scald yourself. I would not see you come to harm, milady."

"But Frida is often in here." Esme folded her arms, not willing to be so easily dissuaded.

"Indeed, she is. And I was most put out about it, when first she came." Agnes threw her the ghost of a smile. "If you are so intent on staying put, you can cut this into rounds."

Esme had no idea what that meant, but she walked forward and accepted the serrated pastry cutter with an outward show of nonchalance.

Agnes rolled her sleeves above her elbows, displaying forearms made strong through years of chopping and stirring. "Do you know what to do?"

Esme eyed the misshapen pastry and took a guess. "Of course."

"Put the tarts on here." Agnes banged a tray down beside her. "You can stud them with raisins from the jar."

Glancing about her, Esme nodded. This had been a mere whim, but now she was beginning to enjoy herself. The pastry was soft and malleable beneath her fingers, the raisins were plump and juicy. She stole a handful whilst Agnes was turned away.

The cook grunted with effort as she pulled something from the oven, wafting steam away from her face.

"'Tis hotter than hell in here."

Esme giggled; she couldn't help it. No one had spoken to her so bluntly since her sister Isabella got married.

"It must be a blessing in the depths of winter," she suggested.

"Aye, and a curse on a hot summer's day." Agnes pushed her long plait out of her way and surveyed Esme's handiwork. "A decent effort," she admitted.

Esme dipped into a short curtsy. "Why, thank you."

The cook's face was briefly transformed with a genuine smile of amusement. "I never thought I'd see Lady Esme de Neville with flour on her nose."

"Have I?" Esme reached to her face with alarm.

"'Tis all over your cheeks now."

"Bother." Esme wiped her palms on her skirts, conscious of the white streaks she was putting there.

"Wash your hands in the sink, milady. Then I suggest you retire for a while. I'll have Jennifer bring you some bread and cheese."

Esme wrinkled her nose. "In truth, Agnes, I do not wish to sit alone in the great hall."

"No more would I." Agnes inclined her head. "Why not join your brother in the solar? He might be glad of your company." She met Esme's eye and gave a conspiratorial grin. "All things may be possible on this day."

"You mean since I helped in the kitchen?" Esme gave a peal of laughter. "'Tis a theory I would willingly test. Alas, Jonah has already gone out. I saw him leave earlier."

"Then you will have the solar to yourself," Agnes said equably. "'Tis a pleasant room."

"You're right." Esme nodded. Why should the solar be the preserve of her brother anyway? He was hardly master here. She poured cold water over her hands at the big sink, flinching at the sudden chill and drying them on a nearby cloth. "Thank you, Agnes," she said sincerely. "I hope I have at least been some help and not taken up too much of your time."

"You are welcome any time you wish."

'Twas a trite sentiment, but Esme fancied it was honestly meant as she wandered back along the stone-flagged passageway.

Once ensconced in the solar, she found herself drawn to the neatly arranged squares of parchment upon which Jonah had inscribed his poems. She read the first, feeling a little as if she was intruding, but the words flowed so beautifully and the images he conjured were so vivid, she quickly picked up the second. When Jennifer brought in a tray of foodstuffs, Esme was tucked up on the settle, deep into the third.

"Thank you, Jennifer," she murmured, unwilling to lift her gaze from her brother's poetry.

When she finally looked up to tear off a hunk of bread, there were tears in her eyes.

Who would have thought her sullen brother could capture such sentiments and express them so eloquently?

Esme shuffled the parchment in her hands, feeling oddly moved. There was no doubt that Jonah wrote of love. Deep love. 'Twas naught like the giddy rush of attraction she had once felt for Crispin.

Nonetheless, his words stirred something within her; connecting her to an emotion she had not dared yet give voice to. Not even quietly, to herself. But now, in the quiet of the solar, her pulse quickened, and a sort of wild fancy gripped her, urging her to look deep within her heart and confess to the truth she found there.

The truth about a man with piercing green eyes and threads of silver in his dark hair.

But as she trembled on the brink, hoofbeats sounded on the cobbles outside the window and she realized she must leave the solar before Jonah found her lurking there.

Tightening her lips, she swiftly gathered up the pieces of parchment and placed them neatly on the desk, hoping she had correctly recalled the order of them. But one glance out of the window told her there was no need for haste. The returning horseman was not Jonah, but merely one of the guards.

Relief made her knees go weak and she sagged against the wooden desk, feeling her heart pound beneath her bodice. Then she frowned and looked again out of the window, observing the long shadows which stretched the length of the courtyard. The hour had grown late, and Jonah had not yet returned.

Her relief was immediately replaced by the first flicker of concern.

Surely, her brother did not intend to be absent for so long? He had given no instruction of his intent to stay away; Agnes did not even know he had gone.

"Oh, Jonah." Esme put a hand to her heart, recalling her harsh words to him that morn.

Had he ridden off in a huff? Determined to demonstrate the meaning and purpose that she had derided him for lacking?

Breathing deeply to quell her nerves, Esme crossed to the window so she might have a better view of the path from the gates.

It was empty.

What should I do?

Panic gripped her by the shoulders. Jonah might have fallen. Even now, he might be laying injured in a ditch. And it would all be her fault. Not only because of how she had spoken to him—words said in temper that had wounded one with such a sensitive soul—but also because she was *his sister*. She had watched him ride away. She should have noticed, before now, that he had not returned. Frida was gone and there was no one else to watch over him.

She wrung her hands and tried to steady her thoughts. As tempting as it was to rush out to the stables, demand a horse and set off in pursuit, she knew this would not be sensible. For one, she had no idea which direction Jonah had ridden in. For another, darkness would soon be upon them and the drop from the cliff tops was severe.

As this thought crystallized in her mind, Esme was obliged to grip the desk to steady herself in a chamber that swung about her.

And then the answer came to her, like a loud horn blast carrying through the fog.

Adam is here.

He would help her.

She had hoped to avoid him, after yesterday's awkwardness. But these concerns now seemed trivial. She swept from the solar, pleased to encounter Jennifer building up the fire in the great hall.

"Where is Adam?" she asked without preamble.

The housemaid looked surprised. "I have not seen him this day, milady."

Esme sought to contain her frustration. "Not at all?"

"Agnes said he was keeping to his chamber." Jennifer's hazel eyes flickered to the logs on the fire, then back to Esme.

"And where is that?"

"His chamber?" The housemaid blanched.

Esme's folded her hands together to stop her flinging them about. "Aye, his chamber. Where can I find it."

"'Tis on the very top floor. I dinna ken which one though, milady."

"No matter, I shall find it." Esme spun around and made for the staircase, but Jennifer called her back.

"You'll need to take the servant's stairs." She pointed to a low wooden door in the far corner of the room.

Esme hid her discomposure. She had never even noticed this second door. "Thank you, Jennifer."

The servant's stairs were small and narrow; in her haste, Esme feared she might trip. She picked up her skirts and ascended as quickly as she could, pleased to emerge onto roughly plastered landing. She took a moment to catch her breath, relieved that high, narrow windows had been carved into the outer wall as she had not thought to bring a torch. But the fading light meant it was hard to make out very much.

Esme looked left and right. To one side of her was a dead end. One the other, a narrow passage led to two wooden doors; one of which stood ajar.

Downstairs in the solar, Esme had felt as if she were intruding in her brother's private space, but that was naught to the trepidation she knew now. She had never been up here. She did not belong here. But surely, she could not be accused of trespassing in her sister's home? 'Twas only that she felt out of place. And back home at Wolvesley; Esme had never once experienced such an emotion.

Swallowing her anxieties, she held her head high and marched toward the pair of doors. By inclining her head at an awkward angle, she could spy a sort of store through the gap of the open door.

Adam's chamber must be opposite.

Esme took a deep breath and knocked.

CHAPTER ELEVEN

To FIND ESME standing on the other side of his chamber door gave him a jolt of pleasure. At first, he blinked at the shadows beyond his chamber, thinking her mayhap a specter conjured by his imagination. But nay. She was flesh and blood; her chest rising and falling after her ascent of the stairs. He was pleased to see her; that was the simple, honest truth of it.

All day, he had assumed she was avoiding him—and for reasons that were good and understandable—*but here she was*! Her golden hair was loose across her shoulders, and she wore a simple gown as blue as her eyes. Just the sight of her eased the band of tension across his ribs as if her brightness might yet banish the darkness inside him.

Then he saw the panic stamped across her heart-shaped face, and his chest grew tight once again.

"Esme, what ails thee?"

Acting entirely on impulse, he put a hand on her arm, squeezing with what he hoped was gentle reassurance.

But the lady's eyes filled with tears. "Forgive me." She sniffed. "I shall be myself again in a moment."

Adam withdrew his hand, unsure of the etiquette of this situation. Good manners dictated that he should invite her inside his chamber. Propriety, surely, did not! But they could not converse on this narrow landing, where the floorboards squeaked whenever anyone moved and the dim light made it hard to see much of anything.

Esme squared her shoulders. "I have come to ask for your help."

"I will do whatever I can," he promised, fighting a strong urge to put his arm around her.

"'Tis my brother Jonah. He rode off this morn and has not returned."

Adam quickly considered this. Jonah was a grown man, and it was not yet fully dark. But Esme's distress was palpable.

Rather than debate the matter here and now, he pulled his door closed behind him. "Let us go downstairs, where we can talk more easily."

He should have fetched a candle from his chamber, he reflected, as they made halting progress down the narrow stairs. The situation put him in mind of the time they climbed the wooden steps to the hayloft, and he had longed to kiss her. Then of the time when they became entangled in the narrow passage beyond the kitchen, and he so nearly *had* kissed her. In contrast to the shadows of the stairwell, the great hall positively blazed with light. The fire was lit, as were a dozen wall sconces, and flickering candlelight cast a golden glow over the wooden paneling. The elegant room exuded an air of coziness, but Esme shivered at the bottom of the stairs. He took her arm and drew her closer to the hearth.

"Sit down," he instructed. "Shall I ring for some wine? To bring some color back to your cheeks," he added quickly.

Esme shook her head, although she obediently lowered herself onto a cushioned chair. "Nay. I cannot bide here long. We must find Jonah." She pressed her hands together, either in supplication or restraint, he could not tell.

Adam forced himself to sit down in the adjacent chair, even though his instincts—as a man—were telling him to put all available distance between himself and this lovely young woman who had seemingly gained control of his heart in the last sennight. All his resolutions of yesterday had dissolved like morning mist, the very moment she asked him for help.

This was dangerous territory, the likes of which he had never known, where sense and reason did not prevail. He should protect himself from it.

But his instincts as a warrior and a protector *of others* ruled overall else. *For now.*

"Tell me what you can."

Esme pressed her pink lips together. "I watched him ride away. He insisted on mounting the horse himself, even though it pained him to do so. He was in a foul temper." She hung her head.

Adam's hand twitched to comfort her. "How do you know that?"

"Because we had an argument." She lifted her chin, and he saw her blue eyes were glassy with tears. "I said things that I should not have said."

"I believe 'tis a common occurrence between siblings," he offered gently.

"Still, there are boundaries one should not cross." Esme's voice carried a tremor.

Adam nodded to show he understood. He was an only child, but the men he fought beside were as close as brothers. He knew all about breaching boundaries.

"Where did he go?"

'Twas the wrong question to ask. Esme all but jumped from her chair in distress.

"I have no idea."

Then how can I find him for you?

He kept this question to himself. "I shall go and speak to the grooms. They may know something more."

He meant for Esme to remain here, where it was warm and light. But she stood up alongside him and straightened her skirts.

"I am coming with you."

She spoke as a lady, the daughter of an earl. He was unable to argue.

"At least allow me to fetch you a cloak."

She gave him a slight smile. "I seem to have requisitioned my sister's cloak. You will find it on a peg outside the kitchen."

Frida's cloak was of serviceable wool. It would keep her warm, he reflected, as he fastened it over her shoulders. 'Twas necessary to keep his mind on the domestic; otherwise, he would gaze at her slender neck and forget who—and where—he was.

As they passed through the arched front door, he grasped a wall torch and held it high to light their way across the cobbles, fixing his gaze at the huddle of outbuildings rather than risk a glance at the beauty by his side. The yard was peaceful, the air sweet with the scent of hay. A tall youth with gangly limbs and freckles was talking to a dapple-grey mare as he bolted the stable door, all the while juggling two large buckets. He startled in fright when he beheld Adam and Esme walking toward him, dropping the buckets which were, mercifully, empty.

Nevertheless, the buckets made a tremendous clatter as they hit the ground and rolled, causing the horse to shy backwards with her ears flattened.

The youth looked mortified. "Beg pardon, milady."

Esme quickly recovered her composure. "Do not apologize, please. We are the ones who gave you a fright."

The youth stooped to collect the buckets and Adam saw that even the backs of his ears were red.

He cleared his throat. "We are here to speak to the man who saddled Lord Jonah's horse this morn."

The lad looked relieved. "That was John, methinks. I shall fetch him for you." He scurried away, leaving Adam and Esme standing alone in the pool of light from the torch.

Settled once again, the dapple-grey munched at her hay, occasionally turning liquid eyes in their direction. Adam was growing increasingly concerned about Esme, whose concern had morphed into an almost frenzied agitation. She tapped the toe of her boot on the cobbles and hugged herself tightly against the gusty wind. He cast about for something reassuring to say, but rapid footsteps announced the arrival of John, who bustled around the corner from the barn, wiping his hands on a stiff apron.

John was short, but from Adam's perspective, so were most men. He looked most alarmed to behold his visitors and gave them both a respectful bow.

"You're here to ask after Lord Jonah's horse?"

Esme swept toward him, her sister's cloak billowing behind her. "My brother has not yet returned."

John scratched at his thatch of red hair. "I was sayin' that just now, to the lads."

Adam intervened. "Do you know where he was going?"

"'Tis not my place to ask." John calmly stroked the muzzle of a pony, who had poked his head over the adjacent half-door to see what the fuss was all about. "And he said naught to me."

Esme heaved a sigh of frustration. Adam would not have been surprised if she ordered her own horse to be saddled this instant.

I cannot allow that.

Searching for a man in the dark was a fruitless undertaking. Especially in lands as extensive as those around Ember Hall. And the steep drop of the cliffs could be treacherous. His stomach churned at the thought of Esme exposing herself to such danger.

"Does Lord Jonah have a regular haunt?" He directed the question to both John and Esme, swinging his eyes from one to the other.

John shook his head, regretfully. "I cannot say so."

"He has not left the house in days." Esme put her hands on her hips, a desperate glint in her eyes. With her cloak swirling in the brisk breeze, she looked almost like a goddess, or some kind of avenging angel.

Albeit one who must be encouraged to stay safely indoors.

Adam spoke up again quickly, needing to deflect her. "And his horse, is it a steady creature?"

"The steadiest." John nodded in emphasis. "Whatever else

has happened, that horse won't have thrown Lord Jonah. I swear it on my life."

"That is reassuring." Adam crossed his arms and widened his stance, feeling a little as if he were negotiating a fragile truce. "We cannot guess where Lord Jonah has gone. But you can vouch for the reliability of the horse?"

"You have it right, sir."

"We should go and look for him." Esme voiced the words he had been dreading.

John scratched at his cheeks. "That wouldn't be safe, milady. Not 'till first light."

Adam swallowed down his surprise. He had not been expecting a mere groom to voice dissent to the Earl of Wolvesley's daughter. But as he recalled, neither Frida nor Callum stood much on ceremony. Before Esme could counter the idea, he spoke up. "Wise words, John. I agree."

Esme spun around, her blue eyes accusing. "You do?"

He met her gaze. "I agree that upon first light, if Jonah has not returned, we should send out a search party."

Her nostrils flared, but her eyes had lost some of their fire. "We should alert the guards."

"An excellent plan." He bowed his head. "John, could you take a message to the guards on the gate? They should look out for a lone rider approaching the hall."

John nodded smartly. "I'll go right away."

As the man departed, Adam turned to Esme. "I can go myself and keep watch at the wall, if you would prefer it?"

He did not want to, not because he baulked at a night in the open, but because he wanted to stay near her side. *To keep her safe.*

At least, that was what he told himself.

Esme looked at him for a long moment, her expression unreadable. He began to fear that she might actually send him to the wall.

"In truth, Adam, I would prefer your company inside. But perchance *a man like you* would not choose to spend his evening with a woman like me?"

Her words did not wound him so much as the depths of feeling in her gaze.

The last woman to affect him so thoroughly, by saying so little, was his mother.

A muscle clenched in his jaw as Adam raced through his choices. It took mere seconds for him to realize that the only option was the truth.

"I am sorry," he whispered, his words floating through the soft air of the gloaming toward her.

Esme said nothing, but the torch showed the flicker of surprise across her face. It seemed that even the horses stood still in their stalls, waiting to hear her response.

"What are you sorry for?" She stepped closer and he breathed in her scent of lavender.

"I showed my anger to you. But my anger was not with you. My anger was at the whole world."

For a brief second he looked away from her, fixing his eyes on the cobbles and his own booted feet. He had erred from the truth, for yesterday, at the standing stones, he had known a rush of anger that was directed toward Esme. Only it wasn't Esme the living, breathing woman beside him. The one whose smile lit up his day.

It was Lady Esme de Neville; daughter of the Earl of Wolvesley.

Consumed in grief and bitterness, he had believed, for a moment, that her title defined her.

But he could not hope to explain all of that out here in the stable yard, with a chill wind, whisking up dust and grit around them. He could only hope that she would forgive him.

Esme touched the cuff of his sleeve. A simple gesture that all but brought him to his knees.

"I came to understand something yesterday."

"What was that?" He longed to take her hand and entwine his fingers with hers.

"You are here as my personal guard, but you are also a man with a past. A very full past."

A man who has seen and caused death.

He winced at the memory of his harsh words.

"Your life has made you the man you are this day, Adam." She took a quick breath. "And the man you are this day, is a man I have grown to like, very much."

Ye Gods, he could not help it. He reached for her hand, and she gave it to him.

How could their hands fit together so well when his was the roughened palm of a worker and her hand was soft and small and white?

How could such an innocent touch send burning jolts of awareness flooding right into his core?

She tilted her lovely face toward him and the temptation to lean down and press his lips against hers grew almost overbearing.

Almost.

At the last moment, he remembered they stood in full view of the grooms, the guards, and any servants who might wander from the house.

And he remembered that Callum—his master and his friend—had charged him with the safekeeping of his sister-in-law.

That did not include ravishment in a stable yard.

Breathing deeply, Adam released her hands. "Thank you for your understanding."

His actions were too rough, his words too abrupt. But he knew not how to temper them. He was lost and floundering; for the first time in almost twenty summers.

Esme only smiled. The smile that could brighten not only his day, but the darkest of nights.

"Let us go inside," she said lightly, "and await my brother's return."

CHAPTER TWELVE

ADAM CLOSED THE door on the wind and the cold and the encroaching darkness. They walked together through the stone-flagged entrance hall, bumping hips accidentally as they turned into the great hall.

Esme smiled an apology, although the sensation had been more than pleasant. Indeed, it felt good and right to stand beside this mighty warrior and see her problems become his as well. As soon as he had opened his door to her, she had felt safe.

When he had touched her arm, upstairs on the landing, such a feeling of relief swept over her that tears had sprung to her eyes.

One word came into her head.

Home.

Not home like Wolvesley. All bustle and chatter and gaiety.

Home in a steadier, more contented way. Somewhere she felt safe. Somewhere she could be entirely herself.

Although right now, Adam was looking at her with concern in his green eyes.

"Esme?"

"I'm sorry." She put a hand to her heart, aware she had been daydreaming.

"I said should I ring for wine? Or refreshments?" They were standing by the fire, and Adam's hand was hovering by the bell rope. "You should eat something," he added.

"I could not face it," she said sincerely. Concern for Jonah's

132

welfare mixed with her heightened awareness of Adam meant that her appetite was much diminished. "I had some bread and cheese not long ago."

She recalled her time in the solar and Jonah's poems which had so evocatively described this altogether new rush of feeling. This peculiar blend of excitement and contentment which made her want to do… all sorts of things.

She wanted to lean into his hard, strong body and feel his arms closing around her.

She wanted to kiss him.

She wanted… so much more! A twisting sensation deep in her core almost made her forget why they were here in the great hall; and why Adam was gazing at her with such anxiety.

Jonah.

Now that she had talked the situation through, Esme couldn't help thinking that her earlier alarm was a trifle embarrassing. Caused, mayhap, by a long day of loneliness and a mind that tended toward exaggeration. Afflicted though he was, her brother was a grown man. Well-used to looking after himself.

But if she said as much now, Adam would waltz back off to his chamber, leaving her alone.

She seated herself in the tapestried chair and smoothed her skirts, realizing a beat too late that she still wore Frida's cloak. "I will take some wine," she suggested, glad that Adam would be distracted by the bell rope whilst she tugged the unflattering cloak from her shoulders.

"Let me take that from you." He scooped up the cloak and laid it on the window seat, stirring memories of the time they had sat here and played chess. "I know you are still concerned for your brother; but try to take comfort from what the groom told us. His horse is steady, and Jonah is an experienced rider. He is unlikely to come to harm."

Esme tugged at a crumpled sleeve, trying to organize her thoughts. She did not wish to exercise deceit or hysteria. But she did want Adam to stay with her.

"You are right, of course." She smiled at Jennifer as the maid carried in a pitcher of wine and two goblets. "But even the steadiest of horses can spook. And even the most accomplished of riders can fall."

He nodded. "'Tis not common though."

She took a sip of rich wine as she considered this. "You do not think so? 'Tis lore in our family."

Adam frowned at her over the rim of his goblet. "Lore that even accomplished riders can fall?"

"Most certainly." Esme sat back in her chair and cradled her wine. "My sister Frida was unconscious for three days after a fall from her own horse."

She was gratified to see genuine interest in his face. "I did not know that."

"'Tis why her hair is now silvery white. She hit her head and her hair was shaved."

"And the hair that grew back was white," Adam finished for her, his eyebrows disappearing beneath his dark curls. "I have heard of such things, but never before seen them myself."

Esme took another mouthful of wine, finding it did much to restore her spirits. "If it were not for a fall from a horse, I would not be sitting before you now as Lady Esme de Neville."

That got his attention.

Adam placed his goblet onto a low wooden table and clasped his hands. "What do you mean?"

"My father was a younger brother. He never expected to be the Earl of Wolvesley. But his older brother died after a fall from a horse in his own stable yard."

Considering the gravity of the subject, Esme reflected that she should not have announced this with such relish.

Adam baulked. "That is a sorry tale indeed. For a man to fall to his death in his own stable yard."

"The girth was not properly fastened."

Adam whistled under his breath and picked up his goblet. "Such a simple thing."

"We were all raised to check our horses' girths before ever placing a foot in the stirrup." Esme drained her goblet and held it out so that Adam could fill it again. "'Tis second nature to us. Even to Jonah." She placed her hand daintily before her mouth as she hiccupped. "I watched him do so this morn."

Mayhap I should go easy on the rich wine.

Adam was gazing at her and the last thing she wanted to be was muddled.

But the wine was in her blood and the warmth of the crackling fire had brought a flush to her cheeks. Esme found she could not sit quietly. There was naught for it but to keep talking.

"'Tis strange, the twists of fate that have such an impact on our lives."

He still had not lifted his gaze from her face.

"'Tis indeed."

"If your parents had not died, you would never have worked for Rory Baine. And you would not be here now."

She thought, but did not say, that if Clara had not been killed, he would never have followed Rory Baine to Kielder Castle.

Instead, she glanced behind him, at the darkening sky still visible behind the open shutters.

Adam cleared his throat. "And if your uncle had checked his horse's girth that day, I might be here talking to the niece of an earl. Not the daughter of an earl."

His eyes burned with an intensity that sent another delicious twisting sensation deep into her core.

She placed her goblet down on the table, lest her trembling fingers betray the attraction she could no longer deny.

"Would that make such a difference?" she asked, staring right back into his eyes. Eyes that were flecked with fire.

Adam opened his mouth and closed it again. His voice had grown hoarse. "In truth, sweet Esme, I do not know."

Sweet Esme.

Her heart began to beat so quickly, she feared he might hear it over the crackling of logs in the fire. "I do not think it would."

Greatly daring, she placed her hand over his, emboldened to link her fingers with his when he did not pull away. A jolt of heat flowed all the way through her body.

"Not at all?" Adam's breathing was becoming heavier, matching her own.

"It might make things simpler." She looked down at their joined hands, because that was simpler than looking into his eyes. "I would have fewer pretty dresses. Fewer ribbons. Fewer bonnets. But I would no longer be troubled by false knaves seeking only my father's fortune."

She heard his sharp intake of breath. "Is that what you think of me?"

"Nay." Her eyes widened. That was not what she meant at all. "I do not think you have a false bone in your body."

"Good." He placed his other hand atop hers. "Because my feelings for you, Esme, are entirely sincere."

His words had stolen her breath. She could only look at him and hold on tightly to his hands, lest she become lost in the whirlwind of emotion rippling through her.

"Misguided, mayhap, but entirely sincere." He gave her a little smile which tugged at her heartstrings.

Esme swallowed, knowing she must tread carefully even as her instincts screamed for her to dive in. "Why misguided?"

"Because you are the daughter of an earl."

"By a twist of fate," she reminded him.

"And I am naught but a servant of Rory Baine. Your sister's father-in-law." He sighed deeply.

"You are a trusted friend of Callum; a man I hold as dear as my own brothers." The fire spat, giving her a glow of inspiration. "He even told me you were like family to him."

Another sigh. Another sad smile. Then he said, "Callum is kind."

He was about to pull away again, she could see it in his eyes. She tightened her grip on his hands, so that he would have to wrench them free.

"And you are not a servant. You are a warrior. Your father fought alongside the Laird of Kielder."

"Your family's enemy," he interrupted.

Esme tutted at that. If she were not holding onto his fingers so tightly, she would have flapped her hands at him.

"You think that should stand between us? When Frida has long been happily married to Callum?"

"There is the difference in our status." His eyes were so full of pain it was difficult to look at them. "And that is before I even think about your tender age to my bitter-long years."

"None of that matters." Esme lowered her forehead until it rested against his.

"I wish it did not," he whispered, his breath hitting her bare neck and sending a delicious tingling down her spine.

"It does not have to, if we do not let it." She placed her palms on his cheeks and gently raised his head until they were once more gazing into one another's eyes.

Only she felt as if she were gazing into his soul.

"I am not so grand as you think," she announced. "My mother was a village healer. In truth, she first went to Wolvesley as a servant."

She did not expect him to chuckle. "You are full of surprises, sweet Esme."

"*Her* mother was a suspected witch," she went on. "Which is why everyone was so worried when Frida used to talk to people who weren't there."

Adam was now trembling with repressed laughter. "I feel I must do something to stop you spilling all the de Neville family secrets."

Esme shook back her hair. She no longer knew whether her daring or her longing were fueling her decisions.

"There is something you could do," she said.

She inched closer, feeling well as hearing his next question.

"Tell me what it is."

"Kiss me."

She half expected him to refuse. But he did not.

Silence fell upon them as they sat close together in the empty hall, by the warmth of the fire. Esme could smell woodsmoke mingling with Adam's particular masculine fragrance. She fancied she could hear his heart beating, a steady thump beneath the raggedness of his breathing.

He wants to kiss me.

She knew this as surely as she knew her own name.

But will he?

His lips hovered less than inches from hers. His cheeks were coated with stubble, which was alternately black and grey. His breath smelled faintly of the wine they had drunk.

His arms, slowly, wrapped around her, drawing her closer to him.

She could not help a sigh of deep contentment and deep, deep desire.

His kiss was soft and gentle, his lips feathery light against her. She moved her hands to his shoulders, then entwined her fingers in his tousled hair, bringing him back for more.

Because she wanted more.

But a heavy hammering on the front door made them both freeze. Esme might have been inclined to ignore it, but after a moment's hesitation, Adam got to his feet. His expression passed from regret to bewilderment, before settling in the fixed lines of duty she was so accustomed to.

"It might be Jonah." His voice was rough.

Jonah.

She had all but forgotten her missing brother.

The hammering came again.

"Whoever it is, they are most keen to gain entry," she observed.

Adam gave her a curt nod and strode over to the entrance hall. "Leave it. I shall get it," he said brusquely, to Jennifer mayhap.

Then came the sound of the heavy bolts being pushed back

and the unmistakable squeak of the solid door being pushed open.

Esme put her hand on her heart. Who would come upon them at such an hour?

She strained her ears, but all she could hear was the crackling of logs in the fire. Suddenly unwilling to sit, she pushed herself upright. Just moments earlier, she had been so happy. But now she could not shake a feeling that something terrible was about to happen.

CHAPTER THIRTEEN

I SHOULD NOT *have opened the door without demanding to know who was there.*

Adam deliberately closed his eyes, momentarily making himself even more vulnerable to attack. When he opened them again, he was better able to see through the dark night into the cobbled courtyard.

Which was apparently empty.

He narrowed his eyes, looking right and then left before walking out onto the upper step. The air smelled fresh and clean, with the same brisk wind billowing about his tunic.

"Who is there?" he demanded in his harshest voice, unable to dispel a notion that their easy days of peace were over.

Have I grown so besotted with Esme that I have inadvertently put her in danger?

A sliding sound made the hackles rise on the back of his neck. Then came a hiccup. Adam spun around just as a hand landed on his leg.

"Adam, my good man. Help me up."

His words were slurred, but it was recognizably Jonah. Adam's pounding heart began to still.

"Milord."

Esme's brother was slumped against the wall of the house, his long legs inelegantly splayed amidst the autumnal remnants of the flower beds.

"I took a fall." Jonah sounded surprised, but not really put out.

The man is drunk, Adam realized.

He extended both hands and grasped him under his arms, pulling him upwards and allowing him time to recover his balance. Jonah wobbled a little, then clapped him on the back.

"I'm most grateful, sir."

"Let us go inside," Adam suggested, leaving one casual arm around the younger man's shoulders to keep him steady.

"Excellent. That is precisely where I was headed." Jonah hiccupped once more, then swung his free arm toward the open door. "Onward."

They made halting progress, with Jonah staggering a little, but seconds later, Adam was instructing Jennifer to refasten the front door whilst leading Lord Jonah to a chair by the fire.

The chair he had not long since vacated.

Regret burned in his veins as he beheld Esme's lovely face. The moment he had longed for had ended scarce before it began.

Esme folded her arms across her chest and shook her head, a dozen emotions chasing across her blue eyes.

"I am glad you have returned to us, Jonah," she said at last.

Although his finely stitched tunic was crumpled and stained, Jonah did not at all cut a sorry figure in the tapestried chair. A smile played across his face as he spied the pitcher of wine.

"We need another goblet," he declared. "If you please, Jennifer."

"Have you not imbibed enough?" Esme asked with sisterly sharpness, crossing the floor to sit beside him. "Jonah, you are more into your cups that I have seen for many a year."

"Ah." He held up a restraining hand, smiling more widely now. "That is for good reason, sister. I shall tell all. Once we all have a drink." He gestured wildly to Adam. "Come and join us."

Adam looked from brother to sister, reassured when Esme caught his gaze and nodded firmly. "Come and join us," she echoed.

Adam carried over a third chair as Jennifer brought in the wine. When he reached them, Esme leaned over and whispered in his ear.

"Do not think to leave me with him."

Her eyes rolled and he felt an answering smile stretching over his face. He longed to know if Esme regretted the interruption to their embrace, as he did. Or if she regretted the embrace and was glad of the interruption.

But she wants me to stay.

That had to be enough, *for now.*

He had positioned his chair too close to the fire for comfort. He perched as far to one side as possible and rolled up the sleeves of his tunic.

A sensible man would decline more of the rich wine that had made his head spin.

But on this night, Adam's sensibilities were being sorely tested. He accepted a full goblet and drank deeply.

Jonah brandished his goblet, spilling a little onto his breeches. "Cheers, friends."

"I am your sister," Esme pointed out.

"We are all friends," Jonah declared grandiosely. "And we have much to celebrate."

But Esme was still displeased. "Where have you been, Jonah? Pray, do not tell me you rode back here in this condition?"

Jonah looked perplexed by the question; his blue eyes roving over the fireplace as if he might find the answer in the finely wrought stonework.

"I have been in the alehouse." He smacked his thigh, pleased with deductions.

"All day?" Esme's voice was dry.

Jonah's eyes became glazed. "For much of it, I would wager."

His sister tutted. "How did you return?"

"By carriage." Jonah snapped his fingers. "The good physician said I should leave my horse in his yard till the morrow."

"Thank all that's holy for the physician," Esme muttered

toward Adam.

"I can still hear you, sister. The ale has not rendered me deaf." Jonah leaned forward, his eyes glittering. "Do you not want to hear my news?"

All Adam wanted was to be alone with Esme once again, but he could hardly demand this.

"Go on then, brother, furnish us with your news." Esme sounded weary as she sipped at her wine.

Jonah's blue eyes fixed on Adam. "Perchance this story affects you more than us," he ruminated.

Despite all that had passed, Adam was intrigued. "How so?"

Jonah's goblet completed another sweeping arc, but miraculously the liquid remained inside. "Roger Mortimer has been arrested."

His words fell into silence. Adam could not, at first, make sense of them.

Esme frowned. "Who could arrest a man with so much power?"

Jonah crossed his legs, looking very pleased with himself. "Only the King himself."

Adam breathed slowly, beginning to realize the import. But quick-thinking Esme got there before him.

"So, the young King is once again leading a united England." She put down her goblet and clasped her hands together. "Roger Mortimer, the usurper, is captured. This is good news indeed."

"As I said." Jonah was languid. "'Tis better news still for the prospects of lasting peace with Scotland."

"Aye." Adam readily agreed. It seemed as though half his body had a fever; he was burning up with heat from the roaring fire. He raked a hand through his hair, forcing himself to concentrate. "There was no telling where Mortimer's greed would lead him."

"He dined with us once at Wolvesley." Esme tapped her fingers on the arm of her chair. "Father said afterwards that he was not a man he was willing to trust."

"Amen to that." Jonah took another large mouthful of wine. "Better a young King than an imposter."

Adam nodded. Rory Baine had once been in correspondence with Queen Isabella's lover. Adam had worried no good would come of it. He was glad naught had come of it at all, as far as he could see.

"The King is not so very young these days." Esme shook back her hair, unaware of the beauty of youth. "How did it happen?"

"'Tis a marvelous tale." Jonah beamed at them both. "The King crept into Nottingham Castle by secret passage and arrested Roger Mortimer in front of the Queen herself." He pressed his lips together, briefly regretful. "How I wish I had been there."

Esme leaned forward, excitedly. "Do you think Tristan was there?"

A shadow passed over Jonah's face. "Our brother is always at the forefront of any excitement. Most likely he was the one to discover the secret passage." He drained his goblet and clumsily placed it down on the table.

Esme touched his arm in a rare show of sibling compassion. "Tristan is tucked up at home with Mirrie, awaiting the birth of their first child. Fear not, Jonah. On consideration, I do not believe he was at the forefront of this particular excitement."

Jonah was not to be dissuaded. "Then most likely he was the one to build the passage."

Esme's response was a peal of laughter. Adam wondered if they were at all aware of their good fortune in hailing from a large, loving family.

He rubbed at his temples and felt the pressing of his years upon him.

"Are you not pleased Adam?" Jonah rose to his feet, unsteadily, and clapped him on the shoulder. "I should think that Callum will be pleased."

"Aye." He nodded firmly and summoned a smile. "I am pleased with any step that takes us closer to a lasting peace."

"Peace and prosperity for all." Jonah swayed, grasping the

back of the chair for support. "England and Scotland united." He yawned widely. "I am going to sleep in the solar."

Without further ado, he began stumbling in that direction. Adam hurriedly went after him.

"Allow me to help you."

Jonah surprised him by grasping his forearm; almost as if they were kin. "Adam Hawker. You are a good man, I think."

"I try." Adam's smile became genuine.

"Be good to my sister." Jonah nodded vaguely in Esme's direction. "We will talk more in the morn. A great weariness has come upon me."

Adam waited until Jonah had disappeared into the solar before turning back to Esme. He wanted to take her in his arms and pick up where they had left off, but an awkwardness clung to him. Perchance she regretted her earlier actions.

One look at her radiant smile told him otherwise.

He stood in the vast hall and grinned back at her, feeling like a green youth.

Esme held out her hand and simply said his name. *An invitation.* He went to her willingly, eschewing the chair to kneel at her feet. The wooden floor was hard, but Adam scarcely noticed. He took her fingers and pressed them to his lips.

"I should walk away from you," he breathed.

She shuffled in her chair until the softness of her breasts pressed against his chest. "Why would you do such a thing?"

"For all the reasons we talked through earlier." He ran his hands through her waterfall of hair, loving the way it slipped through his fingers. He took a breath. "Because we have both drank our fill of wine, and I do not want you to have any regrets come the morn."

Esme tightened her hold on his shoulders. "The only regret I will have is if you do not kiss me again."

The last vestiges of his restraint fell away as his lips molded onto hers. Whereas before, his kiss had been gentle and tentative, now he was emboldened to claim her mouth as his own. Her lips were soft and yielding, her hands, entwined in his hair, pulled him even closer. Adam felt the urgent swell of his desire beginning to overtake all rational thought as he skimmed his palms over her bodice and along her spine.

She felt right in his arms. They slotted against one another as if long accustomed to the fit of their particular limbs and lips and fingers. How could that be? When she was light, and he was darkness?

But it was so.

Kissing her deeply, Adam had never felt so sure that he was entirely where he was meant to be. Her hands ran over his chest, and even though they were both fully clothed, he felt her touch like fire.

He groaned at the back of his throat. "We should take care."

"Just this once, I am of a mind to not take care."

Her playful whisper stoked his desire further. In one smooth movement, he could lift her from the chair and carry her to the rug. "But the servants." He pulled away, his breathing ragged. "We might be discovered."

I must not be caught deflowering Lady Esme de Neville.

The thought was instantly sobering. He rested his forehead against hers and tried to steady the pounding of his pulse.

Esme leaned back, her blue gaze scorching him. "There are other chambers."

He groaned again. "You know not how you torture me."

She swallowed and turned her head, so he regretted his harsh response. But at least his reason was returning. The lady did *not* know how she tortured him. She was an innocent.

Although she does not kiss like an innocent.

She kissed with all the passion and intent that she brought to everything else.

"I do not mean to torture you," she said tightly.

"I know this." He stood up, pulling her up alongside him and resting his hands lightly on her shoulders. She was slender against him. A delicate, beautiful flower that was not his to pluck. "You would not do anything that was ill-intended," he said in a rush. "You are all things that are honest and true."

Her response was to press her face against his chest. He caressed her hair, thinking it was better he could speak these words without the challenge of her all-seeing gaze. "I have never met anyone like you before," he whispered. "You have opened my eyes once again to the beauty of the world."

He felt her deep, shuddering breath. "There is much you have shown me, taught me."

He skimmed his thumbs over the defined lines of her cheekbones. "How to swing a sword?" he offered, half teasing.

"So much more." She tipped back her head, and her eyes shone up at him.

"I would not have you thinking that I am some old, seasoned warrior looking only for a conquest to brag about." He was trying—and so far, failing—to articulate the complexity of his feelings. "When I first met you, you were Lady Esme de Neville. Now you are a bright, guiding light in the darkness of the world."

"I am not anything so grand." She half shook her head.

"You are to me." He had to make her understand. "You are beautiful and pure in a way I have never known."

"What if I am not so pure?" she choked.

"But you are." He smiled down at her. "Kind and honest and pure. There is naught you would not do for another. Naught you would shy away from."

Once again, she pressed her face into his chest so he could not see her expression. 'Twas an invitation to further unburden himself.

"I have become hard and unknowable in these last years. I erected barriers in my heart and hid behind them. But you have begun to break them down."

Esme pulled away and he saw, with distress, that she was trembling.

"I am not the person you think I am."

"I think you are wonderful," he answered simply.

She put the back of her hand to her mouth, her eyes fixed on the floor. Adam realized, belatedly, that his words had pushed her away.

But how?

He had never been gifted with words. What had he said that was so amiss?

"Wonderful and good," he added, tentative now.

"Nay." She shook her head. "I cannot do this."

Of course she could not.

Adam saw the scene unfold in slow motion, as if he was hovering somewhere in the rafters. The beautiful, golden-haired lady. The clumsy oaf who had attempted to romance her.

How foolish he had become. In just one night.

"Forgive me." He backed away and put a hand to his head, immediately seeking to put distance between them.

"There is naught to forgive." Her words sounded sincere, but Esme looked everywhere except at him. "Truly, Adam. The fault is with me."

"I will leave you." His mind still whirred, but his body knew what to do. He gave a short bow, turned abruptly and walked toward the servant's door in the corner; his long legs striding across the polished floor, even as his heart yearned to stay where he was.

Where he had been, just moments ago.

Happy. Or at least, beginning to believe in the possibility of happiness.

You are a fool, Adam Hawker, he told himself grimly as he clambered up the steep, narrow stairs. He could scarcely see where he was going but could orient himself well enough with one hand brushing against the cold stone. He reached the top floor and flung open the door to his chamber so violently that it banged loudly against the wall.

"A damned fool," he said out loud.

CHAPTER FOURTEEN

SME FELT AS if her heart were being wrung from her body as she watched Adam walking away from her. He wrestled with the little wooden door and disappeared from view, without so much as a backward glance.

And she could not blame him.

She had treated him despicably. All because she could not bear to tell him the truth and see the shock of sudden disappointment darkening the glow of affection in his gaze.

She pressed her fingers to her eyes, hoping to stem the tears that threatened to spill.

This was not supposed to happen.

She should not have kissed him, nor entreated him to return to her so she could kiss him *again*. But such was the force of desire he ignited within her. All reason and rationality had fled. She only wanted *him*, mind and body and soul. Now that he had gone—*nay*, now that she had *compelled* him to leave—she felt more alone than ever in her life before.

Esme walked over to the fire and sank on her knees onto the thick rug spread before the hearth. She held her hands toward the flames, seeking some comfort from their warmth. But the heat seemed not to reach her. She was chilled through and could not stop trembling.

How could she move forward now?

Just days earlier, she had blithely considered a life without marriage. Without men. She had even contemplated this future with something like relief. But that was because she had not known what it was to stand in a man's arms and believe she belonged there. Had not known what it was to quiver at a man's touch and long for his kisses.

To feel as if she was not whole without him by her side.

She gazed unseeingly into the burning embers of the fire and felt knowledge twist inside her.

I am falling in love with Adam.

This was the truth she had struggled to admit to herself. The reason Jonah's poetry affected her so deeply.

And she dared hope that he loved her the same. She saw it in the way he looked at her; the way he held her, as if she were the most precious treasure.

But Adam thought her pure and honest and true. And she was not.

Esme hung her head, unable to prevent hot tears sliding down her cheeks. 'Twas all a bitter mess and there was no way out of it. If she told Adam the truth, she would ruin her image in his eyes and her family's reputation, all in one swoop.

But she could not continue to lie to him. Not now.

Esme reached out to grasp the arm of the chair and used it to heave herself to her feet. She felt as drained and weary as an old woman.

Perchance things will look clearer, come the morn, she thought. But she did not believe it.

She jumped in fright when Jennifer cleared her throat. *How long have I been standing in the shadows?*

"Beg pardon, milady. But there's a man here to see you."

Esme put a hand to her heart, which was beating so quickly she feared it may fly from her chest. "A man?" she repeated stupidly.

"He says he knows you." Jennifer avoided her gaze. "John brought him over and Agnes made him wait by the back door, but he said as how he knows you and we shouldn't treat him so poor."

A dreadful suspicion began to unfurl in Esme's belly. She took a breath. "Did he give a name?"

"Aye, milady. He said he was Sir Crispin de Gough."

Esme's world tilted. She held onto the back of the chair and desperately hoped this was not really happening.

All the days I have waited.

'Twas cruel irony that he should arrive now.

"But he dinna look like no knight to me, milady," Jennifer added in a low voice. "Should I fetch Adam?"

"Nay." Her answer came too forcefully, and the housemaid flinched. "The hour is late," Esme added quickly, modifying her tone. "And our visitor is correct. Sir Crispin de Gough is indeed known to me. You can show him in, Jennifer."

Jennifer bobbed into a small curtsy and left Esme alone to frantically gather her composure. She smoothed her hair as best she could; but there was no remedy for the turmoil of her heart. The last time Crispin saw her, she had been bedecked in pearls and ribbons. Now she wore a plain, practical gown, with no adornments. But the biggest change was to Esme as a woman.

She was no longer naïve. And her girlish giddiness had matured with self-reflection.

Moreover, she knew that she didn't love Crispin. The pull she had once felt toward him was one of simple, base attraction, whipped into something more by the secrecy and intrigue that had heightened their clandestine meetings.

She had never loved Crispin.

And Crispin has never loved me.

The realization settled in her stomach to the same beat as the heavy, booted footsteps crossing the entrance hall.

Esme turned to face him, her hands neatly folded and her face composed.

Jennifer scurried ahead. "Sir Crispin de Gough, milady."

But the servant had scarcely finished her announcement when Crispin strode past her and grasped Esme's hands in his, dispatching his heavy satchel by their feet.

"I have come," he announced.

For the smallest of moments, Esme's heart picked up speed. His nut-brown eyes were full of affection as he smiled down at her. His chestnut curls, which she had so loved to run her fingers through, beckoned to her just as loudly as ever. But his chiseled cheekbones gave him an appraising look, and his large hands gripped hers with a trace too much determination.

She looked down to see that his hands bore the mark of long days in the saddle. His fingers were stained, and his nails were dirty.

Esme extracted her hands with some difficulty. She would never again allow herself to be swept away by false promises.

"Crispin. I was hoping to see you some time before this."

"I was delayed, terribly delayed. Events did not go to plan." Rather than seek to renew their connection, Crispin began to pace up and down the great hall, tracking mud on the rugs in the process. He coughed and put a hand to his throat. "Can I have some wine, Esme? I am half-parched."

She quite appreciated the distraction of pouring wine into the same goblet she had drank from earlier. Passing it to Crispin, he drank deeply and gestured for more.

This time, she took a good look at him whilst he was occupied with the wine. His skin had lost its bronzed look, in fact he had dark circles around his eyes and his face, beneath the dust, was pale. His movements were jerky and anxious. His smile, as he placed the goblet on the table and came to stand before here, was entirely insincere.

"My own Esme. 'Tis the memory of you that kept me going."

Esme folded her arms. "Where exactly have you been?"

"'Tis of no consequence." He placed his hands on her shoulders, making her wince at the weight he pressed upon her as well as the sourness of his breath. "What matters now is the future. You and I."

Esme's heart stilled.

I do not want that future.

He must have seen the hesitation in her face, for Crispin's eyes quickly narrowed. "We are betrothed," he said, dampening his lips with his tongue. "You are my faerie queen; the only woman I want to be with."

Esme felt very calm. 'Twas almost as if she was watching this performance from afar. Two principal players stood amongst the low-burning candles in a hall that had already seen so much this night.

Crispin's overtures did not affect her because she knew them to be false.

Now that she had observed true feeling and true emotion, from Adam, she could recognize the counterfeit. Though sparse and sober, Adam's declarations came from a place of truth and honesty.

Crispin said much but meant little.

"I am no faerie queen," she said. "Indeed, this very day I have been working in the kitchen."

Crispin wrinkled his nose. "'Tis a blessing then, that I have come to save you from such a fate."

Esme lifted her chin. The fire in the grate was merely smoldering now, but she no longer felt any chill. Indeed, resolution burned in her veins. She spoke clearly. "I do not need to be saved."

A beat passed, during which she saw surprise and indecision race across Crispin's chiseled features. "I am sure the days must have grown long and dull for you here, sweet Esme."

She could not stand before him any longer. She turned away and walked to the window seat, lowering herself onto the cushions despite the draught from the open shutters. Now that some distance was between them, she could see a somewhat desperate slant to Crispin's shoulders. He held himself ready for battle, she realized, quelling a flicker of fear.

Surely, I have naught to fear from him.

"At first, they did," she admitted. "But I have grown used to the quiet rhythm of life at Ember Hall." Her mind skittered to Adam, but she could not allow herself to think of him now.

"But you must long to return to Wolvesley? With me? As man and wife?" Crispin's questions fell like drumbeats into the echoing hall. He put his hands on his hips and waited for her answer.

She could only answer with the truth.

"I do not. I'm sorry, Crispin. Much has changed for me."

He shook his head, almost disbelieving. "You would go back on your word? Break your promise to me?" He came to stand closer, and she saw a pulse flickering in his neck.

Esme took a deep breath, forcing herself to remain calm. *Aye,* she had given her word. But under circumstances that were extreme.

She rubbed at her temples, feeling her headache beginning to return. She had no wish to refer to *that* night. She would rather never talk of it again for the rest of her life.

"You accepted my ring, Esme." Crispin's voice was accusing.

"A ring made of straw," she bit back.

"It does not matter what the ring is made of." He was shouting now, his cheeks turning puce with rage. "In the eyes of the law, we became betrothed when you accepted that ring. In the eyes of the church, we became man and wife the moment you laid with me."

She flinched toward the window, wounded by the fury in his eyes as much as his words.

Words that she could not believe to be true.

He saw her doubt and smiled, cruelly. "'Tis true, Esme. When we return to Wolvesley, you can ask your father as much. He is still the judiciary, is he not?"

She could only nod as dread pooled inside her.

This cannot not be.

"The Earl of Wolvesley has always insisted his children live within the law." Crispin seemed to be enjoying himself.

Esme thought of her father, of his constant love and kindness to his family. And his intolerance of lawbreakers.

She hung her head, knowing she could not bear to disappoint him.

But memories of Wolvesley gave her a shred of hope, which she clung to like a raft in a storm.

"You know as well as I do, Crispin, that 'tis not fitting for an earl's daughter to marry in secret. We cannot return to Wolvesley as man and wife." She smoothed her skirts, as if nothing else in the world troubled her heart.

"I have no argument with that." He paced toward her, grasped her by the wrists and pulled her, inelegantly, upright.

Esme gasped with shock but would not give him the satisfaction of seeing the depths of her alarm. She regarded him steadily, this man she had once thought she loved.

"We will return to Wolvesley as a betrothed couple and there we will have a wedding grand enough to befit an earl's daughter." His sour breath hit her face.

Before she could frame a response, the servant's door banged open and out strode Adam, in a rage greater than she had ever witnessed.

"What is the meaning of this?" he thundered, his gaze taking in Crispin's hold of her wrists. "Step away from the lady, sir, if you wish to ever walk again." One hand went to the hilt of his sword.

Esme could have swooned with relief, but Crispin did not move. "Your concern does you credit, my good man. However, it is ill-placed. I am Lady Esme's betrothed, recently returned and ready to escort her home."

Skilled warrior though he was, Adam could not disguise his surprise. His eyes flew to Esme.

"Is this true?"

Nay, she wanted to shout.

But how could she do that? If, in the eyes of the law and the church, it was so?

"Tell him, Esme." Crispin's voice had the ring of steel.

She nodded, though it cost her dear. "'Tis true," she half whispered. "Though 'tis also true that I was not anticipating Crispin's return this night."

As an explanation, 'twas woefully inadequate. Adam must think so to. She saw his incredulity do battle with something worse as he sheathed his sword.

He fixed his gaze away from Esme and gave a perfunctory bow. "Forgive the interruption, sir. Milady. I will leave you, now."

"Stay a while." Crispin waved his hand. "We intend to leave for Wolvesley at first light. Can you make sure the carriage is ready?"

Esme winced to hear Crispin give orders to Adam; a man worth so much more than he, in every way that mattered.

But Adam stood firm. "I do not serve the Earl of Wolvesley. Nor do I serve the de Nevilles. I am here only as a favor to Sir Callum Baine. But if my services are no longer required, I will also be leaving at first light."

With that, he swiveled on his heel and was gone.

The only man who might have saved her.

But how can anyone save me, when this trap is entirely of my own making?

Esme wanted to sob. More than that, she wanted to run after Adam and beg his assistance. But she could only stand by the dying fire with the man she must now wed.

Crispin yawned widely. "It has been a long day, but a dare believe it has ended well. Time for bed, sweet Esme."

His hand at her waist made her nauseous. She deftly stepped out of reach. "Very wise, Crispin. Though I am afraid 'tis too late to expect the maid to make up a guest chamber. You must sleep here, before the fire." She was about to add that she would fetch him a blanket, but she changed her mind.

He was not so easily dissuaded. "Will I not keep you company in your own chamber?"

Esme shook her head. "Not until we are married in the eyes

of my father," she said firmly. "Good night, Crispin."

She walked from the room without a backwards glance, not hesitating until her chamber door was bolted behind her. Then she sank back against the wooden panel and allowed her despair to surface.

What now?

She had little choice but to return to Wolvesley on Crispin's arm, as Crispin's betrothed. 'Twas an outcome she would have longed for, just days earlier. But now the prospect filled her with a mixture of dread and grief.

Dread for the loveless years ahead.

Grief for the joy she might have known with Adam.

Esme blinked back her tears, focusing on the glow of candlelight from the dresser to keep her rooted in the present moment.

Her mother had long taught her to face the hardships of life without flinching. "What can't be cured, must be endured," was a favorite saying. But so was, "Fortune's wheel never stops turning."

Esme clung onto the thought, picturing her mother's finely drawn face and kind eyes. "Things have a way of working themselves out," she would say to her children, whenever they railed at some injustice.

Things had certainly worked out for Frida, happily married to Callum even though, for a while, he had been their brother's sworn enemy.

Likewise for Tristan, ensconced in domestic harmony with Mirrie, though for years he was blind to her and the love she had for him.

Esme pressed her lips together. Rather than feeling envious toward her siblings, she allowed these reflections to give her a flicker of hope.

Hope that was born out almost straight away, when a tentative knock sounded at her door.

Esme spun around and shot back the bolt. She did not need to ask who was there.

It must be Adam, come to put things right.

CHAPTER FIFTEEN

I HAVE BEEN *a damned fool, again.*

Adam's satchel was open on his narrow pallet, but he was too agitated to properly gather and fold his belongings. Instead, he gripped the back of an upright wooden chair and tried to regain control of his emotions.

For despite his many years of training and experience on the battlefield; despite all he knew about violence and where it led; there was nothing he wanted more than to swing his fists at the plastered wall.

He should not have allowed Esme into his heart.

Clearly, he had been but a dalliance for her. A flirtation. Something to pass the time.

A plaything.

He could not quell his roar of outrage, which reverberated around the small chamber.

The indignity he could deal with. This was not the first time a beautiful young woman had ensnared a foolish old man with her charms. Nor would it be the last.

What he struggled with, was the pain of rejection. For he had believed the connection between them was real. He had believed they were building something, together. Right until she had pulled away from him, trembling.

Nay wonder she did not want their kisses to go any further.

She was betrothed to a young man. A knight. Adam had

known it from the way the man stood. Entitled. Arrogant. He had met many such a man. Had paid them little heed. Fur mantles and fine clothes would not get a man far in battle.

Although Esme's betrothed had not cut such a fancy figure in his stained tunic and torn breeches. His hair had been combed, hastily perchance, but his face had not seen a washcloth in days. Where had the man been, to appear before a lady in such a state?

Adam turned back to his satchel with a growl.

What does this matter to me? Naught, he told himself, snatching up his good cloak and stuffing it inside. Lady Esme's affairs were no concern of his now.

Although he could not help but recall the strong emotions swirling in her blue eyes.

Fear, he had thought, the first second he barreled into the great hall.

She is scared of her betrothed.

But this had been replaced by something else. *Hope,* he fancied, when first she saw him come. At that moment, his heart had been filled with the urgent desire to protect her.

Just as he had foresworn to do.

But she had not denied the man's words.

And that flicker of hope in her eyes had turned into a desperate resignation.

He paced over to his small closet and flung what was left of his belongings onto the pallet, but his attention was not on the task.

What if I am wrong?

Or rather, what if his first instincts had been correct?

If Esme was afraid of this man, this imposter who had come to Ember Hall unannounced and in the middle of the night, then Adam's duties, as her personal guard, were to protect her.

And instead, he had walked away.

He sat down on the pallet, thinking hard. Callum had said naught about Esme being betrothed.

She is the youngest child of the Earl of Wolvesley. A prize many men would like to claim.

Mayhap this knight was some chancer, come to stake such a claim?

Adam dragged a hand through his hair, trying to recall what else Callum had said that night. He could not explain why Esme so strongly desired to remain at Ember Hall but had suggested some quarrel with an admirer might be the reason.

Adam snapped his fingers. *Mayhap that was it.*

He took a deep breath, not wanting to rush in *like a fool.* But he at least owed her a chance to explain.

Most certainly, I owe that much to Callum, if not to Esme, he told himself sternly.

He rose from the bed and straightened his shirt. If they were headed to Wolvesley at first light, there was no time to lose. But still, he baulked at creeping around a house at night. And to a lady's chamber, no less. Every time a floorboard creaked, he froze, half expecting to feel Jonah's sword pointed at his back. He was sweating by the time he reached the first-floor landing and the family's bedchambers.

Which door is Esme's?

He held his candle high, hoping for a clue and finding none. The smooth wooden panels were all neatly closed and the silvery moonlight filtering through the long window afforded no assistance. Would he have to knock at each in turn, risking Jonah's wrath?

Better a brother's wrath than a sister's distress, he reflected. Jonah might even come to his aid. Perchance he knew something of this knight and his background with Esme?

Then he remembered how Jonah had retired to the solar.

Newly emboldened, Callum strode forward, before a sound from the nearest chamber sent frissons of cold through his veins.

A scuffle. A squeal. The voice, undoubtedly, belonged to Esme.

The lady was not alone in her chamber.

Then came the low rumble of a man's laughter.

Embarrassed and angry, all over again, Adam turned away.

ESME HAD CURSED her stupidity when she opened her door to find Crispin on the threshold. Even more so when, instead, of flinging it shut, she somehow held it open whilst he shouldered his way inside.

"You should not be here," she had said.

Crispin had regarded her coolly. "I am here to make certain of your affections."

Esme felt her spine stiffen. "You must know by now that my affection for you is sorely diminished. 'Tis obligation that forces me to return to Wolvesley. No more."

"Obligation." Crispin walked further into her chamber, his greedy eyes roving over the polished furnishings. "What would the pampered daughter of the Earl of Wolvesley know about obligation?"

"I know plenty." She folded her arms, determined not to betray her growing anxiety. "I know to treat people with respect. I know 'tis wrong to ride away from someone without giving word of your likely return. Especially after—" She stopped abruptly, heat rising in her cheeks.

"After what?" Crispin leaned against the window ledge, a mocking smile playing about his thin lips. "Can you not bring yourself to say the words, Esme? 'Tis odd to display such reticence when you were keen enough to lay with me."

Her hands clenched into fists. She had not been so keen to lay with him. She had scarce known what she was about, nor where her actions would lead. But there was naught to be gained in arguing this point now.

"Are you come to shame me, Crispin?" she demanded instead. "Have you not already had your fill?"

"Not nearly," he retorted, his eyebrows raising beneath his hair.

Hair that was much in need of a wash, she noticed.

"You need to leave." She wrenched open the door and pointed into the hallway. "Now."

"Why should I?" Crispin regarded her steadily. "How are you going to make me?"

"I shall scream." She met his provocative gaze.

"And who shall hear you?" Crispin strolled across the chamber, making her stumble over to the dresser. He calmly refastened the door and turned toward her. "Your family are not here. I was told as much by the groom who took my horse. There is only your brother, Jonah. Do you really think him a match for me?"

There is Adam, she thought. But she knew it was unlikely he would hear her screams from his chamber on the top floor.

Nor would Jonah, as he was sleeping in the solar.

She must find some other way out of this.

"You surprise me, Crispin." She made her voice mild. "I once thought you a man of honor. At the very least, you were a man most certain of his success with the ladies. And here you are, occupying a lady's chamber against her will."

She hoped her acid words would bite but saw immediately that she had failed.

"Forsooth, there is much you do not yet know about me, sweet Esme." He reached out and touched her cheek, forcing her to flinch away. "But fear not, we have the rest of our lives to better our acquaintance."

While he was talking, Esme had reached behind her on the dresser, for the wooden sword which she'd discarded there after her last training session with Adam. She relished the look of surprise in Crispin's eyes as she brandished it before him.

"Get away from me!" she ordered.

The sword was not sharp, but it was sturdy and strong. It formed an effective enough deterrent to make him take a step backwards.

"Further," she said, jabbing at his belly with the tip.

"There is no need for violence, Esme." With one smooth

movement, he grasped her wrist and twisted until she had no choice but to drop the sword. As she scuffled away from him, he chuckled. "But I have to confess, it provided an unanticipated pleasure." He picked up the sword and examined it with apparent interest. "Is this how you have been entertaining yourself whilst I've been gone? With kitchen chores and toy swords?"

His baiting fell on deaf ears. She could only think of how to escape, but Crispin stood between her and the door.

"Now that I am back you can know other pleasures." He pushed her forcibly toward the bed. "Starting now."

Esme railed against him, raining her fists on his chest and kicking with her feet, but Crispin was tall and strong and insistent. He half dragged, half carried her over to the bed and threw her, unceremoniously, on top of it.

"No!" she screamed, biting at the hand that held her down.

"Do not do that." In the midst of unfastening his breeches, Crispin stilled. "Unless you wish to return to Wolvesley with a black eye?"

"You would not dare." She scrambled up the bed, her eyes frantically scouring the chamber for something else she might use as a weapon. "My father would see you in chains if you ever raised a hand to me."

"But you will no longer belong to your father, sweet Esme." Crispin's breeches dropped to the floor. "You will belong to me."

Fear coursed through her veins, but before she could think to respond, her chamber door was kicked open with such force the candle fell from the dresser. An acrid smell of burning came from the rushes and Esme blinked in the sudden darkness. But she did not waste the moment of reprieve. Swinging her legs, she rolled to the other side of the bed and backed her way into the corner of the chamber.

Two men were fighting at the far side of the room, but it was hard to see who was who, much less who was winning. A cacophony of shouts and grunts came from them both. Esme wrung her hands, unable to think how she might help.

It must be Adam, who had come to her aid.

But she could not be of service to him if she could not see him.

With trembling fingers, she fumbled for her nightstand to find a taper. The smoke from the rushes was thickening and making her cough. At last, she secured a flickering yellow light which illuminated the scene. Her frightened eyes took in Adam, breathing hard, tying a length of rope around Crispin's wrists. Crispin was face down on the bed with his hands behind him. He was shouting expletives into the blankets.

As soon as he had the man secured, Adam poured the contents of the water jug over the smoking rushes. With a hiss, the burgeoning fire went out.

Adam exhaled loudly, his gaze travelling at once to Esme. "Are you hurt?"

She shook her head. Her hand was trembling so much the candlelight jumped and shadows startled around them, as if the chamber was packed with people.

"Release me at once, you wastrel."

Adam showed no sign of having heard him. His eyes stayed focused on Esme's face. "Are you certain he did not hurt you?"

"Aye," she whispered. Blood pounded in her ears and her fingers shook. She must secure this taper before she started another fire.

Adam nodded, briefly. "I will take him away." He hauled Crispin off the bed, as if the tall knight weighed little more than a child. "If that is what you want?" he added.

Esme bit down on her lip, alarmed that he needed to ask. "It is what I want."

When they were gone, all the spirit went out of her, and she sank down onto the bed with an audible sob.

In recent days, she had come to doubt Crispin's integrity. But never in her dreams had she believed him capable of such violence and cruelty. To think, she had pledged herself to such a man.

Worse. She had *given herself* to such a man.

Her vision blurred with salty tears, but she could not summon the will to blink them away. She knew not how much time passed before Adam returned and she raised her head to find him standing, awkwardly, before her.

"I have brought you this." He handed her a goblet of the rich wine they had been drinking earlier. "For the shock."

But Esme could only think of how Crispin had drunk from her goblet. Mayhap his lips had touched this very rim? She placed it on her nightstand without touching a drop.

"'Twas a kind thought," she said, unable to look him in the eye.

"Will I leave you then, milady?"

"Nay." Still unwilling to glance upwards, she reached out and laid a hand on his arm. "Pray do not, Adam. I am sorry if I appear ungracious."

Immediately he sat beside her and placed a comforting arm about her shoulders. She leaned into his warmth and strength, and her trembling began to ease. Adam was a patient man. He gave her the time she needed without question, silently passing her a handkerchief when her tears began to fall.

"Where did you put him?" she asked at long last.

"In my chamber." At her look of surprise, Adam pursed his lips. "'Tis the only room for which I have the key."

"Of course." Gratitude washed over for her his thoughtfulness in not alerting more of the household.

"The situation must be addressed again come the morn." Adam tilted his head, thoughtfully. "I would see the man clad in irons and flung over the cliffs." Esme gasped at the vision and Adam grimaced. "Is it not what he deserves for attacking you in your own home, where you should be safe?"

For a moment, Esme thought of Adam's former love, Clara, who had not been safe in her own home.

But out loud, she said, "I cannot think clearly on this at all. Crispin is not the man I thought he was."

She felt him stiffen beside her. When she lifted her head, he was gazing blankly at a tapestry on the opposite wall. Pools of candlelight lit the chamber, and the smell of smoke still hung in the air. This room had always been peaceful—in days past she had railed at the unending tranquility of it—but now its serenity had been severed, and even familiar objects seemed strange and untethered. Tension and high emotion rolled around them in waves. Some of it, she realized, coming from Adam himself.

"I have much to explain to you," she whispered.

He gave the slightest shake of his head. "There is naught you have to explain, least of all to me. You are Lady Esme de Neville."

"And you are the man whose opinion I value above all others." Esme sat up straighter, so his arm slid from her shoulders. As much as she missed his touch, she knew she must speak freely and honestly, not hide behind vulnerability or distress. She pressed her palms together and took a deep breath. "'Twas true what Crispin said to you, downstairs. We were a betrothed couple. But 'twas only very recent."

"Did you love him?" Adam's voice was without expression.

"I believed so. Certainly, at first. Crispin was a hearth knight for my father, and I thought him the handsomest man I had ever seen." Esme plunged on with her tale, knowing her only hope was the truth. "We started meeting in secret not long after yule."

Adam gave her the ghost of a sideways smile. "Secrecy can add excitement to the most commonplace affair."

She felt the reprimand. "I see that now." Tears were leaking from her eyes once more and she impatiently dabbed them away with his handkerchief. "'Tis strange to think of these events. They seem so long ago. So foolish. 'Tis almost as if they happened to someone else."

"You do not have to speak of it, milady. I can guess at the bones of the story."

"Nay, do not say that." Her self-pity was replaced by a spark of frustration. "Do you not see what I am doing?"

Surprise flared in his face. "What?"

"I am explaining myself to *you*." She placed her hand briefly on his chest for emphasis. "Because of all that has passed between us. Because of who you are to me." She looked down, swallowing hard as she replaced her hand in her lap.

"And who am I to you?" His voice was strained.

"Someone important. Someone who should not seek to put distance between us by addressing me as *milady*." She sniffed. "Though I can see why you might want to do so."

It was a heartfelt plea such as she had never made before. Esme's pulse pounded painfully as she waited for his response. When he gently placed his hand over hers, she exhaled with relief.

"Tell me your story, please, Esme."

She turned her palm, so their fingers interlocked. The world around her grew steady and calm once more. She took a breath.

"It seemed as if every man in England was wrangling for my hand. Not for want of *me*, you understand? But in pursuit of my father's coin and patronage." At Adam's nod, she continued. "My parents threw a ball at which it was hoped I would choose a suitor. Crispin did not even turn up." She screwed up the handkerchief in exasperation. "Forsooth, that very night he planned to ride away from Wolvesley. I found him in his horse's stable, ready to leave." Her words dried up as shame rose within her.

"And then?" Adam prompted calmly.

"I did the only thing I could think of to get him to stay."

He was shocked. She could tell as much from his sharp intake of breath. Squeezing her eyes shut, she tried to explain. "I kissed him, freely. I permitted things to go further. Though I did not quite think they would go as far as they did. But nor did I ask him to stop," she added quickly, when she saw he was about to speak. "Nor did I protest."

It is important to be honest.

Adam looked down at their cojoined hands. "And then he asked you to marry him?"

She cast back her mind to that fateful night, but the details were unclear. "He gave me a ring."

"I see." Adam breathed heavily.

"A ring made of straw." A wave of heat rushed through her. "And then he left."

"Oh, Esme." Adam tightened his grip on her hand. "You deserve so much more than a ring made of straw."

She made a strangled sound, somewhere between a sob and a burst of laughter. "I would not care what any ring was made of, so long as it was given to me by someone who truly loved me."

Adam waited—and the room waited—for her to say the most important words.

"I know now that Crispin did not truly love me. Moreover, I have come to realize that I did not love him," Esme quavered. Yet she ploughed on, knowing she might never get this chance again. "I know all of this, because I have learned something of true love since coming to Ember Hall."

Adam's response was to shift on the bed, so he faced her. With his free hand, he lovingly stroked back her hair.

"Because of you," she whispered.

The smile he bestowed upon her was like dawn breaking after the darkest night.

"I have also learned something of love in these last days." He squeezed her hand. "Because of you."

Hope flared in her chest. "But you cannot still feel that way. Not now you know the truth about me."

Adam's gaze did not falter. "If you think that, then you underestimate the depths of my feelings for you, Esme." He put a gentle finger to her lips when she went to speak. "You are the same bold and beautiful woman I fell in love with. Naught has changed. Save the fury I feel toward the knave who so dishonored you."

She placed her palm on his stubbled cheek, her breath catching in her throat as he leaned into her touch. "Let us not speak again of Crispin. He has stolen enough from us, this night."

His kiss was sweet and gentle, and it unfurled all the emotions bound inside her so she feared her heart may crack open. She looped her arms around his shoulders and felt anchored.

Home.

They sat close together, arms wrapped around one another and their hearts beating to the same rhythm. Esme felt tension lifting from her body, until the urge to close her eyes became undeniable.

Adam's lips skimmed the top of her head. "I should leave you to sleep."

"Nay." She tugged at his shirt, keeping him beside her. "Stay with me."

"I cannot." His face was serious.

"I feel safe with you here. All I want is to lay beside you and rest."

For a moment, his arms tightened around her. "I will always keep you safe, Esme."

"I know it."

She did. She knew it with the whole of her being.

"Very well." He lifted her chin and gazed deeply into her eyes. "If you promise to sleep under the covers."

Yawning, Esme did as he bid, slipping under the blankets that he held open for her. "Why do you want me under the covers?"

He waited until she was settled on the pillows before leaning over and kissing her lightly on the lips. "I may be your protector, Esme. But I am also a man of flesh and blood." He threw her a rueful smile as he stretched out beside her, his long limbs kept separate from hers by the layers of blankets between them. "I am not a saint."

She reached up and kissed him, full on the mouth, but only for a moment. "I am glad to hear it."

She was still smiling, minutes later, when she drifted off to sleep.

CHAPTER SIXTEEN

ADAM AWOKE TO the dance of sunlight on his face and the sound of singing in his ears. Immediately alert, his eyes focused on Esme, who was sitting at her writing desk with her little black cat on her knee. For a long moment, he was able to watch her unobserved, admiring her waterfall of golden hair and the grace of her long limbs as she hummed a melodic tune. Then she noticed he was awake, and the spell was broken.

"Good morn," she said with a shy smile.

"I do not usually sleep so late." Adam sat up and rubbed at his face with his hands, encountering a rough growth of stubble.

"You do not usually sleep in my chamber," she responded lightly. "Is this the shape of things to come in our future?"

He smiled at her teasing, even though the idea of a future with Esme caused him equal parts pleasure and pain.

How can I, the son of a poor farmer and the servant of Rory Baine, have any kind of future with Esme de Neville?

But such ruminations were for another day. He must put them aside until the more pressing matter of Crispin had been dealt with.

"I shall have to remember that idleness is a sin." He swung his legs onto the floor, noticing the deep creases in his breeches. Despite the strain of last night's events, he felt well rested. Most likely because of where he had slept.

By Esme's side.

Where he wanted to be.

Unable to deny himself the joy of her proximity, he crossed the chamber floor and dropped a kiss onto her upturned face.

"Good morn," he whispered.

"Good morn." She tugged on his shirt tails as he straightened up. "Is that all I am to receive?"

He feigned amazement. "You want more of my kisses, milady?"

"I do not want them. I command them." Eyes dancing, she wrapped her fingers in his tousled hair and pulled his face back down to hers.

Adam kissed her willingly but then backed away laughing. "'Tis a terrible thing for me to confess, but all I can think is that I have not had my chewstick this morn."

She pretended to pout. "Your concern is all for your appearance. Next you will be complaining that you have not combed your hair."

"Ye Gods, I have not. Nor have I shaved the stubble from my cheeks."

Esme rose from the chair and placed her palms at either side of his face, ignoring the cat's mewl of protest.

"I like you with stubble on your cheeks."

"Do you though? Even when I do this?" He rubbed his cheek alongside hers until she squealed with laughter.

"As it happens, I do," she said airily. "There is naught you can do that displeases me, Adam."

He could have gazed into her eyes forever. "Naught?" He raised a teasing eyebrow.

"Nay indeed. When I am with you, I feel happy and safe."

His stomach contracted with a swell of emotion. "That is exactly how I want you to feel." His words came out gruffly, because she had taken him by surprise.

But they were words that he needed to say.

They must proceed only with absolute truth and openness. Although many more honest expressions of emotion would see him blubbing like a boy.

"This is a grand state of affairs." Determined to make his mood more playful, he put his hands about her waist and spun her around, her blue skirts flying.

"It bodes well for the future, does it not?" She sighed happily, resting her head beneath his collar bone, so that it was the most natural thing in the world for him to cradle it with his hands.

Her hair was slippery, soft and pungent with the scent of rosewater. Once again, he was reminded that he had neither washed nor changed his clothes since yesterday.

And it would be hard to do either with Crispin locked in his chamber.

A beat of silence fell, and Adam realized, belatedly, that Esme was looking at him expectantly.

"Why will you not join me in talking about the future?"

He should have guessed that she would pick up on his reticence. Esme was too quick-minded and alert to his moods for him to hide anything from her.

Instead of prevaricating, he traced his thumb along her cheekbone and looked deep into her blue eyes.

"Because I am the son of a farmer, and you are the daughter of an earl. Because you are in the springtime of your life, and I am well past midsummer."

She frowned. "We have already talked on this, at great length as I recall."

How he hated being the one to ignite such sadness in her expression. But the connection between them ran too deep to countenance falsehoods.

"We talked about why I should kiss you without hesitation." He rocked her slowly, shuffling until they were away from the glare of sunlight coming through the shutters. "We talked about why we should not be ashamed of this bond that has sprung up between us. All of that I own, even in the bright light of day."

"What then?" Esme was gazing at him with such heartfelt emotion he could have begged her to look away.

"We did not talk of a future between us. I am not sure I dare to dream of such a thing."

Esme's expression changed. Adam was braced for her anger, but when she spoke, her voice was gentle.

"That is where you are going wrong. You should always dare to dream, Adam."

A smile stretched across his face as her words resonated inside him. Once upon a time, he realized, he had dared to do just that. "Mayhap you are right."

"I often am." She nodded in a most businesslike fashion. "But now you must leave me."

He blinked at this sudden change. "How so?"

"We have much to do, this morn. First, I must wash and changeout of yesterday's clothes." Her cheeks pinked, prettily. "As much as I dare to dream of a future for us, that does not include me struggling out of my underthings in your presence. Not yet anyway."

He could not help a low chuckle at her boldness. A chuckle that helped to dispel his sharp twist of desire at the picture she painted for him.

"Well, that is a future I look forward to," he said huskily, leaning down for a parting kiss.

"Away with you." She flapped her hands. "If you see Jennifer, pray ask her for a fresh bowl of water. Mine went all on the rushes."

He had all but forgotten the smoke and his sharp fear that the fire would take hold whilst he wrestled with Crispin.

He glanced down at the blackened rushes by the dresser. "We had a lucky escape."

"*I* had a lucky escape," she corrected him. "Because of you. And I will never forget that."

"I would do it all again, a thousand times." His voice near trembled with sincerity.

"Let us hope you do not have to." Esme put her hands on her hips and threw him a glare. "Do you insist on staying to watch me wriggle out of my underthings?"

"Do not tempt me."

Laughing, he went from her chamber and closed the panel behind him. The long gallery was quiet, with dappled sunlight on the plastered walls. Such joy bubbled up inside him that he could almost forget he had an angry knight to deal with.

And perchance an angry brother into the mix, especially if Jonah had any idea where Adam had spent the night.

He must hope and pray that Jonah had slept through all of the evening's drama. And the young lord had drunk enough wine to make that probable.

Adam was not sure whether to go downstairs or up to his own chamber. But he had no wish to face Crispin before he must, and his stomach was rumbling with hunger. Humming to himself, he headed for the kitchen, passing Jennifer on the stairs and relaying Esme's message about water.

If the housemaid was surprised to receive such domestic instruction from a warrior, she hid it well.

The kitchen was warm and smelled of freshly baked bread. Agnes startled to see him, clasping floury hands over her apron.

"Mercy, you gave me a shock. I was beginning to think the place was deserted. Lady Esme is usually down before now."

Adam carefully said nothing. He had already risked Esme's reputation in speaking to Jennifer.

"Is milady awake?" The cook's question was nonchalant, but he felt her eyes upon him as he walked over to the breadbasket.

"I could not say." He crammed a heel of bread into his mouth to avoid further questions.

"Could not or would not?" Agnes crossed to the sink and picked up a knife which Adam eyed warily. "There's not much goes on in this house that the servants dinna know about. And there's plenty that's gone on over the years, if you know what I'm saying."

Adam was not sure that he did.

"What happened to that young knight that turned up out of

the blue?" she continued, pushing her plait over her rounded shoulder.

Adam cleared his throat. He had not anticipated an inquisition. "I could not say," he repeated.

"You'll need drop your airs and your distance if you're going to stay here," Agnes observed, reaching for a turnip and beginning to peel it.

"Am I going to stay here?" His eyebrows raised with genuine curiosity.

Agnes turned to face him. "Do you *want* to stay here?"

Adam's hand hovered over the bread. He could pick it up and flee. But the cook's question made him pause.

He had not properly considered where he wanted to stay—or go, for many a year.

He had gone where his master bid him. But did it have to be that way?

"I have not thought."

Agnes snorted. "I suppose that's better than *I could not say*," she mimicked, with a smile to take the sting from her words. "Think on it, sir. There are worse places to wind up."

Adam fished for words. "I do not know if the possibility exists for me to stay," he said at last, folding his arms and leaning back against the scrubbed wooden table.

"Oh, it exists." Agnes waved her knife airily. "All things are possible up here in the northern hills. People can be who they want to be."

The idea was preposterous to him. How could aught be so simple?

The cook laughed at his expression. "Many a day I had Miss Mirrie in here, miserable as can be over her unrequited love for Lord Tristan. And look at her now! A lovelier bride I never did see."

Adam had only the slightest grasp who she was talking about. He could see no comparison between himself and the ward of the Earl of Wolvesley.

"I am sworn to a Scottish laird," he said, reminding himself as much as Agnes.

She gave him a knowing look. "And my master is the son of a Scottish laird. As I said, all things are possible in these hills. If you want it enough, that is." She turned back to her turnips, seemingly losing interest in the conversation.

Adam helped himself to more bread and slipped through the back door, desperate suddenly for some fresh air. As soon as his feet hit the cobbles, he felt better. Birds sang in a sky that was as blue as midsummer, but the chill of the season kept his senses sharp. He walked through the stable yard, smelling the sweet hay and rubbing the ears of a little grey pony who whickered at his approach.

"Good morn, mister Adam," called John from across the yard, carrying a pitchfork over his shoulder.

Adam nodded his head. "Good morn."

"Lovely day for it," the groom continued. "Whatever *it* is, of course." The man laughed at his own joke as he disappeared into a stable, and Adam's lips twitched upward.

He smiled, even as reality sunk its teeth into his arm and reminded him what the day must bring—a confrontation with Crispin. Mayhap a similar confrontation with Jonah, who surely could not live through this day without learning the truth of Esme's relationship with Crispin?

Nor, perchance, the truth of his own relationship with Esme.

It would be a day of reckoning. But whichever way it turned out, Adam recognized that he was more at home at Ember Hall than he had ever been at Kielder Castle, despite all the friends and allies he had in the highlands.

And was that so strange? When he had grown up just a few hours distant?

As his eyes roved over the green hills, his mind raced at the possibility that the cook's words were right.

Perchance all things were possible.

If he dared to dream.

CHAPTER SEVENTEEN

ESME DRESSED WITH care, knowing that this day was important. It was a time for standing firm and acting with purpose; lace, ribbons and bright colors would not strike the correct note.

Instead, she went again to Frida's closet and brought out a simple gown of sage-green with small buttons and minimal decoration. *Green for Wolvesley*, she reminded herself as she tied the sash. She was Esme de Neville, and she would not be taken for a fool.

When Jennifer offered to dress her hair, Esme dismissed her with a smile. She could manage very well herself, with a comb and hairpins. Once ready, she spent little time gazing into the looking glass. Instead, she walked swiftly through the long gallery and descended to the great hall.

Her stomach was churning with so much anticipation that she could scarcely even glance at the foodstuffs laid out on the trestle table. Her gaze went to Adam, standing ramrod straight in front of the newly lit fire. He turned at her footsteps and smiled, softly.

"You look beautiful, Esme."

That had not been her goal. She pulled a face as she joined him at the hearth. "I hoped to look serious."

"You can be both." He took her hands in his. "You know that you have my full support, whatever the next hours bring?"

"I do." Standing by his side made her feel safe and content, despite the ordeal ahead of them. "I see you have chosen to keep the stubble I so admired." She tilted her head and smiled up at him.

"Alas, I have not had the opportunity to wash or change my clothes," he said ruefully.

"Of course." Her hand went to her mouth. "Crispin is still in your chamber."

"Shall I bring him down?"

Adam was a man of action, but Esme found she had not yet gathered her courage. She shivered and wrapped her arms about herself, glancing toward the solar door. "Has Jonah not risen?"

"I have not seen him." Adam regarded her carefully. Even in his crumpled tunic, he exuded an air of authority. "Shall I knock on his door?"

"Nay." Her answer came too quickly, and she took a deep breath to calm herself. "In truth, Adam, I would prefer that my brother did not bear witness to my shame."

Jennifer chose that moment to come in from the kitchen. She bobbed into a small curtsy when she saw them by the fire. "Beg pardon, milady. Shall I clear the table?"

Esme tried to order her thoughts. "Lord Jonah has not yet broken his fast. Leave it for a while, if you please, Jennifer."

When the maid left the room, Adam once again took her hands inside his. The urge to lean into his strength and comfort was almost overwhelming, but she knew she must stand tall.

"Any shame belongs to Crispin. 'Tis not yours to bear," he declared.

She met this gaze. "My foolishness, then," she amended.

"Nay, Esme. I will not hear this."

"And I will not deny it." She made her voice level. "I made a mistake. A foolish mistake. 'Twould be wrong of me to pretend otherwise."

"You allowed yourself to be deceived by a man who set out to charm you. That is no great crime."

His calm insistence broke through her barriers, and she smiled up at him, some of the tension leaving her body. "Not all would see it that way, but it makes my heart glad to know that you do. I *was* a fool, but I shall know better in the future."

"Forsooth, you are very wise." He paused to push back a tendril of her hair. "You said something this morn that has made me see everything differently."

A warm feeling of pleasure ran through her, at his words as well as his touch. "What did I say?"

"That I should dare to dream." He cupped his palm about her face, looking deeply into her eyes. "I am endeavoring to do so."

Her breath caught in her throat. It would be the most natural thing in the world to stand on her tiptoes and press her lips to his. But a voice spoke in her ear and urged restraint. This was no time for girlish gaiety.

Later, there would be time for kisses and dreams.

Esme placed her hand atop his and took a steadying breath. "I am happy to hear it. This gives me courage to face what is to come."

Adam gave a slight nod, seemingly privy to the run of her thoughts. "Should I fetch him now?"

Her lips quirked. "I suppose we cannot delay indefinitely."

He dropped a chaste kiss onto the top of her head. "Have faith, Esme."

With that he strode in the direction of the servant's staircase, leaving her alone. Esme clasped her hands together and gazed fixedly at the fire. She wanted to pace, to release some frustration by pounding the wooden floorboards, but she would not give Crispin the satisfaction of coming into the room and seeing her ill at ease.

She could not countenance him thinking he still had the ability to make her heart pound.

They are taking an unholy amount of time.

She spun around to face the servants' staircase, willing the panel to open and for Adam to appear, but the door remained resolutely closed. A pressure against her calves made her look down to see Felicity winding about her ankles. The little cat mewed, as if sensing her distress.

"Are you come to give me comfort?" Esme asked idly, reaching down to stroke her.

Felicity purred loudly, arching her back with her tail stuck straight in the air.

Esme was about to scoop her up, when the sound of trampling footsteps made her pause. She had just straightened her back when the door to the servants' staircase opened, and a familiar figure emerged.

Crispin.

The same chestnut curls and glinting eyes which had once made her knees weaken. Though now she fought a wave of nausea at his confident smile.

"Good morn, sweet Esme."

"'Tis not the best of morns, for you," she replied tartly, nodding toward his bound wrists.

But Crispin merely shrugged. "I see my betrothed, looking lovely as ever. And a table fair groaning with foodstuffs." At this announcement, Crispin's stomach audibly rumbled. "I am not an ambitious man, Esme. I do not seek more than that."

She was discomfited, which was no doubt his intention. Esme's eyes traveled behind Crispin's crumpled figure to the doorway which remained stubbornly empty. Crispin followed her gaze and smiled.

"I begin to see how the situation unfolds. You wait upon my jailer, do you? The hulking serf who pretends to be my better?"

"Adam pretends to be naught he isn't," she said hotly.

"Adam, is it?" He raised his eyebrows and Esme wondered why she had never noticed the cruel slant to his eyes.

As if their words had summoned him, Adam now appeared at the bottom of the staircase. He closed the door behind him and came to stand beside Crispin. He had changed into a fresh shirt and fastened a sword belt around his waist. Esme was reassured by the gleam of metal at his hip.

"What are your orders, milady?" His voice was quiet, and his actions were understated, but his eyes were quick and alert.

Esme lifted her chin, bidding herself to remain calm. "Crispin is to leave."

Adam put a heavy hand on the knight's shoulder. "You heard the lady."

However, Crispin seemed hardly to hear them. "Not so fast, dear Esme. We have much to discuss. And I have not yet broken my fast."

"There is naught to discuss." She worked hard to keep her voice from trembling as a feeling of rage rushed through her.

"I have traveled frequently and far in these lands." Crispin strolled to the window and gazed out at the green fields beyond, as if he were an honored guest at Ember Hall. "And wherever I have rested, I have always been welcomed as a knight sworn to the Earl of Wolvesley."

Adam made a strangled sound. "A privilege you have abused, sir."

"A privilege I have enjoyed." Crispin kept his back to them both. "Though one that will pale into insignificance once I am accustomed to my new standing."

Esme's hands clenched into fists. She could not bear to hear him say the words she knew were coming.

"Please stop," she choked out, at the same time as Crispin turned to face them with a flourish that was hardly dampened by the fact of his bound wrists.

"As the new *son* of the Earl of Wolvesley."

"You will never be that," she declared, through gritted teeth. All her carefully gathered composure had deserted her. She thought that she would like to run at Crispin and slap his face.

Adam strode forward before she could do anything she might later regret. "It is time for you to leave." He put his hands on Crispin's shoulders and turned him to face to door. Esme was gratified to see that he stood some half a head taller than their foe.

Nonetheless, Crispin found the strength and balance to resist, seemingly grinding his boots into the polished wooden floor.

"Unhand me this instant." He swatted at Adam as if he were a mere annoyance. "How dare you treat me this way? Do you not know who I am?"

Something had pierced Adam's careful self-control. Esme could see it in the way he held his body, like a hawk about to dive upon its prey. "I have seen many men like you." Anger flashed across his stubbled face as he leaned closer. "Aye, I know exactly who you are."

"I am the son of a nobleman." Crispin glared into Adam's eyes, even though he had to tilt his chin upwards to do so. "And you are nothing. You have no authority over me."

A terrible fear dropped over Esme, like a coarse and scratchy blanket.

Could Crispin be right?

Even if Adam successfully removed him from Ember Hall, there was no telling what harm he might wreak upon her, should he return to Wolvesley.

As if reading her thoughts, Crispin switched his gaze from Adam to herself. Despite all her best efforts, Esme found herself cringing.

"If you insist on me leaving this place, I will go at once to Wolvesley Castle. Imagine, dear Esme, the conversations I will have there."

Sickened, she pulled away from his hypnotic gaze and looked, instead, at Adam. For a brief moment, their eyes met across the vast hall, and she felt as if all might yet be well.

Adam's fingers closed around the hilt of his sword, no doubt longing to draw it free. "You are in no position to bargain, Crispin. You are bound and I am not. If I must take you back to Wolvesley myself to ensure the earl hears the truth, I will do so."

Esme's heart leaped with hope, but Crispin only chuckled—a sound which made the hairs rise up on the back of her neck.

"You will, will you? And who do you think the earl will believe? A knight he has ridden with into battle? Or a Scots servant he has never before laid eyes upon?"

Esme took a breath. "My father will recognize the truth when he hears it."

"Excellent." Crispin nodded sagely. He strolled over to the trestle table and perused the contents with lazy interest. "He will recognize the truth about his daughter, who laid with me freely, in a stable, no less."

Esme hated herself for flinching and hated Crispin even more when he hooted at her obvious discomfort.

"Mayhap he will recognize the truth about that same daughter having transferred her affections to a man worth precisely naught." He raised an eyebrow at her mockingly, before raking his gaze over Adam so there was no doubting his meaning. "I've seen how you look at him, Esme. Like a cat desperate for attention. Like this one, here." Before Esme's startled eyes, Crispin took aim at Felicity with his foot. The little cat had been sniffing his boots; now she flew through the air with a mewl of protest.

"You brute." She ran over to where Felicity landed, relieved to see her recover and then dart away—tail low—to hide beneath an armchair. Esme put her hands upon the back of that same chair, her pulse pounding. "How could you do that to a defenseless creature?"

"To whom do you refer?" Crispin drawled. "Yourself or the cat."

"Enough of this." Adam held up a palm to silence him. "You can accuse me of aught you wish. But I will not hear you slander Lady Esme's good name."

"Then you had best stay away from Wolvesley." Crispin shrugged. "Especially in the days to come. And it matters not how you glower at me, nor how your fingers linger on the hilt of your cheap sword. You are but a servant here. You have no authority. You cannot strike down a knight without facing comeuppance, and you know it."

"I will face whatever I have to." Adam's face was white with anger. Esme knew a thrill of fear that he really would strike Crispin.

And face the consequences.

"Stop it, both of you," she cried, striding between them and holding out both of her arms.

"Now this I long to see." Crispin looked as if he was enjoying himself, despite his hands being bound before him. "You have the status, Esme, but not the strength to stop me. If only your brother was here."

"Oh, but he is."

Esme turned, along with Adam and Crispin, to see Jonah standing in the open doorway from the solar.

He adjusted the cuffs of his shirt and smiled benevolently. "I have no doubt you were referring to Tristan, of course. But I'm afraid you shall have to make do with me."

Her heart sank.

Now my brother must bear witness to my shame.

"It seems I have much to catch up on." Jonah walked steadily into the hall and surveyed the trestle table. "Esme, you can fill me in whilst I break my fast."

CHAPTER EIGHTEEN

ADAM FELT HIS spirits sink along with Esme's. The lass had hoped to be rid of the knight before her brother awakened and heard her sorry tale.

But Adam knew that the truth was best laid out in the open, not hidden away in dark corners to be stumbled over at a later date. Mayhap Jonah's arrival was a blessing?

Certainly, it might save him from running that base knight through with his sword. The temptation had been achingly strong. In truth, it coursed through him still, like warmed wine on an empty stomach.

Esme was white-lipped, but she held herself admirably still. She could face down a battle charge without flinching, that one.

"Pray, do not trouble yourself, Jonah. 'Tis a trifling matter and Adam has it well in hand."

Damnation.

He deliberately folded his arms, clenching his hands so they could not reach for the hilt of his sword.

Jonah's pale blue eyes flickered toward him. "Is that true, Adam? Do you have the situation under control?"

He grimaced, wondering how best to answer without contradicting Esme's claim. A few feet across from him, Crispin leaned his hips against the trestle table. Adam was gratified that he had tied the man's hands in such a way that made feeding himself impossible. Otherwise, he had no doubt that Crispin would be helping himself to grapes right about now.

Jonah took a seat at the opposite end of the table and began spreading a hunk of bread with soft cheese. "Well?" he asked.

"I found this man attacking your sister, last night," he said bluntly. "The situation is under control as you can see. His wrists are bound. He will not hurt her again. The question is, what shall we do with him now?"

He had told the truth.

Though he dared not look toward Esme to see what she made of it.

He expected some show of surprise from Jonah, but the young lord chewed thoughtfully and swallowed. "I recognize you, I think?"

Crispin bowed his head. "Sir Crispin de Gough. I serve your father."

Jonah clicked his fingers, a rare smile transforming his face. "That's it." He cut another piece of bread. "And how fares my father?"

A trace of discomposure showed on Crispin's unshaven face. "Very well, milord."

"You have seen him, recently?" Jonah's gaze traveled over Crispin's stained clothing, but he passed no further comment.

Adam's pulse, which had started to pound when Jonah first claimed to recognize Crispin, began to steady. He risked a glance toward Esme, who had mirrored his stance with her arms crossed across the demure bodice of her blue gown. She felt his eyes upon him; he could tell by the way her body stiffened. But she did not meet his gaze.

"Not recently." Crispin's voice showed some strain.

"He has sent you on some campaign, I think?" Jonah smiled, encouragingly. "You have endured many nights of discomfort, is that not so?"

The knight smiled, relaxing a little. "Perchance, a little discomfort, aye. But I will endure much in the service of milord."

Esme strode forward, placing her hands on the table and

leaning angrily toward Crispin. "You lie. You rode away from the service of my father after the last Wolvesley ball. Whatever you have been doing these last days, 'tis not in my father's name." She gave her head a little shake. "I do not know why this surprises me. One more lie atop a dozen or more."

Jonah pursed his lips and carefully placed his knife down beside his trencher. "And what is this about you attacking my sister?" His voice was soft, but his eyes were razor sharp.

"A misunderstanding," Crispin countered quickly.

"Not so." Esme tossed her hair. "He came at me in my chamber. If it were not for Adam's intervention—" she stumbled to a halt. "Crispin all but started a fire."

Crispin tutted. "I would have saved you the embarrassment of this, Esme."

"She has naught to be embarrassed over." Adam could stay quiet no longer.

Crispin continued as if he had not spoken. "But 'tis true that all will be known before long." He shuffled his feet until he stood beside Esme. Adam fancied that he would have slung an arm about her shoulders, if he were able to. "Your sister has done me a great honor."

"I have not," Esme snapped.

Jonah held up a hand, a plea for peace. "Allow the man to speak."

Esme's face showed her shock. Adam too knew a prickling of fear. Would Jonah side with the knight, after all?

Crispin clearly thought so. He looked down at Esme with the gleam of victory in his eyes.

"She is already my wife, in every way that matters." His voice was silky.

Esme darted away from him as if he had struck her. "'Tis not like that, Jonah." She gripped her skirts and gazed at the floor as if seeking inspiration.

Adam hated to hear the distress in her tone, but he was helpless to assist her. Intervening now would be unseemly at best. He rubbed at his aching temples, hoping fervently that Jonah had just some of the integrity and intelligence he had credited him with.

Or was it to be a case of the earl's son supporting the wealthy knight, even against the supplication of his own sister?

"Already your wife in every way that matters," Jonah repeated, as if reciting some indecipherable rhyme. "Does that mean what I think it means, Esme?"

After a terrible pause, she nodded. Her head was low so he could not see what emotion shone in her eyes, but the air fairly shimmered with tension.

"She laid with me at Wolvesley," Crispin put in. Perchance wanting it to be clear.

Adam stiffened and so, he fancied, did Jonah.

"I see." Jonah's gaze traveled to his sister. Eventually she too looked up and they locked eyes.

Two golden haired, blue-eyed de Nevilles. Could Esme count on her brother's support?

Adam clenched the hilt of his sword, but only out of habit. He could not wield it against Jonah de Neville.

Jonah scratched at his faint growth of beard, his expression thoughtful. "It cannot be said that I am a worldly man." He looked at Crispin, as if for confirmation.

Mayhap taken by surprise, the knight nodded.

"But I do believe that these things, occasionally, happen." Jonah's blue gaze now swung to Adam. "Is that not the case?"

What is happening here?

"I have heard tell of such things." Adam forced out the words.

Jonah nodded. "Esme, do you wish to wed this man?"

She showed only momentary surprise, before casting a withering look at Crispin. "Most assuredly, I do not."

"Then there is naught further to discuss." Jonah opened his palms, as if dismissing them both.

Adam was half-frozen in place with shock, but he gathered his wits and walked purposefully forward. "Shall I escort him outside, milord?"

"I do not know if he should, after all, be flung into the cellar for a while. Any man who moves against Lady Esme de Neville should be punished, do you not think?"

Adam felt a smile pull at his lips. "Very wise, milord."

But Crispin stood tall. "I would advise against that, de Neville. Unless you intend to keep me prisoner here for the rest of my days."

Jonah also rose up from the table. He did not have Crispin's height or bearing, but real anger showed in his finely-boned face. Adam recalled how Esme had lauded his swordsmanship, and fancied that it would not serve to underestimate the youngest de Neville son.

"Do not tempt me, sir," he said.

"Nay, Jonah. We do not want a man like him poisoning the sweet surrounds of Ember Hall." Esme held her head high. "You will leave us, Crispin. And never trouble us again."

A pulse flickered at Crispin's neck. Before Adam could restrain him, he slammed his bound fists onto the table, making the platters of food jump. "That is the trouble with you people. You always think you have more power, more *right* than the rest of us. When will you start listening?" He shook his head, almost regretfully. "You cannot win in this. Esme, you will be my wife. Jonah, you will be my brother." His voice rose with mirth.

"The man is deluded." Jonah wiped his fingers on a linen cloth, his face screwed up in distaste.

Adam knew not whether to bundle Crispin from the room or wait to see how the man might explain himself. It felt wrong to take charge of the situation, when the son of an English earl was also present.

I am but a servant, Adam reminded himself.

His feelings for Esme counted for naught. Forsooth, Jonah may well fling *him* into the cellar, should he discover them.

Watching the scene, Adam began to feel detached from it. He had never felt further apart from Esme, than when Jonah and Crispin faced one another.

Two sons of the English aristocracy.

Whereas he was the son of a farmer.

A Scots farmer, at that.

His muscles and training meant nothing. Without rank or wealth, he could not hope to save Esme from this situation. The realization caused a deadening of sensation within him.

"Explain yourself," Jonah commanded.

Crispin's eyes never left his face. "Your sister gave me her virtue and accepted my ring. We are, to all intents and purposes, already wed. Will the Earl of Wolvesley state this is not so?"

Jonah's gaze flickered.

"The Earl of Wolvesley, your father, is the judiciary, is that not so?" Crispin smiled cruelly.

"The Earl of Wolvesley puts the happiness of his children above all else," Jonah stated.

"Indeed. Does he put it higher than his family's reputation?"

Jonah's eyes glittered menacingly. "Are you threatening me, de Gough?"

"Finally." Crispin widened his stance and threw back his shoulders. "The man realizes what is happening. Aye, *Lord Jonah,* I am indeed threatening you. If I do not get my way in this, every family in England will know how your sister laid back in the straw and spread her thighs for me."

If Jonah had not leaped for him, Adam would have. Crispin's coarse words had reawakened his senses, like a jug of cold water flung over his head. But the fury in the young lord's face gave Adam pause to think.

Closing his ears to Esme's distress, Adam pulled the two men away from one another. "He is not worth it," he told Jonah, shortly, giving him time to find his balance as Crispin stumbled against the table.

Jonah straightened his tunic, his breath coming fast. "I have never wanted to see a man's head roll before this day."

But Adam's mind was speeding quickly in another direction. "Lady Esme accepted your ring, you say?" he demanded.

Crispin nodded. In parting the grappling men, Adam had swung his fist at the knight's face. A steady stream of deep red blood now flowed from a cut on his lip.

"And you wanted to marry her?" Adam laughed, even though the situation was far from humorous. "You certainly seem possessed of the desire to marry her now."

Crispin nodded again, his eyes blazing with fire. If his hands were not bound, Adam knew he would have been obliged to reach for his sword before now—for self-defense if naught else.

"So why did you ride away from Wolvesley?"

His question fell into silence. From the corner of his eyes, he saw Esme swivel her head toward him, her expression wondering.

He pushed his advantage. "Why did you not insist she marry you the next day? If the lady herself was willing?"

Crispin tried to spit away some blood. "The timing did not suit."

Jonah laughed, hollowly. "You all but had the hand of Lady Esme de Neville. A prize far beyond your reach. And you say the timing did not suit?"

"There was something I must do. But that is of no consequence. As I say, Esme must marry me now, else face public humiliation."

The knight's voice was steady, but for the briefest of seconds, his gaze flew beyond his inquisitors to the tapestried chairs by the fire.

Adam turned slowly. There was nothing of note about the chairs, save a dark shape at the foot of one of them.

His pulse quickened. "What is that?" he asked.

"His satchel." Esme was already hurrying toward it. "He brought it in last night."

"Leave it." Crispin's eyes had widened with alarm. He lurched sideways to evade Jonah's grasp and ran with surprising swiftness across the floor.

Adam stuck out a leg to trip him up before he made much

headway. As the knight sprawled across the floorboards, Adam finally unsheathed his sword and held it at his chest.

"Stay where you are," he ordered, trying not to take too much pleasure in the moment. "Esme, search his bag."

"You have no authority to do so," Crispin raged.

"That's the trouble with people like us," Jonah commented mildly. "We always think we have the *right* to do whatever we want."

Adam did not allow himself to smile and consequently, his muscles to relax. He stayed focused, even as his mind whirred.

"There is nothing in here." Esme's shoulders sagged.

"Keep looking." Adam's fingers itched to conduct the search himself, but he dared not step away from the knight.

Jonah seated himself back down at the table and took a swig of ale, his hands shaking. If Adam had entertained any doubts as to his loyalty to his sister, they were now assuaged.

"There is a letter." Cheeks flushed, Esme rose to her feet and carried it over.

"Give it to Adam," Jonah said, surprising them both.

Adam took the parchment with one hand, his other still holding his sword at Crispin's chest.

Was this a test, to see if he was able to read?

Rory Baine had his faults, but he had ensured that Adam's early education was on parr with Callum's.

Adam squinted at the cramped handwriting. The message was short, and the ink blotted, as if it had been written in haste.

"The letter states that Crispin should flee for his life," he finally said.

"Please, can I see?" Without waiting for his answer, Esme took the parchment and stared down at it. His heart clenched to see how her shoulders shook.

"Roger Mortimer is arrested," she murmured. Her gaze lifted to her brother's. "This is the news you brought us last night." As he nodded in agreement, she looked down at Crispin. "Why should that affect you so? Why should you flee for your life because the pretender to the throne has been arrested?"

Realization dawned across her pretty face just as Adam also slotted the puzzle together. Jonah slammed his cup down onto the table.

"God's blood, the man's a traitor," he half-whispered.

"You left Wolvesley to attend Roger Mortimer?" Esme's voice dripped with scorn.

"And Queen Isabella." Crispin, to his credit, did not cower. "They were at Nottingham Castle. I was riding to their aid. But the dratted young king got there first."

"You will speak of the King of England with respect." Jonah pushed back his chair, his face weary now. "Ye Gods, my father will be shocked at this. For how long has he entertained a traitor in his ranks?"

"Roger Mortimer came once to dine at Wolvesley." Esme gasped. "In the early days. Was that when you met him?"

Crispin's face twisted with scorn. "My family has long been aligned with his."

Adam cared little for the loyalties of the English aristocracy. He renewed his pressure on the sword, gratified when Crispin's eyes traveled to its tip.

"This is why you have become so intent on marrying Lady Esme. 'Tis because your family will soon be branded as traitors to the throne, and you wish to enjoy the protection of the Earl of Wolvesley."

"That is exactly the case." Jonah nodded his agreement. "Had things gone differently, you would have left my sister high and dry."

Esme sniffed. Adam thought she was about to say that might have been a better outcome.

"It seems you will get your wish, after all, Crispin de Gough," Jonah said. "You will have your chance to speak before my father. You will do so in chains, as a traitor."

"This changes naught," Crispin tried one last time.

Even Esme laughed. "It changes everything," she chimed in.

"Do you think anyone will believe the desperate rantings of a traitor?"

Walking rather unsteadily, Jonah came to join them. He folded his arms and looked down at Crispin, before his gaze passed over Esme and Adam. "Let us have the carriage made ready at once," he murmured. "We will all travel to Wolvesley."

CHAPTER NINETEEN

O F ALL THINGS, Adam had not anticipated travelling to Wolvesley Castle in a stately carriage, with gilt on the windows and plush velvet on the seat cushions.

Not had he anticipated being seated beside Jonah de Neville, who occasionally turned his pale blue eyes toward him in an assessing manner.

Adam tried to concentrate on the flashes of countryside he could see through the open window; sweeping moorland and green hills that gradually gave way to smooth roads and wooded valleys. Birds called from the trees and the sound of hoofbeats was regular and soothing; but he felt anything but calm.

How could he be calm when Esme sat opposite him. Close enough to touch, but so far away—in every way that mattered—that he might have been back in the highlands.

How could he be calm when Jonah had insisted he travel with them to Wolvesley, for reasons that were far from clear? Thinking of his role as Esme's protector, Adam had offered to travel in the second carriage so he might keep a close eye on Crispin. But Jonah had waved his suggestion away.

"The door will be locked from the outside," he said airily. "With guards stationed at either end of the carriage. You need not concern yourself with Crispin."

Then why am I here?

Adam stretched his legs as much as he was able in the confined space of the carriage interior. Every time they went over a bump in the road, he was obliged to grip the window ledge, for fear of barreling into either Jonah or Esme—both of whom were clearly well-practiced in the art of travelling by carriage and seemed hardly to notice the jolting.

Next time he took a long journey, whatever the circumstances, he would insist on riding a horse.

If there ever is a next time.

Much as Adam took care not to let his emotions get the better of him, he could not help a flicker of fear about this turn of events. He recalled that long-ago day when Callum had spoken with him in the solar, and how sound had drifted through the thin walls from the great hall.

His skin prickled with apprehension.

How much does Jonah know of my relationship with Esme?

Esme had given fleeting mention to Adam's role in rescuing her from Crispin's advances, but Jonah had hardly seemed to notice. Not that Adam was looking for acclaim, nor even thanks. But would this be enough to save him, he wondered.

Or am I also to face the wrath of the Earl of Wolvesley?

It would have been better if he rode to Kielder Castle, just as he had sworn to do last night. But even as the thought occurred to him, he knew the sentiment was false. He could have no more abandoned Esme this morn, than he could have sawn off his own leg.

For better or worse, his fate was entwined with the de Nevilles.

Jonah was looking at him again. Though young—Adam counted anyone who had seen less than thirty summers as young—his eyes held both wisdom and cunning. Adam fixed his gaze out of the window but could not shake the feeling of being watched.

Enough!

He swallowed and turned to face the young lord. "How far is there still to travel?"

Jonah thought for a moment, his head on one side. "You are best asking this question of Esme. She is more familiar with the journey than I am."

Adam took a breath and lifted his gaze to Esme. She met his eyes squarely. "When we cross the bridge, we are almost there."

This was hardly helpful. But Adam could not feel cross with her answer. Not when so much anxiety showed in her face.

"Jonah, are you certain we are doing the right thing?" She pulled at a loose thread on her sleeve, unaware how lovely she looked with her golden hair shining over her shoulders.

"Under the circumstances, I am certain we are doing the only thing we can," came the reply. Jonah folded his arms and made a show of closing his eyes.

"That is hardly reassuring," she retorted.

Adam could not help silently agreeing with her. When her familiar blue eyes turned beseechingly toward him, his heart turned over.

But what could he say?

It was safer to follow Jonah's lead and close his eyes, letting his head tip back against the headrest. It was uncomfortable, but it gave him the space to think.

Or to fret.

If things went against him, he must get word to Callum, he decided.

Esme would be safe in the bosom of her family. *But would he?*

After some insurmountable time, Esme leaned forward and clutched at the windowsill.

"We are almost there."

Adam's eyes felt gritty, and his limbs had grown heavy. He forced himself to look out of the opposite window, noting the graceful turrets of a stone bridge and the distant shimmer of a vast blue lake.

But what are those strange white birds swimming on its surface?

Alarmed, Adam leaned closer, prompting an amused smile from Jonah.

"Swans," he explained.

Ashamed of his ignorance, Adam sat back. "I have never seen them before."

"Most likely they have not yet reached the highlands," Jonah offered.

Adam nodded, slightly relieved.

"They can be vicious creatures, but our father likes them."

"Father likes them because they are so beautiful," Esme added, and the siblings shared a smile.

"Our father likes beautiful things," Jonah cast a sideways glance toward Adam. "Which is why my sister here can wrap him around her little finger."

"That is not true." Esme smoothed her skirts, though Adam could see the idea pleased her. "Isabella is the one who wields power over all the men she meets, including Father."

"Ah well, I have not seen our sister Isabella for some time." Jonah shrugged. "Perchance her much fabled powers have dimmed in my memory."

Adam was late to find his balance as the carriage swung around a sharp corner. He found himself flung forward against Esme's seat, with his head all but in the lady's lap.

"Forgive me," he muttered, his cheeks burning as he righted himself.

Esme's laugh was like a peal of bells. "Do not worry, Adam. You will grow used to the twists and turns of this journey, over time."

Her innocent comment caused a second wave of heat to rush to his face, especially as he felt Jonah's speculative gaze settle upon him once again.

"Indeed," Jonah said.

Adam felt as if he could hardly breathe, but Esme's attention was not on him.

"We are here." She could hardly contain her excitement as the carriage drew to a halt. "Mother is waiting for us, Jonah."

All her reservations seemed to have fled. She wrestled with

the door handle and jumped out, leaving Adam blinking in the sudden burst of light.

Jonah drummed his fingers on the cushions before fixing his face into a smile.

"Welcome to Wolvesley, Adam Hawker."

Adam realized a beat too late that he should have risen first, to help both Esme and Jonah from the carriage. As it was, he descended last, his heart thumping in his chest as he looked about him.

A petite woman with long hair, threaded with silver, had her arms wrapped around both her children. Behind her, a row of uniformed guards marched as one toward the second carriage. It had scarce stopped when the door was unbolted, and Crispin was unceremoniously bundled out.

"Take him to the dungeon," came the barked order.

Before Adam could process the situation, both carriages had been driven back to the stable yard and the guards had dispersed. A gust of wind sent up a plume of dust.

"Let us go inside," said Esme. "I must change out of this dress. It is not at all right for Wolvesley."

"Have you forgotten something, dear?" her mother asked mildly. Esme stared blankly back at her.

"Your friend," her mother prompted.

Esme put a hand to her heart and laughed breathlessly. "Forgive me, Mother. This is Adam Hawker. A great friend of Callum's. And a man who means a great deal to me, too," she added.

"Delighted to meet you, Adam." The countess of Wolvesley extended her hand to him and after a moment's panic, he kissed it. "I am Morwenna."

"Milady," he said, aware of his crumpled clothing and unkempt hair. Morwenna was dressed in a beautiful gown of green and gold. Her fingers sparkled with jewels and her bearing was regal as a queen.

This was the woman Esme had described as a village healer?

A woman who had first come to Wolvesley as a servant?

His mind whirred. He must have misheard. Else Esme had been playing some complicated game, one with rules he did not understand. He looked toward her, but her gaze was turned resolutely away from him.

"I am so glad to be home," she breathed, linking her arm with her mother's.

Her words sliced through him, like a blade wielded in a personal attack. On leaden feet, he followed them beneath a smooth stone archway, coming up short when his gaze landed on a vertical tower of sparkling water.

In Scotland, Adam had seen vast waterfalls, with white water cascading downwards over rocks at an unbelievable speed, roaring and rushing on its way.

Never had he seen water travelling upwards.

Just like the swans, this was perchance another thing that had not yet reached the environs of Kielder.

It was too much. All of it. Esme's chatter. The manicured lawns. The two stone lions guarding an elegant sweep of steps and, most of all, this column of rainbow-hued water, shooting up into the sky.

He placed his hands on the rim of the stone basin and breathed deeply. Though the afternoon sun was warm, he felt a shiver run the length of his spine.

A hand fell onto his shoulder.

"Are you well, Adam?"

The voice was Jonah's. Adam fought for his composure, but his head was spinning.

"I need a moment to myself," he replied, truthfully, his eyes fixed on the shimmering water.

He expected—mayhap even hoped—that Jonah would protest. At the very least, he needed instruction of what to do once this moment-to-himself had passed. But when Adam straightened up, Jonah was nowhere to be seen.

Adam was alone.

And never had he felt more out of his depth.

"I am not so grand as you think," Esme had told him.

She had lied.

Adam had seen castles before. But never had he seen a keep as magnificent as this, with walls so smooth they might have been hewn from marble. His gaze traveled up to the turrets, counting arched windows until he gave up.

I do not belong in a place like this.

Kielder Castle was the preserve of warriors.

This was the preserve of the English nobility.

He shook his head. He could not stay. Blindly, he stumbled in the direction of the stone archway. But once there, he ground to a halt. Three paths threaded in different directions, and he had no idea which to take.

He had no idea where he was even headed.

A soft voice came from behind him.

"Adam, is it?"

He spun around to find a lady with kind eyes standing a few feet away. She stepped forward hesitantly, pushing her light brown hair behind her ears.

"My name is Mirrie." She pulled a face. "I should more properly introduce myself as Lady Mirabel de Neville."

Adam could not place the name. He bowed low. "Pleased to meet you, milady."

"Oh, please do not address me as such." She folded her hands over the swell of pregnancy, making him quickly avert his gaze. "I will never grow used to my title. I am just Mirrie."

He glanced at her cautiously, taking in the sumptuousness of her cloak and the glint of pearls at her throat. She looked like a lady to him.

"I grew up here," she said conversationally. "But I well remember the first day I came. How overwhelming it was. That's why Jonah asked me to come out to you." Adam raised his eyebrows and Mirrie smiled. "Jonah sees and understands far more than he ever lets on."

Just like the time in the carriage, Adam reflected that this was hardly reassuring.

"You must be fatigued after your journey from Ember Hall," she continued, holding her cloak against the pull of the breeze. "I once lived there, you know?"

He was surprised into speech. "I did not."

"With Frida, before she married Callum."

Ah yes. Belatedly, he recalled the comments of Agnes the cook. "I am an old acquaintance of Callum's," he offered, cautiously.

"Oh, I think you are more than that." Mirrie reached a hand toward the stone archway and leaned her weight against it. "Callum wrote to Tristan, telling him he had no cause to worry about Esme. He said he had left her in the care of a man whom he loved like a brother."

It took a moment for him to make sense her words. His initial glow of pleasure quickly faded when he reflected what had happened since Callum wrote that recommendation.

"Callum was wrong," he said gruffly, lowering his eyes from the slanting sunlight. "Esme was in danger, after all."

"So it would seem." Mirrie did not deny it. "She was fortunate indeed that you were there to protect her."

The lady put a hand to her forehead and Adam cursed his ill manners. "May I assist you, milady? Is there some place you can sit?"

"Many." She gave a little laugh. "But what I would like most of all is for you to escort me back to the keep. If you like, I can show you to your chambers and you rest awhile before dinner."

"Before dinner?" He could not hide his surprise.

"Of course." She offered her arm, leaving him with little choice but to take it. "You are our guest of honor, Adam Hawker."

Mirrie walked steadily beside him, but he could not forget her show of tiredness, nor her visible swell of pregnancy. He must not meet her kindness with churlishness.

"I have never been a guest of honor before," he commented, drily.

"A great fuss will be made of you," Mirrie announced, as if she was delivering good news. "I can already tell that you are a great favorite of Jonah's, which is no small achievement."

The idea pleased him, but in truth, he longed for more.

Will she say aught of Esme?

Adam's heart quickened as they reached the fountain and Mirrie turned to him, thoughtfully.

"Try to look beyond the trappings of wealth to see the de Nevilles for who they really are," she murmured, so quietly that he had to lean closer to catch the words. "It took me a long time to learn that lesson."

He blinked at her in surprise, and she gave his arm a little shake.

"Do you promise?" she persisted.

"Aye, milady. *Mirrie,*" he corrected himself at her sharp look of reprimand.

She smiled and picked up her skirts to better ascend the steps. Adam could only follow close behind, wondering what on earth the next hours may bring.

CHAPTER TWENTY

ESME COULD NOT seem to settle anywhere.

She was glad to be home amongst her family. But after weeks of peace and quiet, the constant hum of activity that pervaded the keep did not please her, as she had expected it might. She took no comfort in the music and gossip of the great hall, nor in the attentiveness of the servants, keen to supply her every need. At first, she thought this was a matter of costume; she was simply not dressed for Wolvesley.

Once she was attired more fittingly, she assumed the day would pass more easily.

It did not.

Esme gazed at the tiny pearl buttons of her dusky pink, silken gown, and felt only the restrictions of the tightly fitting bodice. The flowing skirt, she saw as impractical. Aye, the looking glass showed that she was still Esme de Neville. But inside, she felt different.

Her muscles twitched, as if she was waiting for something.

News of Crispin's fate, perchance?

In an effort to occupy her mind, she had taken refuge in the beautifully furnished ladies' solar and picked up some long-since abandoned embroidery. But instead of the colorful swirls of looping thread, she saw Adam's green eyes and the uncertainty that had flickered in them during their long carriage ride.

Is he having second thoughts about me?

Esme's fingers shook so much that her sewing needle plunged into the ball of her thumb. Quickly sucking away the plumes of red blood, she warned herself against dramatic flights of invention, forcing herself to recall how he had staunchly defended her against Crispin. And his emotional response when she told him how he made her feel.

Happy and safe.

She had never been more sincere. And the depth of feeling in his rugged face had told her everything she needed to know.

She had no cause to start doubting him now.

But where is he?

Esme had hoped he might come and find her. Had even arranged herself prettily on the leather-covered settle in the anticipation of his presence. But Adam had seemingly disappeared into thin air.

Giving up on any hopes of tackling her embroidery, she abandoned the ladies' solar and tripped down the wide stairs to the marbled hallway. Smiling in acknowledgement at the familiar servants, she found her way to her father's solar and knocked quickly on the wooden door before her courage failed her.

She had yet to greet her father and knew not, exactly, what Jonah had penned in the message that preceded their return to Wolvesley.

Had he alluded to her indiscretions?

There was no wonder she felt itchy all over with impatience. So much was unknown.

When the door remained resolutely fastened, she knocked again. Louder this time, until a deep voice spoke behind her.

"He is not here."

She turned around, skirts flying, to find her brother Tristan walking toward her.

"Tris."

She closed the distance between them at a run, laughing when he picked her up and spun her around, just as he had when they were children.

"My beautiful little sister. What kept you away for so long?"

She could not answer him honestly. Instead, she made a show of inspecting his neatly combed golden hair and the fine cut of his dark tunic. His breeches were spotless, and his boots had been polished to such a shine, she could all but see her face in them.

"Marriage seems to be suiting you, brother."

"It is a fine institution." His white teeth flashed as he smiled down at her.

"And how fares my newest sister, Mirrie?"

"She is as sweet and lovely and kind as ever."

"I was enquiring as to her health, you doddypoll." Esme put her hands on her hips and frowned. "She must soon be approaching her laying in?"

Tristan put a hand to his temples. "Esme, I can hardly speak of it. I am excited and terrified, both at once."

"Terrified?" Esme's eyebrows shot up.

"Aye." He nodded firmly. "For the safety of both Mirrie and the babe."

"I never thought to see my fearless brother admit to such a thing." Her heart softened and she put a hand to his elbow.

"That is what love can do to you," he said with sincerity. "But we will have the best physician in the land in attendance."

"And Mirrie is young and strong," she put in.

"Amen to that." He took her hands in his. "You have not answered my question."

"I had hoped to avoid it," she said airily.

"Walk with me," Tristan commanded, taking her arm and turning them both until they faced the wide arched doorway.

"Do I have a choice?" she grumbled.

"You could try to run, but I believe I would catch you."

Despite herself, she smiled as they stepped out into the late afternoon sunlight. A guard bowed smartly as they passed, but the inner courtyard was otherwise empty. Tristan paused when they reached the pair of stone lions which guarded the steps.

"Do you need a cloak? The air carries a chill."

"How solicitous you have become." She arched an eyebrow. "In truth, I enjoy the cool air on my skin after so many hours in the carriage."

It made her feel alert and alive, as well as providing welcome distraction from the painful circling of her thoughts.

"Very well. We cannot tarry long, anyhow. I must speak to Father before dinner."

With one accord, they turned toward the rose garden.

Esme took a breath. "Where is Father?"

"He is dealing with Crispin." Tristan's voice was level. She could read nothing into it.

Her goatskin slippers were not appropriate for walking on grass. She winced as the damp soaked through them, realizing they would likely be ruined. But Tristan must have brought her out here for a reason. He must have something to ask—or something to say.

She might as well stay and hear it. He would never leave her be otherwise.

"'Tis a dreadful thing that you and Jonah discovered," he said softly.

Esme fixed her gaze on the almost-bare rose bushes. When she was last at Wolvesley, the last few velvety petals had still clung to the thorny stalks. Now they were stark and barren.

"Who would have thought that Crispin de Gough was a traitor to England's rightful king?" he continued.

Esme still stared at the rose bushes, avoiding Tristan's piercing blue eyes.

"Who indeed," she managed.

Tristan tugged on her elbow, and they resumed their stroll. "We have known him since he was an overly enthusiastic squire. I trained him myself." His voice rose with incredulity.

"Aye."

Esme had a terrible feeling of what was to come.

At heart, Tristan was a kind older brother; he did not make her wait any longer.

"In truth, Esme, I fancied you and he had grown rather close over these last months."

She closed her eyes and tried to keep her breathing steady. She should have known that nothing within the walls of Wolvesley escaped his sharp attention.

"I even fancied that the indifference you displayed to all eligible suitors was underpinned by a liking you had for de Gough." Tristan's voice was conversational in tone, but she was all too aware of the steel running through it.

"You fancy much, brother." She tried to smile, but her efforts at deflection died when she saw how serious his expression had become.

"I need to know this." He turned to face her. "Did he hurt you?"

Warm tears nudged at the corners of her eyes. "Nay, he did not have the chance. Adam reached me in time."

Tristan nodded slowly. "You speak of Callum's man? Adam Hawker?"

The sound of his cherished name on her brother's lips did strange things to her insides.

"He is a good man."

"When I meet him, I shall give him my thanks."

Esme took a shuddering breath, daring to hope that her inquisition was over. But Tristan showed no sign of it.

He cleared his throat. "Do you love de Gough?"

She reared backward and looked at him incredulously. "Nay."

"You are very certain." His voice was insistent.

"I am," she nodded.

"How so?" He put his hands on his hips and his blue eyes seemed to gaze right into her soul.

Esme squirmed for a moment, then decided to speak truthfully.

"Because I know now what real love feels like."

She anticipated some surprised reaction, but Tristan only narrowed his eyes.

He waited until a messenger boy had darted past them, before drawing her closer to the rose bushes. Thanks to the lateness of the season and the sparseness of the foliage, she knew there was no one else about.

'Twas a relief, of sorts, to confide in her brother. Some five years her senior, Tristan had always been a heroic figure to Esme. Someone she could always rely on to smuggle honey cakes from the kitchen and plead her case on the rare occasions she evoked her parents' displeasure.

But still, her pulse pounded at the prospect of revealing her secret.

Tristan once again took her elbow and quietly asked, "Tell me, Esme, what does real love feel like?"

Startled, she threw him a quizzical look, but he only inclined his head, indicating that he would wait for as long as was necessary.

Esme bit down on her lip and considered his question.

When the answer came to her, it made her smile.

"Happy and safe." She could not prevent her lips from puckering further upward. "When I am by his side, 'tis as if I know all will be well. Whatever the circumstances."

She anticipated some further questioning, but Tristan shook his golden head with a chuckle.

"Ye Gods, Mirrie is right about everything."

"Mirrie?" Her voice rose. "I have not seen her since I arrived."

"But she has spoken to Adam Hawker. And she has seen how it is between you."

My secret is already discovered.

Esme smoothed her skirts as her cheeks pinked. "You do not disapprove?" Nerves clutched at her as she waited upon his answer.

"Why the devil should I disapprove of any man who makes you happy? And safe," he added with a raised eyebrow.

She hesitated. "Because he has no title." Her voice wobbled. "And he is older even than yourself and Callum."

"Older than myself and Callum?" Tristan feigned a stagger to one side. "And the man still walks about unaided?"

"Do not mock me, brother." She straightened her spine and tried to look severe, despite a keen gust of wind which made her skirts billow outward. "I am asking your advice, heaven help me."

Tristan folded his arms. "Are those the qualities that you prize in a man? Youth and a title?"

"Nay." She shook her head quickly. "They are barriers that Adam himself persists in putting forward."

"I see." Tristan smiled down at her. "He is right to raise these matters. But if they mean naught to you, then they mean naught to me. From what I have learned of the man, he is no fortune hunter."

"Forsooth, I think he would prefer it if I had no fortune." Esme was earnest.

"Then methinks him a worthy suitor of Lady Esme de Neville." Tristan smoothed back her hair with brotherly affection. "You should go and speak with him. I last saw him by the lake. It seems he has some fascination for Father's swans."

"Is that where he is?" Esme felt a jolt of impatience. "I had hoped he would come and find me."

"Ye Gods woman, go and find him yourself. Do we men have to do everything?" Tristan raised his eyebrows, but she could see he was only teasing her.

Impulsively, she rose up on her tiptoes and kissed his cheek. "Thank you."

"For what?" He looked surprised.

"For not lecturing me."

Tristan caught her hand. "I shall leave that duty to Father."

She gasped. "You think he will be cross?" For a moment, she had forgotten all about Crispin and the turn of events that had brought her back to Wolvesley.

He smiled indulgently. "If he is, sister, he will not remain so for long."

"What will he think of Adam?" Her voice was little more than a whisper.

"I learned a few years since that our father values love above all else. He desires his children to be as happy as he and Mother are. He will care only that Adam is a man who truly deserves you."

"He does." She nodded vigorously.

"Then go and speak to the man, for pity's sake." Tristan gave her a little push. "If Mirrie is right, which she always is, he will have found these last hours more daunting than those on the eve of a battle."

SHE CONSIDERED RETURNING to the keep for more suitable footwear, but Tristan's last words rang in her ears and she ploughed on toward the lake, even as dampness pooled between her toes. The setting sun cast deep orange rays over the expanse of water, lighting up the woods more beautifully than a hundred flickering candles. Esme soon located Adam's commanding figure. He stood just feet from the shoreline with his back to her; his arms were folded and his head was lowered.

She hesitated, but only for a moment. Much as she baulked at interrupting a man so clearly deep in thought, this may be the only chance they had to converse before they were both swallowed up in polite chatter at tonight's dinner.

Heart fluttering, she took the final steps toward him and came to a halt by his side.

"Beautiful, isn't it," she said.

Adam's eyes stayed fixed on the lake. "More so than I ever imagined."

Esme pressed her lips together. "Surely you have lakes in Scotland?"

"Lochs," he corrected, with the glint of a smile. "Aye, we do. But I was not talking merely of the lake. Your home is beautiful,

Esme. You are fortunate indeed."

She glanced at the soft crust of mud beneath her feet, and the dark staining on her slippers. Standing on such unsteady ground made her anxious. And this was not a conversation that required any additional anxiety.

Seized by impulse, she reached down and tugged the ruined slippers from her feet. She sighed happily as her toes sank into the mud, wriggling them for purchase and feeling far steadier.

Adam's eyebrows had disappeared beneath his thatch of hair. "What are you doing?"

"Paddling," she said, deciding in that moment to walk closer to the shore. She squealed as cold water closed over her feet, but the chill was invigorating. "Come and join me." she called over her shoulder.

"Are you touched in the head, lass?" His voice rose higher than she had ever heard it. "Your gown will be ruined."

"I have spent far too long caring about gowns and ribbons," she declared. "In the future, I shall follow Frida's example and wear braccae should the mood take me."

She heard him exhale, then felt him come to stand beside her.

"Your boots will be ruined," she quipped.

"They can stand more than a bit of water," he retorted.

He was so close; she was sure her arm would brush against his if she only leaned a little to the left.

But she could not pluck up the courage to do so.

"I am glad you are here, Adam," she said in a rush.

Now she felt the force of his gaze turn fully toward her. "Are you certain of that?"

"Of course." A small wave caught her unawares and she flung out her hand. But when she encountered the iron hardness of Adam's chest, she pulled it back as if she had been scorched. "Why would you say otherwise?" Her voice showed her hurt.

Adam turned his gaze back to the swans, elegantly swimming in the center of the lake. "When we were at Ember Hall, there were times we seemed almost to be equals," he said, honesty rippling through his words. "But now I see the real Esme de Neville."

"Nay." Without allowing herself to hesitate, she took his hand. As soon as his fingers linked with hers, she knew she was doing the right thing. "You already knew the real Esme de Neville."

"This is too much," he said, his voice strangely small. "Crispin was right about one thing. I am worth naught."

"Do not say that." Tears brimmed at her eyes, but she felt more angry than sad. "How dare you say that?"

Adam smiled, but this time it did not meet his eyes. "One thing I am sure of is my courage, milady."

Esme swallowed and tightened her grip on his hand. "Courage is a quality most admired by my family. Courage, honesty, and a belief in true love." Her voice quavered. "Do you believe in true love, Adam?"

So much time passed she began to fear he would not answer. Her limbs started to shake, though whether that was due to cold or trepidation, she could not say.

"I believe that I am in love with you, Esme," he said hoarsely.

She felt weak with relief. "As I am in love with you." Her knees were all but knocking together now. Adam put his strong arms about her and half carried, half dragged her back to the shore.

"This love makes you do strange things." He rubbed her hands together and blew on them. "I do not even have a cloak to wrap about your shoulders."

"You can wrap your arms about my shoulders," she dared suggest, closing her eyes with joy when he did just that. Snuggled against his warm body, she felt happy and safe, once again. "If you love me, and I love you, then there is no more to discuss."

"Esme." He uttered her name like a prayer. One hand cupped the back of her head, whilst the other stroked the length of her spine. "I am the son of a farmer."

"And I am the daughter of a woman who once sold healing

salves in a village called Escafeld."

He gave a slight shake of his head. "I have met your mother, and this description does not do her justice."

Esme shrugged her shoulders, her body molding into his. "Nonetheless, it is true."

"I have seen at least ten summers more than you," he whispered against her head. "Mayhap more than that."

"Then I will benefit from your wisdom and experience." She reached up to place her hands on either side of his rugged face, loving the raspy stubble beneath her fingers. "So, I am younger and wealthier than you would prefer. I can do naught to cure the first, although the passage of time will come to my aid, God willing." She caught the flicker of a smile across his lips. "For the second, the solution is simple. I will leave my wealth behind me."

He gave a sharp intake of breath. "I cannot ask you to live a life of hardship."

"I would rather live with you, in some drafty shack, than with some lord I do not love, however grand his castle."

Adam rested his forehead against hers and blew out a breath. "I do not live in a drafty shack."

She lifted her chin, so her lips skimmed his jaw. "So much the better then."

"I do not live in a castle, either." She felt his muscles brace when she kissed him again. "Well, in truth, I do. But 'tis not mine."

Esme allowed her hands to roam over his broad shoulders, enjoying the way he shifted against her. "Do you have any further objections?"

He shook his head, closing his eyes and seemingly surrendering to her touch. "None that I can think of in this moment."

"Then kiss me," she breathed.

His kisses, back at Ember Hall, had been featherlight and gentle, but now Adam claimed her lips with a passion that left her with little doubt over how much he wanted her. Esme's feet rose out of the suction of the mud as he hauled her closer toward him, his hands roving over her silken gown and setting her body on fire. She no longer felt cold, she no longer felt anything except the need to have his lips and his hands on her, bringing her to life in a way she had never before experienced. When his palm came to rest over her breast, she gasped out loud.

"Esme," he said in a strangled voice. "You will be my undoing."

Her hands had intentions of their own, tugging up his shirt and exploring the warmth of his hard, muscular body. The flat planes of stomach were a revelation, as was the part of him now pressing against her hip. A delicious tension twisted in her core as she met his smoldering gaze. Keeping her eyes fastened upon his, she traced her fingers on a downward path, knowing she had met her mark when his breathing caught in his throat.

He said her name once more, then seized her shoulders and rained a shower of hot kisses along her neck until his lips met the lacy edge of her gown. His fingers fumbled with the impossibly tiny buttons keeping her from him, and she wasted no time in reaching up to help. As soon as her gown sprang open, he freed her breasts with gentle fingers and feasted his lips upon them.

She wound her fingers in his hair and pressed him closer to her, as the twisting sensation in her core grew stronger still.

"Adam," she breathed.

A mistake.

The sound of his name seemed to break the spell of their embrace. With one final, lingering kiss on her collarbone, he straightened up and held her against him. His heart thudded loudly inside his chest, just like hers.

"Why did you stop?" She could not help the petulance in her tone.

Adam took a deep, shuddering breath. "Because I am yet to meet the Earl of Wolvesley. When I do so, I want to look the man in the eye, without having to hide the fact that I have taken great liberties with his beloved daughter."

She threw him an arched look as she re-fastened the buttons

on her gown. "All I can say is I hope you get this meeting over with soon."

Adam's laughter echoed through the trees as he held her close once again. "So do I, Lady Esme."

CHAPTER TWENTY-ONE

DESPITE THE GRANDEUR of his surroundings, Adam felt light of heart as he returned to the guest chamber which Mirrie had shown him to earlier. He had feared that once he left Esme's side, darkness and doubt might claim him once again. But it seemed that her brightness and confidence had broken through the clouds that had haunted his horizons for too long.

I am daring to dream.

And what a dream it was.

His boots sounded heavily on the polished floorboards as he wound down a wide, well-lit corridor. But instead of the intricately woven tapestries hanging from the plastered walls, instead he saw Esme's face; her blue eyes and her corn-colored waterfall of hair.

She loves me!

She wanted them to be together. Had even said she would turn her back on her fortune, if that was what it took.

Adam cared naught for the wealth of the de Nevilles. That a woman as vibrant as Esme wanted to weave her life into his was fortune enough. He started to hum with happiness as he reached the arched doorway and pushed the panel aside.

Inside was a chamber fit for royalty. Thick rugs covered the floor, with more piled high on the comfortable bed which was hung with emerald green drapes. The long, narrow window looked out toward the lake, upon which he could just about discern the majestic figures of the swans.

He closed his eyes, wondering if it was indeed all a dream.

A knock at the door broke his reverie. He opened it to find a golden-haired giant on the other side.

The man smiled, and instantly Adam saw his striking similarity to both Esme and Jonah.

"I am Tristan de Neville," he said, his voice deep and resonant. "Welcome to Wolvesley."

Adam took his hand, unable to help sizing up his obvious strength. The man's muscles moved beneath his finely tailored tunic, though his stance was relaxed and easy.

"I am Adam Hawker." He stepped aside to allow Esme's brother inside.

"I know." Tristan did not allow a beat to pass. "My wife, Mirrie, has sung your praises. And my sister seems equally smitten." He put his hand on his narrow hips and looked at him shrewdly. "I thought I should make your acquaintance in private, without the distractions of music and food and company."

Adam realized that he was also being sized up, by a knight whose reputation preceded him. He recalled the stories of Tristan that had reached as far as Kielder. His bravery and swordsmanship were the stuff of legend, but Adam had been most impressed by how hard he had worked for peace between England and Scotland.

He was a lord; heir to the Earl of Wolvesley. But he was also Esme's brother. Adam's head spun with indecision as to how he should address him.

He bowed his head. "I was fortunate to meet your wife when I first arrived here. Milord," he added.

Tristan waved the words away, looking mildly irritated to hear his title. "And fortunate to have spent several days in the company of both Esme and Jonah." He arched his eyebrows. "I believe you have grown especially close to my sister."

Adam had not anticipated that the challenge would be laid out so quickly. He took a breath. "Lady Esme means a great deal to me."

For a moment, Tristan's blue gaze clashed with his. Adam fancied the secrets of his soul were laid bare, so piercing were his eyes. But then Tristan relaxed and let out a little laugh.

"I am glad to hear it. For she is well taken with you."

"I am not certain I am worthy of her affection." Adam stumbled over his words in his haste to declare them. "But if I am able, I will spend all the years I have left proving to her that she has chosen wisely."

Tristan nodded, relaxing his weight against the window seat so that shadows fell across the chamber and veiled his face. "I understand the sentiment. It has been more than a year since my dear Mirrie consented to be my wife, and I still count it as a blessing, every day."

Adam found himself inexplicably choked with emotion. He fixed his gaze upon a wooden blanket box until he could trust his voice. "Thank you."

The man strode forward and clasped his arm. "Nay, do not thank me. 'Tis I who should thank you, for saving my sister from the base knave who is now languishing in the dungeon."

Adam took in the gesture of kinship with a warm flush of relief, gripping Tristan's arm in return. It was more than he had dared to hope that Esme's eldest brother would share her down to earth sensibilities. But the thought of Crispin made him pause.

"What will happen to him?" he asked bluntly.

"If it were up to me, he would be horsewhipped," Tristan replied, with equal directness, leaving Adam with no doubts as to his family loyalty. "But my father is a man of the law. As such, Crispin de Gough will be turned over to the king's men. They are already on their way here, ready to arrest him." His head turned toward the window, as if listening out for approaching horses.

Adam nodded, slowly.

"If the man has any sense, he will beg forgiveness of his actions." Tristan pursed his lips. "Do you think he has any sense?"

"Very little, that I could see."

They shared a look, before Tristan gave him a bracing smile.

"But let us not waste our time speaking of de Gough. This is a night for celebration. My manservant is bringing you some clothing as I understand Jonah gave you no time pack before leaving Ember Hall."

Adam opened his mouth to protest Jonah's innocence, but he closed it again, realizing Tristan was too polite to point out Adam would likely have nothing suitable to wear.

It was true enough; and seemed a matter too trifling to take offence at.

"That is thoughtful," he said instead.

Tristan clapped him on the shoulder. "I look forward to getting to know you better, Adam Hawker."

And with that, Lord Tristan de Neville strode from the room.

Sometime later, Adam was dressed in finery such as he had never before seen. There was more golden thread woven into his dark blue tunic than could be found in the whole of Kielder Castle. He had combed his hair and finally shaved the stubble from his cheeks. But still he lingered in his chamber, lacking the courage to step into the keep.

Then he remembered that courage was the key trait that might endear him to the Earl of Wolvesley, and he all but jogged down the torch-lit corridor toward the sweeping staircase. Strains of music caught his ear as soon as he turned the corner. Then came laughter, and tempting aromas of roasted meat and garlic. By the time he reached the bottom of the stairs, his stomach was audibly rumbling.

A liveried manservant stood in the marbled entrance hall, apparently waiting for him. He recognized the slight but genuine smile of the man who had delivered his parcel of clothing.

"Sir Adam, the family is waiting in the great hall."

Adam stilled. He could not get through this night on any false pretenses. "I am Adam," he said, "Not Sir Adam."

The man bowed, not appearing put out in any way. "My apologies."

"There is naught to forgive." Adam took a breath, wishing he had the familiar weight of a sword against his hip to steady his nerves. "May I ask your name?"

"Alfred. I have served the de Nevilles since I was a lad."

"Then you are most likely better equipped for this occasion than I am." Adam's toe tapped against the marble floor. "Do you have any tips?"

"None that you will need." Alfred flashed him a reassuring smile. "Shall I show you the way?"

"I believe I can find it well enough." Adam nodded. "But thank you."

But he regretted dismissing the offer of help as he passed along the high-ceilinged corridor toward the great hall. Not because there was any danger of becoming lost—the music called him onward like a beacon atop the cliffs—but because with Alfred at his side, there was less chance that he might turn tail and run away.

Breathing deeply, he squeezed his hands into fists and tried to take control of his scrambled thoughts. He had stood on the ramparts of Kielder Castle and faced legions of marauding soldiers with less qualms than he felt on passing through the high double doors.

At once he was met with such brightness and bustle, that he could only stand and blink until his eyes made sense of the scene.

The great hall at Wolvesley was vast, studded with pillars and lit with blazing candelabras which dangled from the vaulted ceiling. A trio of musicians played a lively jig in one corner, and a host of liveried men-at-arms swarmed around trestle tables which had been laid out across the stone-flagged floor. Small groups of brightly dressed ladies twirled their fans and threw him inviting glances, but he had already found the only woman he sought.

Esme sat at a long table on the high dais, surrounded by her family. When her blue eyes met his, all his worries melted away.

She stood abruptly and beckoned him forward, smiling happily as she waited for him to climb the steps.

"I have saved you a seat," she declared. "You already know

everyone, so I shan't bother with introductions."

Adam's pulse was pounding once again, but as he glanced over the line of golden-haired de Nevilles and saw their welcoming smiles, he was reassured.

"Sit," Esme urged, returning to her own chair and nibbling at a delicious looking tartlet.

Adam's chair was positioned between Esme and Jonah. Beside Esme, sat Morwenna, who gave him a little wave as he lowered himself down. The chair next to the countess was high-backed, elaborately carved, and empty. Tristan and Mirrie sat at the other end of the table, both deep in conversation. Adam saw the way Tristan gazed into his wife's eyes and remembered how he had spoken of her with such fondness.

Esme had listed courage, honesty and true love as the traits most admired by her family.

From what he could see, she had spoken the truth.

She covered her hand with his, sending searing heat all the way through his body.

"Do not worry," she said in a loud whisper.

"I fancy he will worry less if you do not hold his hand in full public view," Jonah drawled.

Esme scowled at her brother. "Must you always spoil everything?"

"Is that how you would describe it?" Jonah clasped a hand to his chest, feigning heartbreak before reaching for his goblet of wine. "One day soon my siblings will learn to recognize all that I do for them," he said confidingly to Adam, draining the cup.

"Ignore Jonah. He has already drunk his fill of wine." Esme looked with concern at Adam's empty trencher. "Are you not eating?"

Adam had thought he might be too nervous to eat, but the feast was too enticing to ignore. At Esme's urging, he helped himself to a cut of roasted boar, adding glazed carrots and an onion tart. Jonah generously filled his goblet with rich red wine, and Adam drank deeply.

He was beginning to relax when Morwenna turned to address Mirrie, and Adam's gaze landed on the empty chair beside her.

"Where is your father?" he asked Esme, keeping his voice low.

Esme pulled a face. "Mother said he would be coming soon." She shrugged. "I cannot think what's keeping him."

The sumptuous food turned to dust in his mouth.

Is the earl staying away because of me?

Adam took another drink of wine, ordering himself to be stay calm. He had been met with naught but kindness from all the other members of Esme's family. Would her father be so different?

He did not see Alfred ascending the steps to the family's table. When Tristan's manservant spoke in his ear, Adam nearly fell from the dais in shock.

"Lord Angus would like to speak with you, in his solar."

He gripped the edge of the table, trying to steady his breathing. Esme's wide eyes swung to his; she looked as shocked as he was.

"What does this mean?" he whispered, uncaring that both Jonah and Alfred would hear him.

"I do not know," she mouthed back. "But you had better not keep him waiting."

Adam felt as if he had been doused in cold water, but there was nothing for it but to stand up and follow Alfred back through the great hall. He told himself he was imagining the hundreds of eyes watching his progress across the stone flags, and the fact that the musicians had begun to play something that sounded suspiciously dirge-like.

Alfred's back was straight, and his stride was long. Adam emulated his calmness as best he could; finding himself back in the marbled entrance hall before he had properly processed what was happening. Alfred motioned him toward a forbidding door hewn from oak and positioned in the far corner of the spacious hallway.

"The earl's solar," he intoned, solemnly.

He bowed and swept away, leaving Adam to meet his fate alone.

He knocked with all the confidence he could summon, wincing when sound ricocheted off the frescoed walls.

"Come," called a deeply masculine voice.

Adam walked into a square-shaped room which was lined with books and furnished with a large writing desk that took up most of the wall near the window. On the opposite wall, a fire burned in the hearth, beside two tapestried chairs positioned, seemingly, for comfort. The scent of lavender wafted up from the rushes on the floor, helping to relax his nerves.

The Earl of Wolvesley sat at his desk, his head down. Adam's first impression was of a great lion, so golden was his hair, and so mighty was his presence. Then he glanced up, and Adam found himself ensnared in the all-seeing gaze of a man who might be Tristan's double.

Were Tristan some twenty summers older.

Adam bowed as low as he could. "You asked to see me, milord." He spoke carefully, anxious to betray none of his disquiet.

How much does this man know about my relationship with his daughter?

Angus sat back in his leather-bound chair, linking his long fingers beneath his chin.

"Adam Hawker, I believe?"

"Yes, milord."

"The man who saved my daughter's honor. If my son's account is true, perchance even her life."

Adam began to grow hot beneath Tristan's fine tunic. At least he was appropriately attired for a meeting with an earl.

Although there was good chance that the earl recognized his own son's clothing.

He swallowed hard and forced himself to concentrate on the conversation in hand. "I would not make that claim, milord."

The earl gave him an appraising look. "I heard tell of a blaze, which might have swallowed up the whole house."

"It did not properly take hold."

Adam could not bear false praise to be heaped upon him.

"I see." The earl looked down at an open roll of parchment on his desk. "One of my own knights attacked my own daughter." He shook his head sadly, drawing Adam's eye to glints of silver amongst the gold. "'Tis enough to make you distrust any man."

Adam's throat had grown so dry, he could hardly form a reply. "I'm sure it is, milord."

The earl made a noncommittal sound, and Adam thought for a moment that he might gesture him toward a chair.

But he did not.

Instead, he sighed deeply and resumed his perusal of the parchment.

Beads of perspiration sprang out on Adam's forehead. He did not have much experience with peers of the realm, but knew enough to realize he must stand here without question, for as long as the earl desired.

"Shall I tell what else I have heard, Adam Hawker? Another tale of your exploits, one might say."

Blood pounded in Adam's ears.

The earl must know what has passed between Esme and I.

But amidst the rising tide of his anxiety, he heard Mirrie's soft voice.

"Try to look beyond the trappings of wealth to see the de Nevilles as they really are."

Adam refocused his gaze, seeing the man in front of him not as a wealthy earl, but a loving father.

The question asked of him was rhetorical, but he answered it anyway, standing tall and speaking with authority.

"Please do tell."

An indecipherable look passed over the earl's features, which were still handsome, despite his advanced years.

He rose up from his chair with admirable ease and crossed

over to the fire.

"Let us sit comfortably." He waved vaguely toward Adam and the second chair.

Adam had no wish to position himself any closer to the fire, but he could not refuse.

The earl sank down and gazed into the flames, seemingly lost in thought. But when he finally looked up at Adam, his blue eyes were watchful and alert.

"I knighted Sir Crispin de Gough myself, if you would believe it?"

Adam did not think this required an answer. He hoped, quite fervently, that inclining his head in recognition would be enough.

"Sir Crispin de Gough claims that you have an improper relationship with my daughter." The earl's voice was harsh. "What do you say to that, Adam Hawker?"

Courage, honesty and true love.

Adam took a deep breath. "I say that I care for her deeply, milord."

The earl made a sound, somewhere between a grunt and a gnashing of teeth.

"And does my daughter return your affections?"

He gripped the arm of his chair. "I believe she does."

"You believe she does." The earl ran his hands over his face. "So, there is truth to this accusation of impropriety?"

"There has been no impropriety, milord." Adam closed his mind to memories of the passionate embrace they had shared by the lake. "I have naught but respect and admiration for your daughter." His vision began to swim as a preposterous idea presented itself to him. "In fact, with your lordship's permission, there is a question I would like to ask of you."

Do I dare to ask this now? On my first meeting with the Earl of Wolvesley?

Once again, Esme's face came before his eyes.

Her bright smile.

Her invitation that he should *dare to dream.*

The earl's voice came as if from a great distance away.

"And what is that?"

Adam rose to his feet and straightened his spine. His voice, when he spoke, was steady and strong.

"I would like to ask for Lady Esme's hand in marriage."

CHAPTER TWENTY-TWO

E SME'S CHAMBER WAS lit only by flickering candles, for darkness had fallen over the castle like a blanket. Heavy clouds obscured any light from either the moon or the stars, so there was little to be gained by gazing out of the window.

Instead, she paced over the thick rugs on her floor and wondered how she would ever last through the long hours until the morn. Impatience scratched at her skin, making her abandon her woolen shawl and fold her arms over her white night rail. Just like down at the lake, the chill air served as welcome respite from her circling thoughts—but this time, there was no Adam to warm her with his kisses and his embrace.

What has occurred between Adam and Father?

She bit down on her lip until she tasted blood.

Why has Adam not come to find me?

God's bones, why had Tristan insisted on playing game after game of chess; keeping her some sort of prisoner in the great hall so that she was unable to wait outside father's solar until Adam came out?

'Twas as if Tristan and father were in league with one another. *Against her.*

But Tristan had sent her in search of Adam, earlier that day. And her brother was not one to switch allegiance; not unless he identified good cause.

Esme stamped her feet; the sound muffled by the thick rugs.

She wished she could howl out her frustration. But that would only alert the maids, who would likely bring her a sleeping draught.

Mayhap a sleeping draught would not be the worst idea. 'Twould at least see her through the long hours of night.

As if in answer to her inner thoughts, a knock sounded on her chamber door. Esme crossed the floor and flung it open, half expecting to find her lady's maid wielding a medicine goblet.

"Mirrie," she said in surprise.

Her sister-in-law smiled. "I hope I have not woken you, Esme?"

Esme flung out her arms. "I have no prospects of sleep this night."

"That is what I thought." Mirrie nodded toward the tray in her slender hands. "I have brought you some warmed milk."

Perplexed, Esme stood back to let her in. "That is very kind."

Mirrie settled the tray on a side table and turned to face her. "I remember how it feels, to not know how the future will unfold."

Esme twisted her hands over her churning stomach. "You mean, you and Tris?"

"Aye." Mirrie drew her shawl further over her shoulders. "Though back then, I was not certain there would ever be *me and Tris*. So many obstacles stood in our path."

"Surely not?" Esme was incredulous. "The two of you were the best of friends. Then you fell in love and got married. 'Twas the simplest love story ever told."

Mirrie laughed, pushing a long strand of hair away from her face. "That is not how I remember it." She laid a cool hand atop Esme's. "But I did not come here to speak of the past. Only to deliver the warmed milk."

That was not true. Mirrie was no natural deceiver, and Esme could sense the turmoil in her.

She held lightly onto Mirrie's fingers. "I am most blessed to have such a thoughtful sister. But you could have sent a servant.

Next time, pray do not walk about the keep in the dark. Especially not in your condition."

Mirrie's cheeks pinked in the candlelight. "But I have a particular message for you, that a servant could not properly deliver."

Esme held her fingers tighter, anticipation surging within her. "What message?"

Mirrie hesitated. "I hope you will not think less of me, when I tell you."

"I will think less of you if you prevaricate further." Esme smiled to take the sting from her words. "Ignore me, 'tis impatience that puts a barb on my tongue. How could I ever think less of the woman who was such a constant friend to Frida? And now makes a happy man of my brother Tristan? You are a blessing to us, Mirrie." She leaned closer. "Tell me, please, before my heart bursts out of my chest with impatience."

Mirrie breathed out a small laugh. "'Twas I who showed Adam to his chamber, earlier this day."

"Aye." Esme waited, expectantly.

"I took him to the eastern wing. To the chamber with a view of the lake."

Mirrie withdrew her hand and smiled as if in farewell.

"Wait." Esme was confused. "Is that it?"

"That is all I came here to say." Mirrie paused in the doorway and placed her hands on the rounded swell of her belly. The torchlight from the corridor shone around her like a halo.

"But the eastern wing is largely empty?" Esme was beginning to put the puzzle together.

"Indeed, it is." Mirrie nodded, sagely. "Conversations could take place there, especially at night. And no one would be any the wiser."

"Conversations?" Esme arched her eyebrows.

Mirrie nodded firmly. "Conversations." She took a step backwards. "Good night, Esme."

"Good night."

Esme watched Mirrie disappear down the corridor, her mind whirring.

Can I really creep through the keep to Adam's chamber?

A smile puckered at her lips. Mirrie clearly thought she could. And Mirrie was a bastion of good sense and propriety.

At least, that was what Esme had always thought.

Perchance I am not the only de Neville to err from the proper path, after all?

The idea was a revelation, but she did not waste any further time considering it. Instead, she pinned a cloak over her shoulders and lit a taper from her nightstand, sheltering the flame with a cupped hand as she ventured out into the corridor.

The night air carried a chill, but darts of excitement kept her warm as she crept onward. Wolvesley Castle was as familiar as the back of her own hand, and she knew which floorboards would squeak and which would not. She deliberately avoided the main gallery, picking a path through the upper story of the keep, which was less frequented by guards and passing servants. Her breath plumed in front of her, threatening to extinguish the candle on more than one occasion. But she reached the eastern wing without incident.

Only one chamber had a view of the lake. Esme tightened her grip on the candleholder and crept toward it, stepping through the pools of light thrown by the wall torches.

Might he be sleeping?

Might he resent me interrupting his rest?

Esme pushed the thoughts away. She had come too far to turn back now. Her knuckles had scarcely made contact with the grooved wood of the door when it was flung open.

Adam stood in the doorway and gazed at her. He was still fully clothed in the black-and-gold tunic he'd worn for dinner, though his tousled hair looked as if he had dragged his hands through it many times.

"Esme," he breathed. "I hardly dared hope it would be you."

Standing on the threshold, Esme's courage all but failed her.

She swallowed hard and lifted her chin.

"I missed you, after dinner."

"I missed you, too." He gestured with his hands. "By the time I finished speaking with your father, you had already retired for the evening."

"You and father clearly had much to discuss." She tried to keep her voice trembling with a combination of nerves and impatience.

"We did." A smile broke over Adam's face, making him appear younger and more carefree.

Or is that my imagination?

He peered over her shoulder, looking all the way down the empty corridor. "Is it safe for us to talk here?"

"As safe as anywhere." Esme grabbed her courage with both hands and stalked past Adam into his chamber. The sight of his familiar shirt, abandoned atop of the bed, made her pause, her flesh tingling with excitement.

This was Adam's private chamber.

They were alone.

And Lord, how she wanted him.

But beyond all else, she wanted to know what had transpired in her father's solar.

He stood with his back against the fastened door. Esme slowly swiveled to face him, trying to read from his expression whether the outcome was good or bad.

Adam's green eyes glowed like a cat's, but the rest of his face was in shadow. The candle in her hand quivered.

"Well?" she demanded.

"'Tis dark in here." Adam took the candle from her, then used it to light the wall sconces. Slowly, the chamber came to life with a flickering glow. With painful slowness, he positioned Esme's candle atop a blanket box, then he came to stand before her. "This is not how I imagined having this conversation."

"Oh." She was momentarily thrown, but his large hands smoothed her hair from her face, and she found herself melting into his touch. "How did you imagine it?"

"I imagined inviting you for a walk by the lake." He chuckled softly. "I am quite taken with the place."

She half closed her eyes, surrendering to the sonorous pleasure of his voice as well as the gentle pressure of his palms. "I thought it was the swans that had stolen your heart."

"Aye, the swans are mighty fine creatures." He skimmed his thumbs over her cheekbones. "But my heart already belongs to another."

Esme's breath caught in her throat. "And what would you have said, down by the lake?"

Adam gave a low chuckle. "In truth, I have spent less time imagining the words I would use and more time imagining what I might do after I said them." He put his hands to her waist and pulled her closer, so she could feel the warmth emanating from him.

The air seemed to leave her lungs. "What might you have done?"

"I might have kissed you." His lips hovered inches from hers. "Perchance I might have done more than just kiss you."

Esme's lips parted involuntarily. "I would have liked that." She wanted him to kiss her now and wondered why he did not.

He grinned wickedly, his white teeth gleaming in the candlelight. "I would have made certain that you did."

Still his lips remained out of reach, even as his hands spanned her waist, holding her in place.

She linked her hands around his neck. "And what is stopping you now, Adam? Must we walk down to the lake to accomplish all of this?"

"Nay." His breath warmed her bare neck, making her tremble all over again. "But there is a question I must ask of you first."

Her heart started beating so hard she feared it might burst from her chest. He gazed down into her eyes as if he had forgotten what he was about to say.

"Ask me," she whispered.

Hope made her knees weaken, so when he took his hands from her waist, she all but sagged against him.

"Esme de Neville." He took hold of both her hands, and she realized, for the first time, that he was trembling too. "With your father's permission, I would like to ask for your hand in marriage."

She blinked. "You *would like* to ask?"

"I am asking." He tightened his grip. "Marry me, Esme. Make me the happiest man in all the land. And I will spend the rest of my days endeavoring to deserve you."

Joy bubbled up inside her, robbing her of all proper responses so that when she first opened her mouth, no sound came out.

"I will," she managed, gasping for air.

Adam let out a whoop before clasping her to his chest and holding her tight.

"I hardly dare to believe it," he whispered.

"I told you to dare to dream." She smiled tremulously, feeling happy tears brimming in her eyes.

My father has consented to our match!

Naught could stop them marrying now.

"And that is precisely what I did." He gazed down at her with so much love shining from his eyes that they hardly needed the light from the wall sconces. "My bright and beautiful Esme."

Esme cleared her throat. "Adam, there is something that I must ask of you."

He stilled. "Anything."

She rose up on her tiptoes to close the distance between them. "Will you kiss me now?"

His answer was to bring his lips crashing down onto hers, plundering her mouth until all strength left her limbs and she clung to him as wave after wave of desire rippled through her. His hands stroked her spine and cradled her breasts, the thin material of her night rail providing little barrier between them. His kisses were hot, matching the spiraling heat rising through Esme's body. She gasped as his hands cupped her buttocks, bringing her hips into close contact with the part of him that strained hard at his breeches.

"You should most probably leave," he said raggedly.

"Is that what you want?" Esme was busy tugging at his shirt, desperate to run her hands over the warmth of his skin.

"It is the last thing that I want." He lifted her hair from her neck and pressed his lips to that sensitive spot until she writhed against him.

"Then I shall stay." She smiled in victory as his shirt finally came free and her palms could caress the curves of his muscular chest.

"If you stay, I cannot promise restraint." His words were muffled against her neck.

Esme's wandering hands came over his shoulders before trailing a path downwards. "Good," she breathed.

With a groan, Adam lifted her up and laid her gently on his bed. "If you are sure?" He unclasped her cloak, and she sat up so he could pull it away.

"I have never been more sure of anything."

When Adam lifted off his shirt, she leaned back on her elbows to better admire the rippling breadth of him.

"Do I please you, milady?" He put his hands at either side of her and dopped a featherlight kiss onto her lips.

"Very much." She let her head fall back, surrendering to his caresses. His hands moved down over her body, skimming over the place she most wanted him to linger. She felt him grip the hem of her night rail and an intense feeling of anticipation mingled with relief fair robbed her of reason.

She lifted her hips and arms, helping him remove the garment in one smooth moment. He gazed down at her with his green eyes, drinking her in.

"Do I please you, good sir?" she asked impishly.

"More than you can ever know." Adam's weight gently came down on top of her as he kissed and nibbled his way over her breasts and stomach. When she realized where his kisses were leading, she half sat up in surprise, but Adam lowered her back down with a firm but steady hand.

"Stay there," he almost growled.

Never had she anticipated such giddy heights of sensation. Esme could not help calling out when the warmth of his tongue first entered her most secret place. She clenched her hands into fists as her hips bucked beneath him, unable to control the spiraling tension which released into spasms of pleasure and left her limbs tingling.

He kissed his way back up her body, giving her time to catch her breath as he wrestled with his breeches.

"Can I?" he whispered into her ear.

"Can you what?" For a moment, Esme did not understand. But then she felt the tip of him against her stomach. Instead of answering, she instinctively moved him into position, matching his deep sigh of contentment when he slid deep inside her.

Almost at once, her pleasure began to build anew. She clung to his shoulders as he rocked, slowly at first, but quicker and quicker as her desire exploded once again. Adam took a great, shuddering breath and then collapsed against her, murmuring her name.

"You're mine now." He rolled to one side and cradled her to his chest.

"I have been for the longest time." She traced a hand over his shoulders, loving the contrast between his strength and gentleness.

"I want to marry you right away, before anyone can change their mind."

"No one is going to change their minds." Contentment washed over her and Esme closed her eyes. "Though to make sure, I should stay here all through the night and ensure the housemaids find me in your arms."

"Naked?" His voice was teasing.

"Entirely," she confirmed.

Adam tensed and she thought he was about to protest, but

then she realized that he was laughing quietly. "I am minded to think that is a most excellent idea."

"Good." She snuggled against him, feeling entirely at home as his arms wrapped around her.

She was happy and safe.

Forever.

CHAPTER TWENTY-THREE

Six weeks later…

SNOW HAD FALLEN overnight, and a white dusting covered the sweeping lawns of Wolvesley Castle. The temperature had not risen above freezing for several days and long shards of ice had transformed the fountain into something both beautiful and forbidding. Esme could not ignore a twist of unease in her stomach as she gazed through the latticed window of the ladies' solar.

"Will she still be able to come?"

Her mother smiled serenely. "The snow is not so very deep, dearest. I am certain the Felsham carriage will find a way through."

Esme nibbled at her fingernail. "She should have set off sooner. We might have known snow would fall this close to yule."

"'Tis hardly a surprise." Morwenna stepped away from the window with a shiver, drawing her fur cloak over her shoulders. "You know, you could have had a springtime wedding."

Esme pursed her lips as she sank down onto the plush window seat. "We didn't want to wait that long."

"We are all very aware of that," Morwenna commented. Her tone was dry, but a flicker of amusement danced behind her eyes.

Esme leaned forward and touched her mother's arm, concern flooding through her. "I'm sorry. Has it all been too much? A wedding coming so soon after Tristan's babe and the news of Rory Baine's passing." She shook her head, her blonde plait falling over one shoulder. "I should have known better, Mother."

"Nay, child. A wedding is a happy occasion. And none happier than when the two people involved love one another as much as you and Adam." Morwenna sat down beside Esme and held her hands out toward the fire.

"I do love him." Esme's heart lifted as she snuggled closer to her mother. "And I long to be his wife."

"Which you will be, in just a few hours." Morwenna's eyes filled with emotion. "To think my youngest child is about to be a bride."

"Only if Isabella is here," Esme interrupted her. "I love Mirrie, and I'm grateful she is with us. But I will not marry without at least one of my sister's present."

"Oh Esme." Morwenna cupped her daughter's face with her palms. "I hope you never change."

A log crackled in the fire whilst Esme processed this. "Is that really true?" Her eyebrows disappeared beneath her hair.

"Of course." Morwenna frowned.

"At the last ball, you reprimanded my so-called indifference." Esme folded her hands across the simple woolen day dress she had donned that morn. "I have long imagined that you and father both wished for me to change."

Morwenna's pink lips hung open. "Change how?"

"I do not know." Esme shrugged. "Mayhap to grow wise and sensible, like Frida. Or kind and good, like Mirrie."

"You are already wise and sensible and kind and good." Morwenna put an arm around her shoulders and held her close. "Your father and I only ever wanted you to be happy, truly happy, as we have been."

Esme breathed in her mother's familiar citrussy scent. "Then you have your wish, for I could not possibly be happier."

The two women smiled at one another in the pleasant solar before Morwenna held up her hand.

"What's this? I think I hear a carriage approaching."

"Isabella," Esme squealed, kneeling on the window seat so she could see as far out of the window as possible. Sure enough, a stately carriage pulled by two chestnut horses was making slow but steady progress toward the keep. Relief washed through her. "Now everything will be perfect."

"I am pleased to hear it." Morwenna rose to her feet and reached up to check her silvery blonde hair. "I shall go down and greet your sister. You should go to your chamber and prepare for the ceremony, my dear."

"But, Isabella," Esme protested.

"I shall send her up to you." Morwenna's voice was firm. "She can help you dress. What could be more perfect than that?"

It had been almost two winters since Esme last laid eyes upon Isabella, who had once been her closest friend and confidant. She could hardly believe that the straight-backed woman who walked uncertainly into her chamber was the same girl who had danced about the keep, charming everyone in her wake. When Isabella removed her veil, Esme all but gasped at how drawn and weary looking her beautiful face had grown. Were it not for her thick, golden hair and familiar blue gaze, Esme might have thought her an imposter.

She swallowed her dismay and smiled as brightly as she could manage. "Bella. I'm so glad you're here." She darted across the room and flung her arms about her sister, who felt as frail as a little bird in her arms.

"I am so glad to be here." Isabella hugged her back, fiercely. "'Twas a most taxing journey, but I have arrived in time to see you wed and that is the most important thing."

Esme nodded, unable to speak for the swell of emotion in her chest. "Can I ring for refreshment?" She thought mayhap some warmed wine would put color back into Isabella's cheeks. As it was, her peacock-blue gown was the brightest thing about her.

Isabella waved her offer away. "Mother said she would send something up. But in truth, I am not hungry. We stayed at a comfortable inn last night and I ate my fill at dinner." She crossed the chamber and stood before the window, perchance avoiding Esme's sharp eyes.

Her sister had always been slender, but now the bones of her collarbone were protruding above the lace-trimmed neckline of her expensive gown.

"You look tired." Esme could not help but speak the truth, but she regretted it almost immediately. "Was your bed at the inn not so very comfortable after all? Mayhap the mattress was lumpy?"

She was rewarded with a small smile over her shoulder. "It was not lumpy." Isabella turned fully to face her sister and leaned back against the window ledge. Outside, the sun had emerged from behind the winter clouds and its soft rays crowned Isabella with a halo of light. "Tell me about the man you are to marry."

The request was quietly asked, but Esme still blushed furiously.

How could she profess such full-blooded happiness before a sister who seemed washed out with weariness?

"His name is Adam," she began.

"That much I know," Isabella interrupted, carefully lifting Esme's wedding gown so she might sit down on the bed. "Come." She patted the coverlet beside her.

Esme took her seat and, after a moment's thought, took hold of her sister's slender hands. "He makes me very happy," she said sincerely. "I love him more than I ever thought possible."

"I can see in your eyes that you speak the truth."

"I do." Esme nodded vigorously.

"But what kind of a man is he?" Isabella crossed her long legs at the ankle. "How did you come to meet?"

Esme divined that her titled sister was carefully avoiding asking anything about Adam's wealth or status.

"He is a warrior," she answered, bluntly.

"A knight?" Isabella sounded hopeful.

"Nay." Esme recalled that night at Ember Hall when she had asked the very same question. "He served a Scottish laird. Callum's father." She glanced at Isabella to ensure she was following. "In fact, Adam and Callum grew up together."

Isabella nodded, but Esme could tell this meant little to her. She had only met Frida's husband on one occasion and all the family had born witness to her surprise at Frida's choice.

Not that Isabella had voiced her disapproval out loud; she was far too well-mannered for that. But from her own choice of husband, Isabella had made it clear to the world that title and status meant all to her. She was the Countess of Felsham; mistress of a grand castle with great wealth at her disposal.

But looking at her now, Esme was far from sure that this choice had made her sister happy. And that was hardly surprising.

Happiness, Esme had learned, was found in smaller pleasures than castles and coin chests.

"Adam taught me how to wield a sword, up at Ember Hall," Esme said, smiling at the memory. "Do you recall how we once petitioned father to allow us to learn?"

"I do." Isabella's full lips curved into a smile that transformed her, fleetingly, into the beautiful woman once heralded the 'Rose of England'. "Tristan and Jonah had lessons. But we were never allowed." Isabella twisted a heavy ring around her finger. "I was exceedingly envious."

Esme nudged her with her shoulder. "I could teach you, if you like."

Isabella's laugh was like a peal of bells, but it ended abruptly. "I would like that very much. Alas, I must return to Felsham on the morrow."

"As soon as that?" Dismay filled Esme's voice. "I thought we might spend some time together."

Isabella arched her eyebrows. "I do not think your new husband would like that. Forsooth, he will want you all to himself, once you are married."

"He has already had me, all to himself," Esme replied without thinking. She clasped a hand to her mouth as her cheeks pinked all over again and Isabella's blue eyes opened wide with shock.

"Esme." Isabella seemed to fumble for words. "I hardly know what to say."

"You need not say aught." Esme collapsed backwards onto the high mattress and swung her legs, suddenly feeling carefree. "In a matter of hours, we will be man and wife, and all will be respectable between us." She glanced sideways at her sister and could not help giggling at her frozen expression. "Bella, I never knew you would be so prim and proper."

Isabella swallowed and Esme noted with surprise that her sister was beginning to blush. "'Tis not that."

"What then?" She sat up leaned closer in a show of sisterly closeness.

"'Tis just that I never dreamed of doing such a thing for pleasure." Isabella shrugged her slender shoulders, fixing her gaze on the patterned rug on the floor. "Instead of duty."

"Duty?" Esme wrinkled her nose in distaste.

"Or to conceive a child." Isabella's voice wobbled, making Esme concerned for her all over again.

"Are those the only reasons why you and—" she paused. She had never been entirely comfortable referring to Isabella's husband by his given name. "Charles," she managed, on an outward breath, "lay together?"

Isabella sat so still that Esme feared she had offended her. But at last, she gave a small nod.

"Though I have not yet managed to conceive a child," she said flatly. "And time is running out. My husband has been confined to bed these last weeks. He is not well. And his nephew, his current heir, has no fondness for me."

"But you do not need to conceive a child," Esme declared, grasping her sister's hand once again and trying to inject some warmth into it. "You are the Countess of Felsham."

Isabella laughed bitterly. "Only until my nephew becomes earl. Then I will be naught and no one. A widow without a child has no place in the world." She crossed her arms over her belly and crouched forward as if she was in pain.

Esme gazed at her blankly, unable to comprehend the weight of sorrow on the shoulders of a woman who had always gotten everything she wanted in life.

She swallowed hard, realizing for the first time that Isabella must have nursed these sorrows, in secret, for many years.

"Whatever happens, you are the daughter of the Earl of Wolvesley." Esme's voice was firm. "You can come home, any time you please."

"Nay. There is no place for me here, either." She held up a hand to silence Esme's protest, her rings glinting in the sunlight. "I know that Father and Mother would welcome me. But what am I to do, year after year, whilst the rest of you have families of your own." Isabella's voice broke and she sprang up from the bed to stand near the window, clearly reaching for her composure.

"Isabella, I had no idea you were so unhappy." A knock at the door made Esme startle, so deeply was she drawn into her sister's tale. "Come in," she called.

A round-cheeked serving maid walked reverently into the chamber and laid a heavy tray on a side table. "Mead and honey cakes for the bride and her sister," she said, smiling brightly.

"Thank you, Molly." Esme summoned a smile for the maid who had served their family for many years. Molly wasn't to know that her words had struck a wrong note.

But she was quick to read the situation. "I'll leave you, milady." She bobbed into a small curtsy.

As Molly left the chamber, Isabella dabbed at her eyes with a lace-trimmed handkerchief. "Forgive me, Esme. 'Tis not right that I bring you low on your wedding day. We should talk of brighter things." She walked over to the tray, poured a goblet of mead and held it out toward her. "Let us make a toast to you and Adam."

Esme accepted the goblet and drank deeply, but she could not forget the sadness in her sister's eyes.

"Things could have been very different for me," she said suddenly. "Not so long ago, I thought my future lay with Crispin de Gough." She winced as the taste of the sweetened mead turned sour in her mouth. Just saying his name made her nauseous.

Isabella looked at her over the rim of her goblet. "The knight sworn to father—"

"Who betrayed the King," Esme finished for her.

"And you had a fancy for him?" Curiosity filled Isabella's voice.

"More than a fancy." Esme pulled a face. "Though I should say no more than that. I believe I have shocked you enough, this day."

"Mercy, sister." Isabella placed her goblet back on the tray with a small shake of her golden head. "It seems much has happened in these last months."

"Much indeed. Which is why I know that things can change." Esme looked at her imploringly, "Do not give up hope, Isabella."

Her sister smiled, but it did not meet her eyes. "What will happen to Crispin?"

"He is under house arrest at Windsor." Esme picked up a slice of honey cake but found she had no appetite for it.

"Ye Gods." Isabella put a hand to her chest. "Will he be put to death?"

Esme shook her head. "Father says 'tis unlikely. Crispin's line is long and noble. His father will secure some arrangement with the King."

Isabella nodded slowly, before straightening her shoulders and fixing Esme with an appraising stare. "We have chattered enough, I believe, on all subjects but the most pressing one. What are you to wear for your wedding?"

"My dress right here, laid out on the bed," Esme laughed.

"I am surprised you are not already wearing it." Isabella picked up the silken gown with utmost reverence and hung it on the door of the closet. "'Tis beautiful," she said.

The dress was pale green and studded with small pearls. As testament to the season, it had a fur-lined hood and a full skirt which swept the floor.

"I have learned that there are more important things than pretty gowns," Esme replied. "I would marry Adam wearing a sack and still be happy."

Isabella put her hands on her hips and frowned with mock severity. "Well, I for one would not be happy about that."

"Seriously, sister." Esme went to join her at the closet, threading their arms together. "Happiness is not the preserve of others. It is out there somewhere, waiting to be claimed and enjoyed. By you," she added, with a nudge of her elbow.

"Well, I shall be sure to look out for it." Isabella was brisk as she studied the gown. "But for now, let us concentrate on turning you into a bride fit for this man who has made you so very happy."

GREAT BOUGHS OF pine had been strung from the rafters of the chapel, so Adam breathed in the scent of yule as he stood by the altar, waiting for the ceremony to begin. His breath plumed ahead of him, for the chapel was high-ceilinged and draughty, but this only heightened his sense of anticipation.

He had dared to dream. And now his dreams were coming true.

Beside him, Jonah gave a small cough, pulling his sumptuous cloak of emerald green closer over his shoulders.

"The final guests are arriving. This is perchance your last chance to make an escape," he commented, drily.

Adam clapped him on the shoulder, knowing that the slender man was a lot stronger than he looked. "Why would I do that, pray tell? I am about to become the happiest man in England."

Jonah nodded, a small smile playing about his lips. "I am just making sure."

"And I am exactly where I want to be."

He spoke the truth, although Adam was careful not to raise his gaze further than the first family pews. Beyond them, all the way to the back of the chapel, sat the great and good of the

English nobility, wrapped in silk and furs, flashing with jewels, and no doubt exclaiming to one another over Esme de Neville's startling choice of husband.

Upon waking that morn, Adam had been unable to quell a faint hope that the snow would keep at least some of these guests away. But the brightness of the sun—together with the lure of Wolvesley Castle—had brought them all out, in their finery.

"I thought we were to have a small wedding," he had murmured to Esme, a sennight prior, as she and Morwenna deliberated over seating arrangements.

She had gazed up at him, bewildered. "This is small."

Standing in the chapel, Adam took a deep breath and focused on the intricate detail of the frescoes on the opposite wall. He would not allow any doubts, insecurities *or other people*, to spoil the wonder of this day.

Jonah cleared his throat. "I am sorry that 'tis I stood beside you, not Callum. I am but a poor substitute for the friend you have known since childhood."

His words were heartfelt; Adam could see as much in his blue eyes.

He grasped his arm. "I am glad you are here, Jonah. In fact, I am honored by it. 'Tis no small matter, to be accepted by the mighty de Nevilles."

Jonah inclined his head. "'Tis no small matter to see my sister so happy." He glanced down the aisle as if looking for a glimpse of Esme, but there was so sign of her yet.

Adam knew this without looking; every fiber of his body was strained with awareness as to her presence or absence.

"I will remain a while here at Wolvesley; to give you and Esme some time alone at Ember Hall," Jonah continued.

Adam's heart leaped at the prospect of having his wife all to himself, but he shook his head. "Nay, you do not have to do that. Ember Hall is your home, and that should not change. Esme and I are only looking after the place until Frida and Callum return."

"You know better than I that Callum will be required in the

Highlands for a long time yet. He is the Laird of Kielder and has duties there." Jonah's voice was low. "Your arrangement benefits all and I do not seek to spoil it."

The sound of fretful crying made all eyes swing to the second pew, where Mirrie rocked her new baby son in her arms. Comforted, the babe went back to sleep, and Mirrie and Tristan exchanged a look of relief.

The babe had been born on the night of the first frost. He was a strong, healthy boy with a lustful cry and a hearty appetite. His name was Lucan, after his grandfather's older brother.

Adam turned back to Jonah. "After today, you will be my brother. I never had a brother before, but I am certain my mother would instruct me to share whatever I have."

Jonah's face was momentarily transformed by a wide and genuine smile. "Your mother must have been a wise woman."

"Aye, she was."

Adam swallowed a lump in his throat. His humble parents would have been overjoyed to see him here. Not because of the wealth of Wolvesley; but because he had found a woman he loved—and been accepted by her large and loving family.

He thought back to the day he first met Esme. He had sat by the window at Ember Hall, all but struck dumb by the beauty and vivacity of the golden-haired girl who teased her siblings and mimed a sword fight.

So much had changed since then.

Nay, *everything* had changed, since then.

Esme's brightness had banished the darkness inside him. She had shown him the light, and he would never deviate from it again.

A commotion by the double doors saw the congregation rise to their feet.

Jonah straightened his shoulders. "This is it."

Adam had no words to reply. His gaze was fixed on Esme as she appeared in the holly-strewn doorway, on the arm of her proud father. She was resplendent in green silk, with her long tresses of hair swept high on her head. When her eyes met his, she smiled, and a feeling of warmth washed over him.

Aye, I am exactly where I want to be.

Tears of joy brimmed in his eyes as he took Esme's gloved hand from Angus and escorted her on their final steps to the altar.

"You are beautiful," he whispered to her.

She squeezed his hand. "That is because I am so very happy."

"I will make sure you are always happy, my love," he promised.

And so he did.

THE END

About the Author

Elizabeth grew up in a rambling old farmhouse high on the Yorkshire moors, where a sense of history was never far away. She studied English at university, specialising in mythology and folklore and often bemoaning the lack of sword-wielding heroines. After graduating, she spent several years moving between northern France, southern Germany and London, where she worked in travel publishing and PR.

She now lives a stone's throw from her childhood home, with her husband, children and a feisty black cat who enjoys interrupting her writing. She plots most of her novels while walking in the rugged Yorkshire countryside, finding endless inspiration in the rolling hills.

9 781969 349782